Praise for

A Wee Murder in My Shop

"Peggy Winn brings a bit of Scotland home to her Scottish-themed shop in Vermont, but this time it's more than she bargained for in this enjoyable debut. A great start to a new series!"
—Sheila Connolly, *New York Times* bestselling author of the County Cork Mysteries

"The very first paragraph of *A Wee Murder in My Shop* hooked me. . . . It is the town of Hamelin, Vermont, however, that charms its way into the readers' hearts . . . a fun start to the ScotShop Mystery series." —Fresh Fiction

"[A] strong start to what is going to be a fabulous series. [Stewart has] created very memorable characters, full of charm and mischief, and readers will be fondly recalling this adventure long after they turn the last page."
—Cozy Mystery Book Reviews

"Scotland, a seven-hundred-year-old ghost, a hunky police officer, and [the] murder of a cheating boyfriend. What's not to like in the new ScotShop Mystery series?"
—Lesa's Book Critiques

"An interesting concept that you might expect in a time-travel romance, only it is a cozy mystery—which provides a completely different flair." —Mysteries and My Musings

A Wee Homicide in the Hotel

Fran Stewart

BERKLEY PRIME CRIME
New York

BERKLEY PRIME CRIME
Published by Berkley
An imprint of Penguin Random House LLC
375 Hudson Street, New York, New York 10014

Copyright © 2017 by Fran Stewart
Penguin Random House supports copyright. Copyright fuels creativity, encourages
diverse voices, promotes free speech, and creates a vibrant culture. Thank you for buying
an authorized edition of this book and for complying with copyright laws by not
reproducing, scanning, or distributing any part of it in any form without permission.
You are supporting writers and allowing Penguin Random House to continue to
publish books for every reader.

BERKLEY is a registered trademark and BERKLEY PRIME CRIME and the B colophon
are trademarks of Penguin Random House LLC.

ISBN: 9780425270332

First Edition: February 2017

Printed in the United States of America
1   3   5   7   9   10   8   6   4   2

Cover art by Jesse Reisch
Book design by Kelly Lipovich

*This book is lovingly dedicated to my sister, Diana,
who gave me my first book of Shakespeare
and thereby lit a fire.*

Acknowledgments

Excuse me for inventing politicians right and left. Believe me, none of the ones in this book are real. I'd like to thank Millar Brown, a piper with the Firefighters Honor Guard of Gwinnett County, Georgia, who spent time showing me the finer points of bagpiping and introduced me to "the Green Book," which is what pipers call *The College of Piping Tutor for the Highland Bagpipe*; Mary Stone, who was the highest bidder at the "Murder on the Menu" silent auction in Wetumpka, Alabama, and who asked me to use the name Windsor Stone in this book; Eric Varner, who won the "Your Scottie's Name in Fran's Book" contest sponsored by the Scottish Terrier Club of Greater Atlanta (STCGA), resulting in the introduction of Silla; Rhea Spence of the STCGA, who verified that a Scottie could dig through a wall; Peggy Dixon, who suggested the name Cord; my editor, Michelle Vega, who took a rather chaotic manuscript and helped me hone it; and the entire production staff of Berkley Prime Crime, who turned an electronic file into something beautiful. Most of all, though, I'm deeply indebted to the independent bookstore owners who've helped to spread the word about the ScotShop Mysteries. I have the greatest respect for you.

All text headings are taken from *Hamlet*, in *The Complete Works of Shakespeare*, Cambridge Edition, as edited by William Aldis Wright, © 1936, Garden City Books, Garden City, New York.

1

You come most carefully upon your hour.

ACT 1, SCENE 1

Nobody expected to die attending Hamelin's sixty-third annual four-day Highland Festival.

Everybody expected kilts and bagpipes, porridge jelly beans (a specialty of Sweetie's candy shop—believe me, they taste better than they sound), caber tossing and hammer throws, with a sheepdog demonstration and a little sword dancing thrown in for good measure.

That's what everybody got from Thursday to Sunday. Everybody except Peggy Winn, owner of the ScotShop. That would be me.

People were expecting to load their stomachs with good food and junk food, and load their cars with kilt pins and lengths of tartan in their favorite clan plaid.

That's what everybody bought from Thursday through Sunday. Everybody except me.

Everybody wanted a spectacular opening ceremony Thursday night, exciting competitions on Friday and Saturday and a part of Sunday, and a spectacular bonfire Sunday evening at the closing ceremonies.

That's what they got those four days. I guess I got some of it.

What nobody expected, though, between the Highland dance competition and the pipe bands, between the Celtic harpists and the solo drummer, was death.

But I'm getting ahead of myself. There are some other things I'd rather mention first. Like the fact that my ghost was throwing a hissy fit that Thursday morning in early August before the ScotShop opened. An angry ghost is nothing to fool around with. Unfortunately, the object of his ire—my employee and, incidentally, my cousin Shoe Winn—wasn't aware of the storm cloud building on the ghostly horizon.

"Ye havena practiced the chanter enough. I canna tell any the difference betwixt your leumluath nor your taorluath." Dirk shifted his plaid in irritation, and it settled on his massive shoulder like a hound curling up for a long winter's nap. "And to put the fillip on it, ye tuned the bass drone as badly as aulde Grandda Gosham."

Shoe played on in blissful ignorance. His *loomlooah*s and his *torlooah*s certainly weren't distinguishable to me, either, maybe because I had no idea what Dirk was talking about. With the A.T.T.T.F. that was generally in process—that's what I called the Automatic Trans-Time Translation Factor that had to be at work here, since Dirk had last taken a real breath during the time of Chaucer, when English sounded totally different—I could usually understand him, but occasionally he'd use words that didn't seem to have an American equivalent.

Covered by the sound of the pipes, which filled the ScotShop with earsplitting cacophony, I ignored the unknown terms and asked, "Couldn't your grandpa Gosham play very well?"

"Nae, that he couldna. He was tone-deaf as a hedgehog."

"How do you know a hedgehog is tone-deaf?" I asked into the sudden silence as Shoe stopped playing. Well, it wasn't quite silence, since the bags had to empty themselves of their excess air in a wheeze that always made me think of a dying dinosaur.

"I dunno," Shoe said. "Something to do with hedge funds?"

Dirk looked at Shoe in disgust. "This isna Twenty Questions, wee manny." He'd been intrigued when I'd told him about that game. It didn't seem like the sort of thing fourteenth-century Scots would have played back then. They were too busy tending gardens and hunting deer and taking care of the family goats and hens. Or were they? When had such games started? And where? I suppose I could have asked my ghost. When nobody else was around to hear me.

". . . anytime you're ready."

"Huh?" I looked up to see Shoe peering at me over the deflated pipe bag.

"Are you going to give me the answer?"

"To what?"

He raised his eyebrows, and I couldn't help but notice that Dirk had almost the same expression on his ghost-face. "To your riddle," he said with exaggerated patience. "How do I know a hedgehog is tone-deaf?"

"I don't know," I said. "I just thought you might know something about hedgehogs."

Dirk didn't even try to damp down his guffaws. That's one of the distinct advantages to being a ghost nobody can hear. Nobody except me.

"Put that thing away, Shoe." I checked my watch. "We have to open the door in seven minutes."

Shoe ran his finger along the braided cords that connected the drones to each other. "I could pipe the customers into the store." His voice was wistful.

"If ye dinna learn any the better, ye would send them running for the wee hills."

"Mountains," I said.

"Huh?" Shoe says that a lot when Dirk and I are around.

I waved him off. "No," I said. "You may most definitely not pipe in the customers. Not until you work on your tor-looahs some more."

I love it when my gangly cousin is at a loss for words. Not for long, of course. "How—where did you learn about taorluaths?"

I smiled, even though I didn't have a clue what I was talking about. I must have said the weird word the right way. "Oh"—I waved an airy hand—"here and there."

"Ye didna give me the credit, forebye?" At least my resident ghost was smiling when he said it.

"You can leave your bagpipes in the back room for

today, Shoe, but don't you dare forget to take them home this evening." I'd gotten tired of walking around what I was beginning to think of as his souvenirs. *Shoe's junk pile* would be a better term. His second-best baseball gear had cluttered up the place last summer, until the bat was used to murder my ex-boyfriend, and now it looked like his piping materials were trying to invade. At least nobody could kill anyone with bagpipes. Blast out their eardrums maybe. My head was still ringing.

"Hills," Dirk said. Because he came from the Highlands of Scotland, his impression of the venerable Green Mountains of Vermont was less than awe-filled. Despite the fact that every road heading out of this picturesque town went steeply upward, even the one that eventually led to Burlington, Dirk refused to think of these wonderful old mountains as anything other than pipsqueak lumps of dirt and stone.

I glanced out the tall plate glass windows and saw yet another travel trailer, towed by yet another pickup truck, headed for the meadow outside town, where the Hamelin Highland Games would commence tomorrow, but the opening ceremonies and the first rounds of the Highland dance competition were scheduled for this evening, so most of the people were here already. The meadow looked like a little city, with the various clans setting up their tents around the perimeter. Some of the people who attended each year were drawn as much by the nearby Appalachian Trail as by the all-things-Scottish theme of Hamelin.

Taking advantage of the fact that Shoe had disappeared into the back room, I turned to Dirk. "You have the shawl,"

I said, referring to the ancient fabric his fourteenth-century ladylove had woven, the one that had allowed me to see Dirk when I first put it on. With the shawl in hand or, in this case, wound securely around the hilt of his dagger, he was free to roam anywhere he wanted. When I held the shawl, though, he couldn't stray more than a few yards away from me, except when we were at my house or here in the ScotShop. Don't ask why—there seem to be certain ghostly rules nobody understands. And who on earth could I have asked about them anyway? Maybe my great-grandmother, if she'd still been alive. My grannie had told me long ago that her ma claimed to be able to talk to ghosts. Or maybe it was only one ghost. I really couldn't remember. It was something of a joke to most of the family; but when my twin brother, Drew, and I turned ten, my wish as I blew out the candles was that I'd have a ghost of my own someday.

And here he was. Last year, when I'd acquired the shawl he was attached to, the woman who'd sold it to me said it had passed from great-grandmother to great-granddaughter for umpteen generations. But then she'd said something that had intrigued me ever since. She'd said she had no children of her own, and the shawl would have to pass to her sister in Nefyn. I'd looked up Nefyn when I got home to Hamelin. It was a town in Wales. Wales was where the Winn family had come from. I even had a whole outfit in the burgundy-toned Wynn family tartan. And Grannie said her mother had died in Scotland on a visit there. Why hadn't I listened more closely to all those old stories?

"What would ye be thinking of wi' such a rimple across your brow?"

"Rimple?"

He scrunched his eyebrows together in illustration. I guess I had been thinking pretty hard. I'd figure it all out later. "Why don't you wander down to the meadow," I said, "and see if the Farquharson clan tent is up yet?"

He considered my question. "D'ye think there will be Farquharsons here, foreby?"

"Of course there will. People come from all over the States to attend the Hamelin Highland Festival."

"I know that," Shoe said from behind me.

"So," I countered, recovering quickly, "do you think we'll sell out of all this extra merchandise this year?"

Luckily, the bell over the front door announced the arrival of Gilda Buchanan, my assistant manager, with her blond curls bouncing around her face, followed closely by Sam—my third employee—with Gilda's dog Scamp, who sported a bright blue collar and leash. Scamp stopped in the doorway to look behind him. When a Scottie digs in his heels, even someone as tall and strong as my cousin Sam tends to pause. "Whatcha lookin' at, Scamp?"

As if he had to ask. A tiny Scottie—a female, I knew for sure—had stopped in the middle of the sidewalk beside the sunken courtyard outside the ScotShop. She eyed Scamp from beneath her perky Scottie eyebrows and sniffed the air delicately. Her human came up the last step, and the dog moved considerably closer to Scamp. I heard the distinct *click* when the man pressed the button to stop the leash from extending any more.

I halfway expected fur to fly, but Scamp had been neutered, and was very well trained. Apparently the other dog was just as well behaved.

They sniffed noses, unable because of their respective leashes to reach the other, more interesting end. More interesting to dogs, that is.

"Your dog is lovely," Gilda said.

The gray-haired man beamed. "And that's quite a handsome fellow you have there."

Gilda blushed. "He's pretty special."

"So are they all." He gazed at his dog for a moment. I knew love when I saw it. "Scotties are a breed apart," he said.

I recognized the man and—wonder of wonders— remembered his name, even though I'd never met him. Big Willie Bowman had been a regular competitor—and winner—at the Hamelin Highland Games, although I hadn't seen him for several years. I'd never seen him with a dog, though. I couldn't resist. So what if the store was a little late in opening? Anyway, it wasn't like I had customers lined up waiting to get in.

Tomorrow and Saturday they'd be lined up out to the curb, if past festivals were any sort of guideline, but today so far, most of the visitors were still dribbling into town, getting settled in the hotels, B and Bs, or camping sites. By midafternoon today, though, the shop would be packed.

I stepped past Sam and Gilda, who both seemed rooted to the spot. "You're Big Willie, aren't you? Do you mind if I pat your dog?"

"Not at all, not at all."

Hearty. That's how his voice sounded. Like Santa Claus, but without the reindeer. And with considerably more life. Maybe *exuberant* was a better word. I smiled in response and reached down a fist. The little female licked the end of my thumb and turned expectantly to Dirk. He backed up a step. Anyone who made contact with Dirk tended to get dizzy.

"What's her name?"

"Officially, her name is Dunedin's Drusilla."

"Drusilla? Wasn't that Cinderella's sister?"

I saw his mouth twitch. "That was Drizella, I believe." He looked down at the petite black dog. "Drusilla is nothing like Cinderella's sister. For one thing, Drusilla has a very nice singing voice."

"Who would be Sindrella? And what," Dirk asked, "does singing have to do wi' wee doggies, forebye?" Naturally I couldn't answer my ghost.

I wasn't sure whether or not the man was pulling my leg. But something still bothered me. "Drusilla," I said. And then the light dawned. "From *Buffy the Vampire Slayer*?"

Dirk opened his mouth again, but shut it when the man said, "No, no, no. Drusilla is a historical character. She was a member of the Roman imperial family; she was aunt to Nero and sister of Caligula."

I glanced quickly at Dirk, but he shrugged his shoulders. Apparently Brother Marcus, the one who had taught Dirk *some Latin and a little Greek* almost six hundred years ago, had neglected teaching him about either Nero's fiddle or Caligula's senatorial horse.

I reached for Drusilla's broad back. She was almost as silky as Tessa, my twin brother's service dog. "Welcome back to Hamelin, Big Willie. I don't recall having seen you for the past few years."

He ducked his head in a surprisingly shy gesture. "I've been . . . gone. It's good to be back, though."

"I assume you're here to take part in the Games again?"

"Caber toss and stone put," he said without fanfare. "Weight toss and hammer throw."

I wondered if he was too old to compete in such strenuous sports where the average age of the competitors hovered somewhere around the mid- to late twenties. Fine lines were etched across his face, and his gray hair had wisps of pure white streaking his temples, but the legs showing beneath his kilt were still as massive as tree trunks, and his shoulders were even wider than Dirk's. He'd been the consistent winner, year after year, as long as I could remember until he abruptly stopped coming to the Games. Come to think of it, the guy who usually came in second place to Big Willie looked almost as old as this man.

Ropes of muscle running along his forearms rippled as he lifted the tartan material at his left shoulder in a move reminiscent of what Dirk had done a few minutes before. A glint of something bright red twinkled on his hand. A ring. "I do a bit of solo piping as well, but I've never won a thing there." He grinned down at his dog. "Silla—that's what I call her—enjoys it when I practice, even though I'm no good at it."

"But a dog's ears are awfully sensitive. I should think she wouldn't like the pipes."

"Ah, but she's a Scottie. They're a breed apart, as I've said before. Often she sings along with me."

I must have looked skeptical.

"Truly," he said. "Scotties have a special song we describe as an *aroo*." He grinned. "There's nothing quite like it, and the sound of the pipes seems to call it out of them." He glanced from the sign above the door to the kilted mannequins in the display windows. "ScotShop," he mused. "Is this your store?"

"Aye, 'tis so," Dirk said.

The man looked at me expectantly, and it took me a moment to remember he couldn't have heard Dirk's answer. The only other one who could see and hear my ghost, besides me—and every animal in town—was my good friend Karaline Logg. "Yes," I said.

The temps I'd hired on for the duration of the Games—all four of them—came running down Main Street, and I directed them to talk with Gilda. She'd give them their assignments.

Big Willie strolled toward the window that overlooked the little courtyard, and the retractable leash reeled out longer and longer. It almost looked as if the Scottie was walking the man. "I see you have Clan Graham kilts." There was a twinkle of delight in his rich voice.

"You're not a Graham, though, are you?" I couldn't recall his last name.

"No. That would be my wife, bless her softly departed soul, the only woman I ever truly loved. I'm William Bowman, of Clan Farquharson."

Dirk's kilt swirled as he strode up before the man and studied his face. "Aye. He looks as though he could be a Farquharson." Dirk should know, since it was his own clan.

"Everybody calls me Big Willie, as you may have heard." He winked at me, and I had the distinct impression that

Big Willie must have been quite a charmer in his younger days.

I studied his face. People show—or hide—grief in myriad ways, but Big Willie looked like a man who may have grieved, but he'd kept on living. "Would you like to see inside the store?"

He shook his head. "I wouldn't want to leave Silla outside." He touched his hand to his chest, right over his heart, and the deep red stone on his big ring twinkled in the early-morning sunlight. "I'm all she's ever had."

"She's welcome in the ScotShop," I said. "After all, Scamp there is our mascot." I glanced around toward Scamp. His leash trailed on the ground. Sam and Shoe had abandoned Scamp and disappeared into the store along with Gilda and the four temps. Good thing, too. I looked at my watch again. We weren't too late. Two of the temps and one of my cousins needed to leave right away, though, to staff the Tartan Tie booth down in the meadow. I sold a lot there each year.

I picked up the end of Scamp's leash and unhooked it from his collar. He knew it was time for him to supervise, so he led me into the store, followed closely by Silla. Big Willie stopped to look at the neatly lettered sign on the glass pane of the window, and Silla's retractable leash kept reeling out.

Well-behaved Scotties and poodles are welcome.
Thank you for keeping any other dogs outside.

"Scotties and poodles?"

I nodded. "They're the only breeds I know of who don't shed. Dog hair would ruin . . ." I gestured to the low-hanging racks of sweaters, tartans, and poet shirts —they were a big seller, since they made any man look fabulous. I glanced at Dirk. In his homespun shirt, crafted four hundred years before the Industrial Revolution, his already broad shoulders were poetry in motion.

I could have gone on thinking such thoughts for a long time, but the little female whined. I couldn't spot her, and Scamp had disappeared as well.

"I'd best retrieve her before she gets into trouble." Big Willie issued a low whistle, and sure enough, I heard doggie toenails on the hardwood floorboards from the other side of the shop, as I followed the retracting leash. Toenails turned to silence when she hit the carpet, and within moments a sturdy black head rounded one of the kilt racks. Her pert ears swiveled, as if to say, *I came because I wanted to—not because you called. Just like my cat,* I thought. Shorty was willing to be with me; in fact, he tended to follow me around the house, but only on his own terms.

Silla ducked beneath a rack of Fair Isle sweaters and turned so her head peeked out. I laughed. "That's one of Scamp's favorite places, too."

Big Willie leaned over and unhooked the leash. "So she doesn't get tangled up," he said.

People had begun drifting into the store, and I excused myself. Even with all three of my employees—and four temps—working, the days before and during the games tended to be extra busy. Overwhelming at times, in fact, but I wasn't about to complain. This was my main source of income. Main source of headaches, too, sometimes, but that came with owning my own business. And the Hamelin

Highland Games weekend was one of the most important sales times every year.

A woman who'd been coming in regularly, although she hadn't bought anything yet, caught my eye as she and a wide-shouldered man I assumed to be her husband—he had his hand on the small of her back—walked into the shop. They headed straight to the glass case where we kept jewelry. Gilda approached her, and I heard the undercurrent of a brief conversation. As I knew would happen, Gilda unlocked the case and brought out a necklace. Why was I not surprised? The woman had been trying it on at least once a day for the past week. This was the third day in a row she'd asked to try on this one particular necklace, and I seemed to recall having seen Gilda showing it to her last week as well. I sure wished she'd make up her mind to buy it. For the past two days, she'd been bringing this man with her; Gilda thought that meant she was getting more serious about paying the rather substantial price. Oh well, if anyone could sell it to her, Gilda could. Gilda had actually suggested that I charge more for it—a lot more—but I'd never taken her seriously.

I smiled at a man carrying a violin case; he was probably a fiddler hired to lead the dancing tonight. Or one of the strolling minstrels who'd be walking through the throngs, playing such crowd-pleasers as "Scotland the Brave," "Isle of Skye," and "Killiecrankie." Before I could ask, a group of white-haired women walked in, full of oohs and aahs. Love that sound. Especially when the music of cash or credit cards follows shortly thereafter.

Almost everyone I saw wore some sort of tartan. Many of the men were in kilts—military kilts, they were called, with the pleats sewn into place, unlike the hand-pleated kilt Dirk wore—and quite a few of the women wore plaid skirts. It was too warm a day for tartan shawls, but we did a brisk business in lightweight tartan scarves. I knew from past experience I'd see many a plaid headband or belt tonight made from ScotShop items, and once people discovered how cool the evenings could be in Vermont this time of year, we'd sell plenty of the shawls on Friday and Saturday.

"Excuse me," said a voice on my left. I expected to see an ordinary customer with an ordinary question. Instead, I saw the governor of Vermont.

I'd met him once before a couple of years ago and had invited him to visit our Highland Games. Naturally, he'd said yes. Naturally, I hadn't believed he would actually show up here.

"It's good to see you, Ms. Winn," he said. "As you can see, I've taken you up on your offer, even though it's taken me several years to follow up on my promise." I nodded, wondering what sort of Farley File he had to be able to remember my name. "Now, I'd like to see what I look like in a kilt."

"Your name doesn't sound like you have any Scot heritage," I said doubtfully. "Maybe through your mother's line?"

He wiggled his hand back and forth in that universal sign of *maybe, maybe not*.

"Still," I said, "a lot of non-Scots wear kilts, just because they like them. There's nothing to stop you from wearing any plaid you like. Just say you're honoring that particular clan."

"Ayuh," he said. That particular word was favored by

old-time Vermonters. It cropped up at odd times here and there and was almost impossible to reproduce in print. I'd tried writing it in texts and e-mails, and somehow it lost the flavor. It was surprisingly close to the way Dirk said the word *aye*. "I could always try on the Royal Stewart," he went on. His eyes twinkled, so I was pretty sure he was joking. Actually, he would have looked quite presentable in that bright red, and I soon found out he had very nice knees. He ended up buying a generic plaid in muted shades of brown, teal, and beige.

"I'll just keep this on." He transferred the contents of his pockets to his new sporran as I clipped off the various tags. "As long as I'm speaking tonight, I might as well look like I belong, wouldn't you say?"

I smiled at him and took his credit card. "I don't think you'll have to worry about that, but it will be nice to see a ScotShop kilt on the platform."

"Two kilts. As soon as Leonzini shows up, I'm going to send him here. He needs all the help he can get."

The governor's aide didn't even crack a smile. The governor was obviously being true to his party, but I did wonder if the aide felt the same way I did about our congressman.

The Games wouldn't open officially until tonight. Events were scheduled for all day beginning Friday, ending with a big farewell bonfire Sunday night. Our congressman was scheduled to speak briefly at the opening ceremonies. He had a respectable Scot heritage through his mother's side of the family, but with an Italian last name like Leonzini, he had to explain himself when he showed up in Hamelin to campaign every election year.

Politicians were standard fare at the Games. I

wondered why the governor had never come to them before this. Had my question shown on my face? He spoke almost as if he were answering me. "I've been here before, but never as governor. This was one of my family's favorite outings each year. I'm sorry I missed it the past few years."

Old-timers still talked about the time Eleanor Roosevelt came to the Games in 1958, while she was promoting her most recent book. There was no Fala, FDR's Scottish terrier, left at that time, but I guess Mrs. Roosevelt had a soft spot for Scotties, because word was she'd stopped to talk to every person in town who'd had a Scottie on a leash.

This year, Vermont senator Josie Calais was on the schedule for the closing ceremonies. It was good to know the senator had recovered completely from the knifing she'd received last winter. She'd speak early in the evening and be available to hand out awards to the winners, just before the bonfire was lit.

I had to admit, the bonfire was one of my favorite parts of the Games. To start with, there'd be a pile of dry wood at least ten feet high stacked in the middle of the meadow, and the leader of the clan with the largest number of members in attendance would have the honor of lighting the fire.

Tonight and Friday night, each clan would have a campfire, or two or three depending on how many people attended. I loved the way people always wandered from fire to fire the first two nights, sharing stories and trading clan pins, and trying to figure out who'd win the Traveled the Farthest to Get Here prize, which was always awarded shortly after the lighting of the bonfire. On Sunday, the campfires paled in comparison with the big bonfire. People sat around on blankets, chairs, campstools, sometimes tailgates, but everyone faced the fire. Even small children seemed entranced—for a little while, until they fell asleep in their parents' arms.

Shay Stone Burns and her committee had been working for the past year, ever since the last Games ended, to make this the smoothest-running Games ever. As far as I knew, they'd planned a spectacular fireworks display to end the Sunday night festivities. Each year Shay hoped for the best, but each year something tended to go wrong, almost as if there were a curse of some sort on the Hamelin Festival.

Four years ago, there had been a big ghost scare in the old Sutherland house on the edge of the meadow, but it turned out to be police chief Mac Campbell's nephews, up to their usual antics. Shay missed it all. It was a good thing she was gone. If she'd been here, she probably would have killed those boys. That was the year her sister died. Shay had to leave Hamelin the first day of the Games, along with her brother Robert and her niece, Andrea Stone, my *former* best friend.

The year after that, several people came down with food poisoning from one of the new vendors. Luckily, nobody died, but that vendor hadn't been back since, as far as I could tell.

Year before last, a boy from Rhode Island fell out of one of the big sugar maples on the edge of the meadow Sunday morning and broke one of his legs; that put a pall over the final day, and his clan leader dedicated the bonfire to the boy and his family. I'd been reminded at the time of when I was in high school and a bratty little boy—a fifth grader, I think he was—pushed a friend of his out of that same tree during the festival, and the kid ended up with a broken arm. I'm not sure why it had made such an impression on me, but I still remembered the brat's name. Bobby Turner. He wasn't much of a friend, at least not the way I defined friendship.

At least it wasn't anything tragic last year. One of the competitors from New Jersey lost his kilt during the sword dance. A lot of people got a great big laugh when his belt broke, and it certainly answered the question of what a Highlander wore beneath his kilt. Come to think of it, I hadn't seen that particular contestant around so far this year. I hoped to high heaven nothing bad would happen this time around, especially with the senator in attendance. We'd run the risk of losing participants next year, and Shay would be devastated if anything bad happened while Senator Calais was here. Or tonight with the governor on the stage.

As if my thoughts had conjured her, Shay stormed into the ScotShop, her bright red tartan skirt swinging in the turbulence of her anger. "There you are! I heard you were in town!" She headed toward Big Willie—he was easy to spot with his head towering above the milling customers.

The aide stepped closer to the governor. "Sir? We should leave now." His voice was unobtrusive but insistent.

The governor extended his hand. "Thank you, Ms. Winn. I appreciate your help." With that, the two men moved to the door and out of my sight.

Every customer in the shop had turned at the sound of Shay's voice, and I wished yet again that she'd learn to moderate her volume. Some people in town called her a powerhouse. Others claimed that *She sure knows how to get things done.* Karaline's opinion was less complimentary: *Pain in the tutu.* Maybe it was a blessing in disguise that Shay never shopped in my store. I'd never seen her brother, Mr. Stone, in here, either, come to think of it. I don't think they had anything against it—or me—but they just never seemed to turn up here. Except today, when loudmouthed Shay showed up. Today, when I had a lot of customers who'd never been here before, and I wanted them to have a good first impression of the Scot-Shop. She wasn't helping me.

I hadn't completely made up my mind yet about her, although at the moment I was leaning toward a big negative. She was older than I, but something about her seemed— I hated to say *juvenile*, but she was just such a *cheerleader* kind of person. Her birth name was S-e-a-s-a-i-d-h, a good old Scottish name, pronounced *Shay-see*, regardless of the way it was spelled. It meant *god is gracious*, but Shay Burns was about as gracious as a chain saw. I did have to admit that usually she acted like she was all sweetness and light, but—occasionally—she could be absolutely virulent. She'd have to be sweet to get everyone in town to cooperate with the Games. I just wished she didn't have to act so obnoxious all those other times.

Of course, the Games brought loads of tourists—and loads of money—to town, so most of the merchants around here were delighted to ignore Shay's less desirable qualities and to help get the job done. But we all were tired well before the end of the first day and exhausted by the end of the fourth one. I didn't need Shay in here braying like a donkey.

People parted as she plowed her way between hanging racks of clothing. Scamp and Silla converged in Shay's wake, looking like stalkers in a horror movie. Cute stalkers.

2

I might not this believe
Without the sensible and true avouch
Of mine own eyes.
ACT 1, SCENE 1

I headed toward Shay, who, after that first outburst, seemed to be keeping her voice level fairly low, which in itself was a minor miracle. She tended to be a full-volume kind of person. All I could hear at the moment was a hum of monologue. Her monologue, of course. But what was she saying? Where was Dirk when I needed him to spy for me? I spotted him in the front corner, peering between mannequins out onto the square.

Two more customers waylaid me. By the time I made it to Big Willie's side, Dirk was there, too, but Shay had fallen silent.

"Thank you," Big Willie told me as he clipped the leash on Silla. He seemed to be avoiding looking at Shay. What was that about? "I hope to see you down in the meadow."

"You definitely will." I swept my arm around, indicating

the store. "I have to be here most of the time during the day, but I have a schedule of the events, and I'll try to show up when you're competing. I hope it's in the morning, because in the evening, I may need to help out at the Tartan Tie booth we have down on the Game grounds."

"I understand. I'll be happy to see you anytime you can make it."

I bent, and Silla licked my hand. She ignored Shay, who strode out through the door, and studied Dirk momentarily. Scamp gave a funny *whiffle* sound, and Silla seemed to decide against trying to lick Dirk, almost as if Scamp had warned her not to. She walked quietly away beside Big Willie. When she reached the door, she swiveled around and gave one good-bye *woof* that turned heads yet again. The bark of a Scottie is something of an anomaly. Such a small dog and such a huge sound, as if a German shepherd had somehow been compressed into a short-legged body with a fringe of black hair reaching to the ground. I watched Scamp leap onto his ottoman, the one in the display window.

Gilda materialized beside me. "Do you believe the gall of that woman?"

"What are you talking about?"

"She ordered that nice man, the one with the Scottie, to leave town. She accused him of—"

I raised my hand to stop her indignant voice. "Not here, Gilda. Not now. We have customers." I shouldn't have had to remind her of that. My curiosity about what Shay Burns was up to would have to wait.

Gilda turned abruptly. She was seldom one to get her dander up, and I certainly hoped she wasn't about to start now. But then I saw that she'd been responding to a raised voice I hadn't even heard. Was I losing my touch? I'd been so concerned about Shay, I'd gone off into la-la land. I debated whether or not to head after Gilda, but she seemed to have the matter in hand. A couple of teenagers looked like they were having a little tiff about what to buy—or not to buy. That was the question. I smiled to myself as memories of my dad's love of Shakespeare came to mind. To be or not to be—to buy or not to buy. I shook my head and went to straighten a stack of shoeboxes that looked in danger of toppling over. On the way I passed the jewelry counter and noticed that the chunky plastic necklace was still in place. Gilda hadn't talked the woman into buying it after all. Who did Gilda think she was kidding, asking me to charge more for the thing? If it wouldn't sell at this price, who on earth would pay more for it?

The price of that necklace was a low priority, though. I needed to do something about the crowd of potential customers I could see gathered around my window.

I walked out through the open front door. A red-haired man asked if the dog was for sale—I got that question a lot. "Everything except the dog," I said. "Come on in and look around." As people swarmed toward the door, I saw an unmistakable figure across the street. He looked like he'd just walked out of Sweetie's. Harper. I knew the depth of his dark gray eyes, but I didn't know what his favorite candy was. One more thing to learn. I waved, but he'd already turned away.

Harper watched the tall man and Shay Burns emerge from the ScotShop. He turned his back, as if to study Sweetie's display of Highland jelly beans in the most disgusting flavors—porridge, haggis, and some red-and-green-striped ones called Purty Plaid, which sounded to Harper like they should have been at the Games in Georgia instead of here in Vermont. But his mind wasn't really on the jelly beans. He studied the reflection of the lopsided pair—one so short and one so tall—as they turned uphill. What was Shay doing with him? And was he really the one? The mug shot hadn't been that clear, but the height was right. Why would he bring a dog along, though? Maybe as camouflage?

Mac—Hamelin's police chief Mackelvie Campbell— had stationed Fairing down in the meadow, dressed in civilian clothes, making her way from vendor to vendor, but keeping an eye on the well-traveled path from town. Easy for someone, even someone as noticeable as this fellow, to just happen to be there during some of the noisier events. Harper grinned to himself; all the events were noisy when that many Scots came together.

Except for that magic moment when the closing bonfire was about to be lit, when silence descended like a blanket of snow, broken nine heartbeats later by the sound of a lone bagpiper from the base of the Perth Trail. The piper was preceded by a stick-wielding man—the silver-headed stick was called a mace—in full Scottish regalia. His outfit included an imposing furred "bearskin" hat, complete with white horsehair tassels, that increased his normal six-foot height to a towering seven and a half feet. He would lead the procession of kilt-clad men representing every clan in attendance down the trail, around the field, and into a wide ring around the stacked wood. For a number of years now, the drum major leading the procession had been Mr. Stone, one of the most impressive-looking men Harper had ever seen, even when he wore khaki slacks and a polo shirt; but put him in that enormous hat, and he looked not just impressive, but fierce indeed.

He turned to follow Shay and the stranger at a discreet distance, but caught a movement from across the street. Peggy had stepped out of her store to greet a crowd of people ogling the display window. Ten to one that dog had climbed onto the ottoman they kept there for him. He was the best advertisement the ScotShop could hope for.

As Harper watched, Peggy gestured everyone inside. He hoped she'd make a lot of sales today.

By the time he looked back up the street, Shay and the man were out of sight.

Not a problem. Harper's orders were to keep the fellow in sight but not to approach him. They'd probably gone into Cameron's.

But they hadn't. Inside the hardware store, he listened for the sound of dog toenails on the creaky old wooden floor. He listened for customers clucking and cooing over the cute little canine. He peered down each aisle, hoping beyond hope that his quarry was sequestered behind one of the tall shelf units. All the hope in the world, though, couldn't make the man in the mug shot materialize. Harper had lost him and was going to have to answer to the Secret Service.

Harper couldn't understand what Shay had to do with this mess. Maybe it was just a coincidence? He checked his watch. The agents should have been there by now. He hoped Mac wouldn't alienate the agent in charge too much.

Mac would either storm or grovel. Either way, it would be irritating.

I stopped to help a woman find the right clan tie for her boss back in Connecticut, who was, as she said, "very proud of his Scot heritage." A few months ago I wouldn't have known which tie to sell her, and I would have had to ask my ghost, but I'd found a chart online that listed Scottish names in one column and the clan to which they belonged in the second column. I'd printed it and had the pages laminated. When she told me his last name was Gillespie, I sold her a Macpherson. Easy as pie, although I had no idea where that saying had come from, since the pies I'd tried to make over the years had all turned out to be disasters. But at least with this chart I didn't have to rely so much on Dirk to keep me straight.

"Isn't there a Gillespie clan?"

"Not a Scottish one. As far as I know, Clan Gillespie is an Irish clan. If your employer is Scot, then he's in Clan Macpherson."

Next, a middle-aged woman wanted to know why ghillie brogues had no tongues. I held one of the narrow shoes and turned it from one side to the other, wondering how to answer her. I'd never thought much about it. "Simplicity of design," I finally said. She seemed satisfied and urged her husband to try them on.

Beside me, Dirk lifted a foot and studied his sturdy handcrafted boots. "I dinna see for why any the one would wear such triffle traffle. Yon wee shoon are nae built to last."

"They're primarily dress shoes," I explained to the woman—and to my ghost. "They're meant to be worn with the formal kilt."

"Can't see wearing them any other time," her husband chimed in. "They're not very comfortable."

"They should be. Maybe you need a different size."

Once that was settled and I'd sold the couple two complete Highland outfits—one for him and one for her—I got caught up in a flurry of incoming customers. I couldn't believe how many people asked if I sold bagpipes. Nobody had asked for months, and now a dozen or so wanted to know. When I first opened the ScotShop, I used to waste a lot of time explaining how bagpipes couldn't be learned quickly. People had to start by learning to play the chanter before they ever dealt with the actual bag. Unfortunately, people's eyes generally glazed over before I made it to explaining the drones, the long "pipes" that stuck up from the bag. Those were what created the constant underlying notes that never changed—was that where the phrase *he droned on and on* came from? I finally got smart and ordered a store copy of the Green Book, which is what the standard piper's bible was always called. When I showed it to potential pipers, it scared most of them away. I supplied the ones who seemed serious with the URLs of several really good bagpiper stores, and—during the Games at least—I always reminded them of the piper's tent down in the meadow.

It was funny that a Scot-themed tourist town like Hamelin didn't have a bagpipe store. On the other hand, there probably wouldn't have been enough of a demand to cover the overhead a storeowner would have to pay. For a product like bagpipes, an online store made more sense.

And Porter Macnaughton, one of the best pipers in the Northeast, gave lessons. I thought of Shoe and his lum-thingies—what had Dirk called them? I did know Porter had started Shoe with the Green Book a couple of years ago, but it sounded to me like Shoe still had a long way to go. Why was I not surprised? Practicing regularly was a novel idea that Shoe didn't seem to have absorbed, unless it was practicing baseball—that he'd do in a heartbeat.

Dirk, of course, had never seen a copy of the Green Book, since he'd been born in 1329, well before the printing press was invented. He peered carefully over the shoulder of one particularly obnoxious man in a bright plaid Windbreaker who seemed determined to read the entire book while his wife waited anxiously. "What," Dirk asked, "would be a semiquaver?" Apparently musical notation wasn't a lesson he'd learned in the fourteenth-century Highlands. Music scores might not have been invented yet. I had no idea.

The man brushed at his ear, almost as if Dirk's breath had tickled him.

I turned away to answer a customer's question about kilt pins. A few moments later, Dirk's voice rang out. "Ye canna take the wee book, without ye pay for it, ye miswenden manny."

I spun around in time to see the man withdraw his hand from the front of his jacket. "That's a store copy, sir," I said quietly, so as not to disturb other customers.

He put on an affronted air and spread his Windbreaker open. "I don't know what you're talking about."

"It isna in his coat," Dirk informed me before I could apologize in the face of the man's obvious innocence. "He gave it to the wee woman to hide in her—" He pointed to the oversized handbag slung over the woman's shoulder.

I held out my hand to the wife. "Thanks for returning it without creating a scene," I told her. Before she or her husband could claim otherwise, I said, "I wouldn't want to call in the constable." Good grief. Dirk's language was invading the twenty-first century. "The cost of a new book, with a CD to accompany it, is less than thirty-five dollars. I assure you, the fine for shoplifting is considerably higher than that." I kept my voice pitched low. "If you return it now, I won't press charges." My tone—and my expression—told them that if they didn't, I would.

"What would be 'shop lifting'?"

Hush, Dirk, I thought. This was no time for me to play dictionary.

The husband still looked like he was going to try to get away with it. "I have a witness," I said, a spur-of-the-moment inspiration.

"There's nobody close enough," he said, and his wife cringed. Most likely it hadn't occurred to him that his comment was an admission of guilt.

"Hidden camera." I couldn't very well say *hidden ghost*.

The woman glanced at her husband and sheepishly withdrew the book.

Dirk and I ushered them out of the store, although they weren't aware of the ghostly half of their escort. I wondered yet again if there was any way I could hire Macbeath Donlevy Freusach Finlay Macearachar Macpheidiran of

Clan Farquharson. There weren't any employment forms with a long enough blank for his full name. No wonder I'd opted to call him Dirk. Anyway, his first name had enjoyed a truly cruddy connotation ever since Shakespeare, and I couldn't very well call him Mac—that was the Hamelin police chief's first name. Dirk sure was handy to have around, though, no matter what I called him.

As we returned from the front door, I smiled at him and whispered, "You're a darn sight better than a security camera." He sketched a brief bow, which necessitated his having to adjust the fall of his plaid over his shoulder. I couldn't blame him for looking a bit smug.

Then he sidled up beside me. "What would be a *sakoority kamra*?"

3

Stay, and speak.
ACT 1, SCENE 1

Although Andrea Stone, my former best friend, hadn't darkened the threshold of the ScotShop ever since that day last year when I'd found her in, shall we say, a compromising situation with my former almost-fiancé, that didn't mean she'd phased completely out of my life. This was too small a town for that to be possible.

Now, of course, with the excitement of opening day, Andrea, a would-be reporter, seemed to be everywhere. That wasn't fair of me; she *was* a reporter. Of sorts. She had some kind of news blog. She did human-interest spots for a local radio station, only I didn't think they were very interesting. Of course, I might have been a wee bit biased against her. She had a regular column, which I tried to ignore, in the *Hamelin Piper*, our town newspaper, complete with a prominent photo of herself. Why hadn't I ever noticed how self-serving she was?

Right at the moment she was interviewing somebody in the courtyard. She'd bought a little handheld recording device. I could see her reach down and adjust it every once in a while.

"For why are ye standing here gazing through the window?"

"Uh . . . I'm just looking around."

Dirk looked from me to Andrea and back at me. He lowered his voice. I'm not sure why he ever does that. Nobody else can hear him. "Who is yon woman, and why d'ye study her sae oft?"

"I don't . . ."

"Excuse me?" A rather stout man in an unfortunate pair of khaki shorts stopped beside me and peered through thick glasses. "You don't what?"

I cleared my throat. "I, uh, don't see anyone helping you. Could I be of service? Were you looking for anything in particular?"

"If ye would stop dithering, Mistress Peggy, mayhap he could answer ye."

I gave that unfair comment the attention it deserved, which is to say absolutely none. But I *did* grind to a stop.

"Yes, well, now that you mention it, I was rather hoping to find something to do with Clan Forrester. For my wife."

A scarf, I thought. *All he'll want is a scarf.*

"You wouldn't happen to have one of those long skirts . . ." His voice faded.

I brightened considerably and reminded myself not to

make negative assumptions based on what people were wearing. "Yes," I said, motioning him to follow me, but he stared past me, out the window.

"Look! Is that Andrea Stone? Her column is a favorite of mine. I recognize her from her picture." He adjusted the rather limp collar of his polo shirt. "I'll, uh, I'll be back later."

I watched him almost stumble in his haste to get out the door, across the pavement, and down the two shallow steps into the courtyard.

I turned my back on the window and went to help some real customers.

Silla pranced beside her person. She did not like the other one, but she enjoyed the walk along the winding streets. She tried not to listen to the two people. When they moved between two houses, left the buildings behind, and entered the forest path, she fairly quivered with excitement. This was a new place, one she had never seen before.

"Okay, you win," her person said, and Silla heard the sadness in his voice. "But after that, I want you to leave us alone."

Us. That was right. Silla and her person. *Us.*

Silla wanted that other person to go away.

"You don't have to worry about that," that person said. "I never want to see you again. Not after what you did to *her.*"

Silla looked around. To who? She didn't see another *her* anywhere. Only an empty path.

Her person looked at that shiny thing on his hand and

then he reached into the place where he kept Silla's treats. Silla's ears perked up, but all her person took out was that other thing he kept with the treats. Silla had tried to chew on it once when he left the little bag on his bed, but he had taken it away from her.

"Here they are," her person said. "And I never want to have to deal with you again."

The other person said something, but Silla had lost interest as soon as her person closed the treat holder. She saw a squirrel cross the path up ahead, so she ignored all the rest of the words.

Harper turned left outside the hardware store and headed uphill into the residential area, moving slowly, hoping to look like he was out for a leisurely stroll. He wasn't wearing a uniform. That would help, but people who were on the run often had a finely tuned radar for spotting cops. He'd learned that when he worked undercover in Poughkeepsie.

He'd already passed a dozen houses when he remembered the apartments above the hardware store. Would they have gone upstairs? He knew Shoe lived in one unit and Sam in another, but had no idea who rented the other two.

A quick phone check with Martin Cameron, owner of Scotsman Hardware, which everyone in town called Cameron's, quashed that idea. Both units were empty. And locked.

So, where had Shay taken the tall man? Did she live up here in one of these quiet-looking houses?

Moira would know. Moira, the Southern-born dispatcher, not only knew everybody in Hamelin—she knew what most of them ate for breakfast and who was carrying on with whom. Harper had no idea how she came by all her information, but she was certainly a handy person to have in the station.

She answered with that drawl he loved. "Hamelin Po-leece. What kin ah do fur yew?"

"It's Harper. Where does Shay Burns live?"

She paused for only a moment. Harper could almost hear her counting. "Third house," she said. "Third above Cameron's on the same side of the street; it's beige with dark blue shutters. Next to that empty lot. You want her cell number?"

"Please."

He called. No answer.

At the blah-colored house, nobody responded to his knock.

I took a quick look around to be sure nobody was close enough to hear me answer yet another of Dirk's questions. It sure would be convenient if Dirk could read my mind. Then I considered some of the things I thought about on a regular basis. *Cancel that wish.* It was worth it for him to have to hear me out loud. "No, Dirk, shoplifting isn't all that common. At least not here in the ScotShop. We don't usually attract the thieving sort."

"How would ye know, if ye didna see them? If I had nae told ye what those twa did, ye wouldna ha' known 'til 'twas too late."

"I would have noticed. Just not fast enough to have stopped them." I headed toward a skewed hanger on the skirt rack.

He looked at me. He seemed expectant about something.

"You're right, Macbeath. I haven't thanked you."

"I am right pleased ye used my proper name for the once, but I didna expect any thanks."

"Thanked me?" A woman's head peeked over the low-hanging rack of Fair Isle sweaters. "For what?" She raised herself—it looked like she'd been kneeling. "And how did you know my name?"

"Your name?"

"Mary Beth. I don't think we've ever met."

Dirk chuckled. I ignored him. "What were you doing on the floor? Are you okay?"

"My tennis shoe laces were too tight." She stepped from behind the rack and rotated an ankle experimentally. "Much better."

"Can I help you find anything?"

"I need a scarf or something. This is the first time I've been to the Highland Games, and I didn't realize how underdressed I'd feel not wearing plaid."

"Don't worry. It's not required. I'm sure you've seen plenty of people not wearing tartans." I couldn't remember seeing many, come to think of it, except for that short guy who was fixated on Andrea and the husband and wife who'd looked at the necklace.

"I think I might have some Scottish family way back when."

"Do ye no ken your family?" Dirk sounded aghast.

"What's your last name? Maybe I can help you figure it out."

"Armstrong?"

Wasn't she sure? It sounded more like a question than a statement. "Let's go look at the clan chart. I'm not sure—"

Dirk interrupted me. "Armstrong would be Clan Fairbairn."

"But," I adjusted my sentence with the ease of long practice, "I think maybe your family is in the Fairbairn clan."

"Really? You sure are knowledgeable."

"It helps to have a—" I couldn't very well say *a ghost.* "It helps to have a chart to look at frequently. I guess the names sort of sink in eventually." I lifted the laminated chart and pulled it to the length of its light chain. After having had three of them misplaced, lost—okay, stolen— I'd resorted to attaching this one permanently to its wall rack. I hated having to do that.

Mary Beth eyed the chain. "Are you afraid somebody will take it?"

"If it's not attached, I can never find it," I said.

Dirk harrumphed.

We located her clan, which was indeed Fairbairn, and a lovely green tartan scarf. After she paid for it, I removed the tag for her and watched as she wound it around her ponytail. "I hope you'll come back to the ScotShop soon."

"Sure." She flipped the tail of the scarf forward over her shoulder. "You still haven't told me how you knew my name."

She hadn't forgotten.

Scamp, with impeccable timing, let out a low *woof,*

and Mary Beth bent and held out her hand for him to sniff. "I love your dog."

"He's not mine." I could hear a wistful tone in my own voice. "Scamp belongs to my assistant manager. His job is official greeter." I beckoned to a nearby man who held a stack of merchandise. "I can help you here, sir." Mary Beth moved out of the way. I met so many people so briefly, and then they were gone.

Once I'd finished ringing up that hefty sale, Dirk stepped behind the counter. "Have ye noticed that yon wee doggie seems to ken whenever ye dinna care to answer a question?"

I nodded. I couldn't say anything, what with a line of customers waiting to pay, but Dirk was right. Scamp always seemed to break in at just the right moment. Uncanny. I wished, yet again, that I had a Scottie of my own.

Harper checked Shay's backyard. Fenced in, no lock on the gate, no guard dog, no noticeable alarm system. Back door locked. Curtains open. Lights off.

He might as well give up. Go back to the station. Take his licks for having lost the guy.

He let himself out through the side gate and noticed a well-trod path leading across the empty lot beside Shay's house. It disappeared into the woods. No harm in giving it a try. They could very well have come this way.

He hadn't gone far when he spotted the relatively fresh, unmistakable calling card of a small dog off to one side of the path between two low clumps of woodland shrub. So, they'd passed by here recently.

But when the path forked, Harper couldn't tell which way Shay and the mug shot guy—and the dog—had gone. The ground along that stretch was stony in both directions, and he couldn't find a single footprint or paw print. He consulted his inner eeny-meeny-miny-moe and headed to his left.

4

How weary, stale, flat, and unprofitable.
ACT 1, SCENE 2

Sergeant Marti Fairing's mouth watered as the smell of grilled sausage wafted past her nose. She felt vulnerable without her duty belt, but the chief didn't want the man targeted by this operation to be scared off by a blue uniform. Even without her uniform, she found herself occasionally holding her arms akimbo, the way she'd learned to hold them to avoid bruising the inside of her arm on the butt of her weapon or brushing into any one of the half a dozen items she carried around her waist on a daily basis. Today her pistol was in an ankle holster under her wide-legged pants, but with that as her only resource, she felt . . . undressed. She watched, hoping she looked like an idle bystander, as dozens of tourists poured into the meadow through the flower-bedecked arches at the end of the path from town. The mug shot hadn't been that clear.

How was she supposed to spot one person in this horde? It would only get worse, too, once the scheduled events started. Of course, by then there'd be dozens of agents milling through the crowds.

She smiled to think that the agents hadn't caught the guy. They'd had to ask the Hamelin cops for help. She bet that stuck in somebody's gullet.

A group of musicians, most of them laden with small cases for violins or flutes, arrived and headed for the bandstand close to the path. One of their fellows brought up the rear, carrying a bulky bass violin. Why would anyone ever take up such an unwieldy instrument? Of course, a good bass player slapping those low notes could get feet tapping like nobody else.

The cop part of her brain wondered if maybe they had a rifle hidden in one of the cases. Maybe one of the fiddlers was the one they should be questioning. Maybe she was paranoid, seeing danger in everyone who walked into the meadow. Still, as a police officer, she was trained to look for the possibles before they became problems. Two fiddles, a couple of flutes, and a stringed bass. Too many places to hide a weapon. But none of them looked like the guy in the mug shot.

Without really thinking about it, she checked for abandoned backpacks near the stand. That's where the president would be in a few hours, and the tragedy at the 1996 Olympics was etched into every police officer's memory.

The musicians climbed up on the stand, shoved the chairs out of the way, and pulled out their instruments. Music wasn't on the schedule. Heck, the schedule hadn't even started yet. But the musicians began to play a lively reel. Sergeant Fairing felt her toes begin to tap, seemingly of their own accord. She looked around at the smiles. She noted the dollar bills being tossed into the conveniently placed open case at the front of the platform. Smart musicians.

Marti applauded when the music ended. She did a quick pivot, checking out who was where. She noticed a man, one of the wandering musicians, she supposed, disappearing into the woods near the old Sutherland place. Hadn't he seen the Porta Potties? There were three different lines of them. No excuse for anyone to look for a tree. She shrugged. Some men couldn't resist the chance to water the landscape. Her brothers were like that, peeing off the back porch just for the fun of it. It drove her mother nuts, but Dad thought it was funny.

She checked her watch. The agent who'd called Mac was probably already here. She'd meet him soon enough. And his backup people. The Hamelin force was ready, though. And wouldn't it be great if she could spot the guy in the mug shot first?

It wasn't even ten thirty yet, and I was already running short of ones and fives. Some days everybody paid with plastic. Other days, like today, cash ran rampant, and nobody seemed to have anything smaller than a twenty. I hated to go by the bank; this time of day there'd be a long line. Oh well, it wouldn't hurt to make a quick run home, where I tried to keep a good stash of smaller bills.

I waited until Gilda finished a sale and told her where I was going.

"I will go wi' ye," Dirk said. "Ye needna be roaming about the wee town w' money for the taking."

"I'll be perfectly safe," I said.

"I know that," Gilda told me.

"If someone would try to thieve a wee green book, would they no be tempted more by—"

I interrupted him. "Right. We'll be back soon."

"We?"

Whoops. "Sorry, Gilda. I meant, *I'll* be back soon." I bent to scratch beneath Scamp's chin.

"Guard the shop weel, wee doggie," Dirk admonished him. Scamp made a sound halfway between a woof and a growl.

Gilda made a hand signal. "Hush, Scamp. What's gotten into you?"

"Maybe he's saying good-bye," I suggested.

"Mayhap he was agreeing to do as I asked," Dirk said.

The sunken courtyard between the ScotShop and the Logg Cabin was filled with what looked like a family reunion. Adults of two or three generations sat on the benches, while children overflowed the rest of it. A block farther on, the street was empty. That wasn't surprising. Although tourists overran the town every year, most of them avoided the residential areas, except for those places where townsfolk rented out rooms. Hickory Lane was always fairly quiet, though.

My elderly neighbor greeted me from his front porch. "Did you decide to take the day off?"

"Just picking up some supplies," I called back. "Why aren't you down at the Games?"

"I was. I came home to have an early lunch."

A bowl of Wheaties. That, I knew, was what he usually ate. No wonder he was skinny as a fence post. "There's some wonderful food in the meadow."

"I know. I'll indulge tomorrow. Would you like me to mow your . . . uh . . . grass this afternoon?"

Poor Mr. Pitcairn. He'd been about to say *weeds*. Or maybe *jungle*. He kept offering to mow, and I kept refusing. I loved my expanse of wildflowers and bumblebee-friendly weeds. Dandelions ran rife throughout my yard; the bright yellow flowers always looked so happy. Luckily the direction of the prevailing breeze blew the puffy seeds away from Mr. P's yard. He would have had conniptions if all those seed heads ended up on his pristine lawn.

I laughed my refusal and headed up the ramp.

Mac paced the police station's large front room. He knew the Secret Service—or maybe the FBI—would be showing up at any moment. He planned to be the first one to greet them. Never knew when they might be hiring. He had a lot of years of policing under his belt. Experience, that's what counted. They could probably use a good steady man like him. He shifted his duty belt to relieve some of the pressure against his hip. It had bothered him ever since he broke his leg last winter. But that wouldn't make a bit of difference in how he could carry out his duties in the White House. Maybe he wouldn't mention his leg on the application form. He'd just stride right up to that agent when he walked in.

No, maybe it would be better if Moira had to call him. He could wait in his office. Nothing wrong with seeming like he'd been busy.

Maybe he should be out on the street looking for this guy the agents were hunting. No, he was the Chief—in his mind, the capital letter was automatic.

He walked back into his office and shut the door. Opened it. Shut it. Closed the venetian blinds on the window to the squad room. Opened them. Closed them.

I opened the bottom drawer of my desk and pulled out a small metal cash box. I usually bundled the bills into fifty-dollar stacks so I wouldn't have to count them out each time I needed some.

Dirk made a disapproving sound. "Ye think such a wee box is a good hiding place? A wean could find it."

"I don't have many weans running around my house," I said. This was an old argument between us, and he hadn't convinced me yet. "I lock the doors whenever I leave. You know that."

"Ye didna used to."

"That was before." Before the disturbing events of last summer. But I didn't want to think about that. I wrapped the money in a legal-sized sheet of paper and tucked it into the cloth bag suspended from my heavy black belt. Much more convenient than a purse. "See? Perfectly safe."

"Unless a cutpurse comes upon ye."

I shortened the string so the bag wouldn't bang against my knees and draped the plaid folds of my arisaidh over it. "Is that better? Does it meet with your approval?"

He nodded grudging agreement and we left the house. He paused outside the front door, blocking my way.

"What's wrong? Why did you stop?"

"Ye didna lock the door."

Oh. "Sorry."

He opened his mouth, but apparently decided not to berate me.

I turned around and locked up.

When we reached the ScotShop, I opened the door and waited for Dirk to precede me, but he stopped. "I will go to the wee meadow to look for Clan Farquharson."

"That's a good idea," I muttered, careful not to move my lips too much in case somebody was watching me. "I'll be down there later. Have a good time."

I waited, pretending to study the display window, but I was actually watching the swing of Dirk's kilt as he strode down Main Street. His shoulder-length black hair always seemed to be moving slightly, even when he was standing still, as if a fourteenth-century breeze stirred his locks, but when he walked, his hair really swayed, the same way his kilt did. I shook myself and walked into my shop. He was a ghost, for crying out loud. Nothing could ever happen with a ghost. But then I remembered that time I'd cried in his arms. I sighed. And then there was Harper. *As if anything would ever happen there.*

Eventually the path turned from the hard stone outcropping back to soft earth, and Harper realized his eeny-meeny compass had led him astray. He'd taken the wrong fork. He retraced his steps, considered trying the other path, but decided they had too big a lead on him. Better to head back into town. The big guy—and certainly the dog—couldn't hide indefinitely.

Meanwhile, he'd have to let someone know about the possible involvement of Shay Burns. Just in case.

He wondered if Moira might have an insight into what was going on. You never knew what that woman had tucked under the reach of her bright red fingernails.

He stopped and pulled out his phone to make a note. He'd just remembered that Amy had called him about a surprise birthday party she'd planned for her husband. Harper's brother. How long had it been since they'd talked?

5

This above all: to thine own self be true.
ACT 1, SCENE 3

Moira Pettis kept an eye on the front door, the phone, the computer, the officers, the chief, everything that moved, and a lot that didn't. She smiled to herself as Mac's door—and then his blinds—did a little dance. She couldn't blame him for being nervous. It wasn't every day the feds moved in on a small town. Wasn't every day the president came to visit, either.

If anybody from Washington came for a visit, though, she'd rather have had it be her nephew Russell Fenton. He'd left Cuthbert, their small hometown in southern Georgia, twenty-five years ago, about the same time she had, and all she'd known of him since then was from his chatty letters about the quiet life he lived in the nation's capital. He worked in a bank or something—he'd never been too specific, but then Moira hadn't been too specific about what sort of job she'd gotten. Her bootlegger relatives wouldn't appreciate her working with the enemy. Better they thought she owned a fabric store.

She pulled open her top right-hand drawer, careful not to nick her red polish, and removed a framed photo. She balanced it on the clutter of notepads, pencils, call sheets, phone directories, paper clips, and maps that constituted her daily work environment. Ignoring the mess, she studied her family. Her whole family. Her parents, grandparents, all the siblings, nieces and nephews, everybody lined up in front of the high school on Russell's graduation day. He sure did look like his daddy. She compared that picture to the latest one he'd sent her last Christmas; she'd stuck it in the corner of the frame. Russell, two and a half decades older, in front of a Christmas tree. No wife, no kids, not even a dog. She sure did hope he liked the bank, since he didn't seem to have too much else going on. Of course, who was she to talk? No husband, no kids, and no dog, either.

She still had the picture in her hand when the front door opened and the photo came to life.

"Aunt Moira?"

What happened to his Southern accent? "Russell?"

"What are you doing"—he looked around him—"here?"

"I could ask you the same thing." Only she didn't have to ask. The careful dark blue suit, the subdued tie, the hint of a wire dropping from his ear and disappearing into his collar. She unhooked her headset and stood to embrace him. "So this is your bank job, huh?"

He hugged her back and swept his gaze around the station again. "Nice sewing shop you've got here."

"There's usually a lot of dark blue fabric around this place." She smiled when he chuckled.

Over his shoulder she saw the blinds on Mac's office door part. "Uh-oh. We've been discovered."

"We could always keep people guessing, don't you think?"

"Moira!" Mac's voice boomed across the open space. "What do you think you're doing?"

"Why"—she increased her drawl to maximum ooziness— "ah'm jest makin' shore this little ole agent feels raht welcome hyeah."

Mac scowled, and Moira felt her nephew's shoulder shake with suppressed laughter as he turned to meet the Hamelin police chief.

This was looking to be one of our most successful Games. Gilda had already sold three full kilt outfits this morning, and I'd sold two to the man and his wife who asked about the ghillie brogues and, of course, the one for the governor. I gave a quick look around. The shelves seemed to be pretty well stocked, no empty places I could spot. "I'm going to run down to the meadow and check on the booth. They may need some change, too." Gilda nodded, and I headed for the door. "I have my cell. Call me if you get an inrush."

"Don't we wish," she said.

Gilda had a tendency to worry too much. We'd been pleasantly busy, although at the moment there weren't many people in the shop.

"If I were you," Sam said, "I'd take a few minutes to

check out all the booths down there. You might not have another chance once the Games open officially."

"You sound like a tour guide," I told him. "But I may take a quick turn around the place."

Scamp barked from his ottoman throne, and I'd swear it sounded like *good-bye*.

I glanced over at the Logg Cabin before I turned to my left to head down to the meadow. Six tables filled with people sat outside under the wide overhang of the roof. Whenever had Karaline thought about outside dining?

In the meadow, nothing official was going on, of course, but that didn't mean nothing was going on. I decided to make the circle first and end up at the ScotShop Tartan Tie booth at the end of the circuit. Scarves and ties had always been a big seller during the Games, and they were easy to display in the tent. I turned to my right after I went through the flower-covered arch, but I glanced the other way and was happy to see money exchanging hands. Another tie sale, another boost to staying in business.

Dirk must have seen me enter the grounds. By the time I spotted him, he was striding straight toward me. I'm always faintly surprised at the way crowds of people simply move aside in front of him, as if they're encountering an unseen wave of energy. And nobody's ever aware of doing it. They just veer slightly off course and converge again once he's passed by.

"Are ye enjoying the sights?"

Nobody was close enough to hear me, so I answered him. "I just got here, but it looks like everyone's happy."

He turned and walked with me. "Aye. There is much laughter and many smiles."

"Did you have events like this back when you were alive?"

"Och, aye. We had market days that were something like this. And for certes, the Gatherings."

I could hear the awe with which he said that word. "They must have been wonderful." I was about to ask him to tell me about them, but a group of youngsters sidled by, eyeing me doubtfully. No wonder. I'd been talking to myself out loud. Or so they must have thought.

Dirk didn't need any encouragement, though. "'Twas at a Gathering I first saw my Peigi."

Even after 654 years of being dead, Dirk still spoke of her with a gentleness that caught at my heart.

A group of musicians left the stage as we approached it, and a bagpiper mounted the stairs. He pulled a massive amount of air into his lungs and inflated the bags in one big blow. Slapping at the bag and reaching overhead to tune the drones, he received a tentative nod from Dirk. "Aye. This one knows what he is doing."

"He should. That's Porter Macnaughton, the lead piper in the Hamelin Pipe and Drum Corps." I waved at Mr. P, my next-door neighbor, but he didn't see me. He must have headed out as soon as he finished his Wheaties. Wisps of thin pure white hair peeked out from under his light brown-and-blue-plaid tam. I tried to connect the tartan with a particular clan, but couldn't remember. Holyrood, maybe? I'd never seen him wear it before. I wondered where he'd bought it. I sure hoped he'd bought it at the ScotShop.

He was staring in my direction, but he didn't wave back. I looked behind me. Nothing but a slightly plump woman in a long tartan skirt eating a meat pasty, a couple of teenage boys throwing mock punches at each other's shoulders, and three kilt-clad men conferring in a circle.

Silla was delighted with such a long walk. Especially when that other person turned around and went back the way they had come. Then it was just Silla and her person. And squirrels. And bushes to sniff. And deep leaf mold. And the fragrant footprints of raccoons and even a skunk.

Her person's footsteps got slower and slower. When he finally stopped walking altogether, Silla went back and leaned against his leg. Her nose, so full of exciting smells, caught the whiff of sadness. And of pain. And of anger. Silla stood, stretched her legs wide apart, and growled, even though she was not sure what she was growling at.

Her person laughed and reached down to stroke her back. Silla liked that. She liked the fresh happy smell. She liked being able to change her person's unhappy to gladness.

"As long as I have you, Silla," her person said. "As long as I have you, all that other stuff doesn't matter."

Silla could have told him that. If he had asked her.

6

All the noble substance of a doubt.
ACT 1, SCENE 4

Around one o'clock I looked up at a commotion near the front door. Congressman Leonzini, flanked by four burly men—*bodyguards, not aides*, I thought, and the word *goons* came to mind—swept through my store, shaking hands with everyone he encountered. I motioned to Gilda and Sam to keep working and headed toward the throng. "Welcome to the ScotShop, Congressman."

"What kind of name would be *Kongrissmun*?"

Naturally, I ignored Dirk, and Leonzini shook my hand as if I were the only other person in the room, which surprised me. No wonder he kept getting elected, if he could make people feel important with just a handshake. I'd always managed to avoid meeting him during his previous campaign swings. "My good friend the governor said I should stop by here and get a kilt."

Good friend, my foot, I thought.

"He sounds verra sincere," Dirk said. "Too sincere. I dinna trust him."

Neither did I, but this wasn't the time to say anything like that out loud. "Mm-hmm," I said.

Leonzini turned from me and fingered a royal Stewart plaid.

Delusions of grandeur, I thought. That bold red would clash with his hair and skin tones. If he stood next to the governor, who looked elegant in his new brown plaid kilt, the congressman would look garish by comparison, rather like what had happened to Nixon in that infamous TV debate my US history teacher had told us about, only Nixon had looked tired while Kennedy looked fresh. In this case, Leonzini would look like a puffed-up bantam rooster standing next to a panther. If panthers wore brown plaid, that is.

I let him buy it.

Harper looked across the cramped room at Fenton, the agent who stood at the board examining what few puzzle pieces they'd managed to collect. Next to him, Mac groveled. Did he think Fenton would tap him as a Secret Service recruit? Mac was old enough to retire, had a gimpy leg after that accident last winter, and would make a lousy team player. Of all the ridiculous things to wish for. But Harper could see the look of hope on Mac's face.

The duty room had never before felt so stuffed, not when it was just Harper and Fairing and Murphy and maybe two or three others from the Hamelin force working on a case.

But within the last hour the room had filled precipitately when the Secret Service contingent invaded. That's what it felt like. An invasion. Fenton was obviously competent, but he had that indefinable attitude, the one that said agents trump locals any day.

Still, Harper thought, *you couldn't pay me enough to want to work Secret Service.* Harper didn't want the safety of the president hanging over his head. The president who had decided on a whim to visit the opening night of the Hamelin Highland Games. He'd attended the Hamelin Games once when he was a kid and thought it might be fun to show up unannounced. While he was here, he'd probably do a little campaigning for Leonzini, who was running for his fourth term.

The only trouble was, a guy suspected of having sent threatening letters to the president had been spotted at the Burlington airport. Somehow he'd evaded the agents who tried to apprehend him. Harper would be willing to bet they'd played their hand too soon at the airport, moving in to corral him while they were still too far away and giving him plenty of time to slip out of their noose and disappear.

But who was he to judge? He'd spotted the guy. And lost him.

"Why would somebody who was after the president bring a dog with him?" Harper thought that was a logical question.

Fenton scoffed. "You'd be surprised what sort of nuts are out there. Anybody can have an agenda. Even people with dogs."

"Ayuh," Mac said, and headed toward the men's room.

The phone rang, and Harper was vaguely aware of Moira's voice. *Hamelin Po-leece.*

Harper had to admit he didn't want the big guy with the dog to be the one Fenton was looking for, partly because Harper didn't want to be the one to have lost track of their only lead. But mostly because—if he were honest with himself, and he tried to be most of the time—the guy looked like Santa, even though his white beard was considerably shorter than Santa's pictures always showed—and who'd want to arrest Kris Kringle?

He looked around the room. If push came to shove, that agent over there at the round table could just as easily be the fellow in the mug shot. Tall, sandy-haired with streaks of a lighter blond at the temple, square face, wide shoulders. A heavy five-o'clock shadow, even this early in the day, gave him the look of someone with a blond beard.

Fenton pointed to a rectangle on the big wall map. "What's this place?"

"A lovely old empty house," Harper said. "Three stories and an attic, in pretty good shape. Local lore says it's haunted. People who buy it usually put it back on the market within two or three months. Hard to believe. It's one of the finest old houses in town. There's nothing inside to steal, and I guess somebody got tired of replacing broken locks, so they don't ever lock the doors."

Fenton traced an imaginary line from the house to the spot where the president would be speaking. "Great place for a sniper, then, wouldn't you say? He could be there already—or he might have made some preparations." He eyed the two agents sitting at the round table. "Check it out." They abandoned their Pepsi cans, opened and almost full, took a quick glance at the map, and left the room. "Try not to give yourselves away this time,"

Fenton said to their departing backs as Mac returned from the john and Moira disconnected the call.

A few minutes later, there was an unexpected lull. Gilda herded one of the temps, the one who'd worked for me a number of times in the past, into the storeroom. Within moments he reappeared, his arms full, and began replenishing the stock. I decided to take advantage of the quiet. "I'm headed to the Cabin for a quick lunch. I'll eat as fast as I can."

"We can handle it." Gilda's curls wiggled as she gave a quick survey of the room. "Oh, by the way, I wrote you a note to reorder paisley scarves. We're a little low on the red ones and we only have one green left."

It always amazed me how people seemed to buy in lumps. One month it would be nothing but blue kilts, and the next everybody wanted red. This past spring I couldn't keep enough brown paisley scarves on hand, but here it was August, and everybody seemed to want green. "Thanks for keeping up with details like that, Gilda. I sure do appreciate you." It was her job, but I'd been trying to show my appreciation more, ever since she'd returned from the rehab facility.

She beamed, which only served to reaffirm that I was on the right track.

"I'll sit at one of the outside tables if I can," I said. "If I see a flood of customers, I'll get a doggie bag."

The day was still a little brisk, so I lifted my plaid around my shoulders as I stepped outside. Across the small courtyard, Big Willie sat at one of Karaline's outdoor tables. I headed their way. "Mind if I join you two?" I bent and scratched Silla under her hairy chin.

Willie stood and pulled out a chair for me. "I'd be delighted."

Dolly appeared at my elbow. "The usual?"

I laughed. "You know me too well."

She filled a coffee cup and placed it in front of me. "I saw you coming and already put in your order."

"What if I'd changed my mind?"

"Hasn't ever happened yet."

Willie watched her walk away. "What's this *usual* she referred to?"

"I love breakfast for lunch. Of course, I eat it for breakfast, too, when I'm here at the Cabin. Maple pancakes with extra-crispy bacon. Nothing better."

Silla made a muffled sound, as if she agreed with me.

I unfolded my napkin. "Have you been down to the meadow yet today?"

It looked like a shadow crossed his face, but maybe it was only my imagination. Or his trim beard. "I was . . . detained."

Shay. He must have been referring to his run-in with Shay.

"That's too bad," I said. "I like to see what I can before the crowds get too thick."

This time I was sure of the shadow. "You have many years ahead of you to do that. For me, though . . ." His voice trailed away to nothing.

Even with all that white hair, he was too young to be thinking about dying, but I didn't know quite how to say that without its being awkward.

Silla let out a little gurgle of protest, and I laughed. "Do you take her with you whenever you travel?"

"Oh, yes. I couldn't leave her alone." He leaned over and scratched Silla's head. "I don't have anyone to leave her with."

That was sad. I waited as Dolly set down our plates. When I went on buying trips to Scotland, I could always count on Karaline to take care of Shorty and water my plants. If she was otherwise occupied, my twin brother was a good backup.

Silla woofed gently.

"Wonder what she's trying to say."

"She's thirsty." He was so matter-of-fact, it sounded like he'd read her mind. Of course, come to think of it, I can usually tell what Shorty's various meows mean.

"Silla and I took a long walk this morning. And I've promised her another one this afternoon—just the two of us this time. I have a lot to think about." He pulled a bottle of water out of a leather pouch he had slung across his body—it reminded me a little bit of the scabbard in which Dirk kept his dagger—and lifted a collapsible bowl from a pocket on the front.

"That's a handy contraption."

"It pays to be prepared when you're traveling with a four-legged companion."

We listened to the *lap-lap-lap* of Silla's little tongue, surprisingly loud in the afternoon air. Between bites—ours, not the dog's—Big Willie filled me in on the padded dog bed he toted with him, the dog seat belt that allowed Silla to look out the car window and still be safe, and the special behind-the-passenger-seat carrier he'd designed for all her dog food.

"Luckily, there are plenty of hotels that allow dogs."

"How long have you had Silla as a companion?"

His brow furrowed. "She was a rescue from a puppy mill. I guess I saved her life, but you could just as well say she saved mine."

"Oh?"

"I went through a really bad spell a few years ago, and Silla came along just in time to pull me out of it." He paused for such a long time, I thought the conversation might have been over. I couldn't think of anything to say. Finally, he sighed. "I wish my wife could have known Silla. And I wish Silla could have known Lorena."

"Lorena? Your wife?"

"Not just my wife. She was the love of my life. Everything's a little grayer since she died."

"I'm so sorry for your loss."

"It's been four years. I still feel bad about not going to her funeral."

He hadn't gone to his wife's funeral? My shock must have registered on my face.

"I couldn't," he said. "I was so broken up after sitting with her day after day, watching her go down like that. Even though she was . . . considerably older than I, she was still far too young to go." He rubbed the flat of his palm along his jawline. "I just fell apart."

"I guess I can understand that," I said.

"I wish a few other people felt the way you do."

I raised my eyebrows, but he didn't elaborate, and I didn't want to push it; his grief still seemed to be so raw.

"After she died, I laid myself down on our bed and hardly got up for three weeks. One of her brothers picked the coffin, her sister planned the service, and they both cursed me to the end of forever. I didn't even care. Not until Silla came along, my brave little trooper."

Trouble was, I could see both sides of the argument. Lorena's siblings must have been the ones he'd mentioned a moment ago—the ones who didn't understand. I wouldn't be surprised. On the other hand, grief could be paralyzing. I studied the piece of bacon I held. "Did your sister-in-law sit with Lorena while she was sick?"

"No," he said slowly. "She was too busy."

"What about her brothers?"

"No. They had their own families."

Armchair psychologist that I was, I had to say, "Then what the heck have they got to complain about?"

I shoveled in a bite of maple pancake, waited a moment until I could swallow, and said, "I was planning to attend the caber toss tomorrow to cheer you on."

He sort of shook himself. "I'd be honored to have you rooting for me." He thought for a moment. "Would you be willing to watch Silla for me while I compete? That way I won't have to leave her in the hotel room."

"I'd be happy to." He thanked me, and we ate the rest of our meal in companionable silence.

He insisted on paying for my lunch. "I like to keep my cheering section happy." He gave a little wave. "See you around ten tomorrow?"

"I'll be there, but I'm sure I'll see you this evening at the opening ceremonies. Bye, Silla."

Big Willie smiled and gave me another friendly wave before he bent to pat his little dog.

7

Something is rotten in the state of Denmark.
ACT 1, SCENE 4

Fairing couldn't stand it any longer. She headed for the Porta Potties. Halfway there, though, she pulled up short. Two guys, one of them a dead ringer for Mr. Mug Shot, strode across the meadow like they owned the place. Made sense. Anyone skulking around would look suspicious, so why not stand up straight and act like you belonged here? Nobody had said anything about two men working together, but she had to stay open to the possibilities. That's what Harper always said.

Look at the structure of the face, she'd learned at the police academy. Cheekbones don't change. She checked this guy's face, the left side. The only side she could see. Yep. Could be. He'd shaved his beard, and cut his hair shorter, but it was still light colored, and she could detect even lighter hair at his left temple.

They were headed toward the piper's stall, a low structure off to one side where the strident sound of bagpipes wouldn't disrupt the main events too much. She followed, staying far enough behind them not to be spotted, but close enough not to lose them. She wasn't surprised when they skirted the pipers and headed straight toward the old Sutherland place. The more she thought about it, the more she was sure she had them. The top floor of that old house was a perfect spot for a sniper to station himself. Without her uniform, without her duty belt, she felt helpless. She was certainly in no position to apprehend a big guy like that alone—and since she knew he had a confederate, she was even less willing to confront them.

Her cell was dead. Damn. She should have checked it. She should have plugged it in last night. She backtracked to where she'd last seen Murphy. He wasn't there, but she found him a few minutes later. "I've got them," she said under her breath. "Two men headed for the Sutherland place."

It didn't take Murphy any time at all to see the possibilities. "Sniper."

Fairing nodded. "Good chance. I'll head back to the piper's stall and keep them in sight. You round up the troops. Tell them to come in from the back."

Murphy headed off toward the path, pulling out his phone as he went.

For just a moment, Fairing considered what might happen if she could sneak up on the men and catch them in the act of setting up a scope mount of some sort.

Murphy stopped, turned around. "Don't do anything stupid."

Mind reader.

* * *

I double-checked that we had enough sets of Urquhart Castle bookends. Those had been a big seller so far this year. Luckily, I'd gotten in a big order just last week. Five sets sitting out, with another set next to Scamp's ottoman in the display window and almost two dozen pairs still in the storeroom. Four of the big coffee-table books, three copies of each in tasteful stacks. We didn't sell a lot of those—the prices were fairly hefty—but they sure looked good. I doubted I'd order any more for a while, though. As I passed by the Fair Isle sweater rack, I couldn't see Scamp's feet peeking out the way they usually did. That meant he was either hiding deeper or else he was out winning friends and influencing buyers—I hoped that was the case.

Sometimes I wondered where I got the energy to get through all these days of the Games. Although the flow of customers tended to ebb and then surge, there was hardly ever a moment when we didn't have a bunch of folks looking at merchandise. Fortunately, a goodly portion of those people who looked ended up buying. Especially during the Games, when shopping seemed to be one of the major goals. With all the different kinds of people who came in, though, we all had to be constantly ready to shift gears. Sometimes we just rang up sales; sometimes we answered questions about everything from how to strap on a *sgian-dubh*—the small knife that fits into the top of the long stockings men wear with their kilts, although for people who'd flown to Vermont for the Games, we had a fake version without a blade so they could make it through airport security—to the geography of Scotland. I'd fastened a detailed topographical map to the back wall near the bookcase, and I can't tell you how many times I pointed out just where the Lowlands ended and the Highlands started. The good news was that most everyone seemed to be in a good mood. This early in the Games, people weren't tired out yet. Sometimes there were people who got cranky by Sunday afternoon.

Gilda was back at the jewelry counter, showing earrings to a group of teenage girls, who seemed to have their squeal-meters tuned to high. Every time one of them held a pair up, the rest would practically gargle in glee. Had I been that silly at that age?

Probably.

Sam seemed to collect the stares of the women shoppers as he walked through the store in one of his favorite kilt sets. He certainly looked imposing, and I smiled at the undercurrent of sighs that followed his progress. I had to admit, though, that I got plenty of admiring comments about my arisaidh. Women coming to the Highland Games either had their own arisaidh, or were primed to buy one. All I had to do was match the right name up to the right pattern of tartan and let the Highland magic in the air do the rest—that and a little judicious coaxing on my part.

I circled the store again. Four bookend sets. Good. We'd sold another one.

Harper didn't want to stand around waiting. "I'll head back out—see if I can spot the guy."

A small muscle lifted at the side of Fenton's mouth. "You're just going to hope you run into him?"

Harper made an almost painful effort to unclench his fist. "In a town this small, it's a possibility."

While he was out, he'd check at the hotel. See if anyone there had seen the fellow. It was about the only place Harper hadn't looked. And he wanted to locate Shay Burns. Maybe he'd see her on the way. Or maybe she and Mug Shot were still together.

Fenton waved him away. Harper gritted his teeth and headed for the Hamelin Hotel. Something about Fenton rubbed him the wrong way. Lots of things about Fenton. Harper didn't like the way he'd taken over. He didn't like the way Fenton looked at Moira, like there was some sort of secret between the two of them. Of course, Moira could take care of herself, but Harper still didn't like it. And that wave of Fenton's hand, like Fenton was the queen of England dismissing an incorrigible subject.

If Harper caught the guy in the mug shot—or even if Fairing or Murphy caught him—maybe Fenton would see the light. See the value of a local crew. But, he reminded himself, it really didn't matter who caught the guy. What mattered was stopping him before he did any damage. Especially to the president.

Harper passed the hotel practically every day for one reason or another, but he seldom paid much attention to the details. Like the elaborate marble cornerstone with *1927* carved in a four-inch font. *What a time to start a new business,* Harper thought. Just a couple of years before the Great Depression hit. He wondered how close, and how often, the hotel had come to closing its doors.

He glanced up at the decorative sign above the imposing entrance. He knew Peggy's woodworking father had
made the sign, but somehow having a bed on one side of
the sign and bagpipes on the other didn't advertise a very
restful stay.

Fairing had to pause as Shay Burns crossed in front of
her. She wondered what Shay would think about the possibility of a presidential assassination attempt. They'd had
quite a long discussion about it at the station when they'd
first learned there might be an assassin in town. Harper
had been in favor of telling Shay, but Fairing and Murphy
had convinced him that she was probably the worst person in the world if one needed a secret kept—well, secret.

Everything she was thinking always showed on her
face. And if Shay looked worried, people would start to
get antsy, and then there was no telling what would happen. The town relied on the reputation of the Hamelin
Highland Games as a fun event, one to bring the family
to. What if people didn't trust that anymore?

But here was Shay Burns looking positively forbidding.
What was she unhappy about? The news of the mug shot
guy couldn't have surfaced. It had to be something else.
But what? When Shay was upset she looked like she'd
just swallowed too big a bite of sauerkraut. Maybe she'd
been turned down by somebody she was trying to charm
out of a big chunk of money for her precious Games.

This wasn't the time to worry about Shay Burns,
though. Marti Fairing had a job to do, keeping her eyes
on the mug shot guy and his buddy—his coconspirator?

How lucky she was to have spotted him. Now, if she could just keep him in sight until backup could get in place.

I hoped Dirk was enjoying the festival. *He must be relieved,* I thought, *to find something in twenty-first century America that is so similar to those Gatherings he's mentioned.*

Of course, thinking about Dirk reminded me of what he'd said. *If I hadna told ye what those twa did, ye wouldna ha' known 'til 'twas too late.* He was right, doggone him. I wouldn't have known. I looked around the shop. People picked up books and ties and scarves. They tried on shirts and sweaters and shoes. They examined bookends and kilt pins and clan badges. Every single person in the room was a potential shoplifter, and I felt woefully inadequate to stop it. To protect myself and my shop. Where was Dirk when I needed him?

A woman with rich chestnut hair nodded at me and smiled. "I love your store," she said. "I come to the Games every year, and I always stop by here."

"That's lovely."

"My whole house—and my closet, too—is full of Scot-Shop merchandise."

"I hope you—" I'd been about to say *I hope you paid for it all.* "I hope you enjoy all of it."

"Oh yes!" She held up a set of a dozen padded hangers, each one with a different plaid pattern on the padded part that clamped together to hold skirts or slacks. I thought they were incredibly hokey, but Gilda had talked me into ordering them, and I was constantly amazed at how many sets of them we sold. "Won't these be perfect for my tartan skirt collection?"

"I should think so." Berating my wild suspicious thoughts, I rang up the sale and wished her a pleasant day. "Come back again."

"Of course." She walked away smiling.

Right behind her was an older woman with a brown paisley scarf in hand. I thought she might have been the woman I'd seen in the meadow earlier, the one eating a Cornish pasty, but I wasn't sure. The way people swirled around town, how could anyone keep track? I rang up the sale, wished her a pleasant day, and smiled at the next person in line. I loved it when business was brisk like this.

Fairing ducked into the shadow of the piper's tent. She nodded briefly to the men gathered around a selection of piping accessories spread out on a green felt cloth, but they hardly noticed her. She was fairly sure none of them would serve as a dependable witness if—when—they caught the two men up ahead.

She watched the two suspects separate to approach the Sutherland house from opposite sides. She lost sight of one when he ducked toward the back. The other one, the one who looked like the mug shot, glanced around as if making sure nobody was watching, then disappeared through the front door.

He hadn't even tried it to see if it was locked. How had he known it was open? Only the locals knew that. So he must have cased the building earlier. Where was Murphy? Couldn't he hurry up?

There! She saw movement. Good. He'd brought plenty of backup. Unfortunately, it looked like Mac was one of them. She sure hoped he'd be quiet.

The high-ceilinged lobby of the Hamelin Hotel still looked like something out of the 1920s with overly elaborate couches squeezed into tight seating areas. All the lamps had off-white shades hung about with loops and doodads. Harper shuddered. Too busy for his taste.

"Ayuh," said the redheaded guy at the front desk, a new hire Harper hadn't seen before. "That could be the fellow in 124, Mr. Bowman. Little black dog?" Harper nodded. "Cute little thing," the clerk continued. "That's why he wanted a ground floor room on the back." He took another look at the mug shot. "Doesn't do him justice. The hair's not the same, either, and the beard's a little different. I'm not even sure it's the same guy, but"—he tapped the photo—"if you say this guy's in town, then it must be him."

I didn't say that, Harper thought. "Thanks. Know if he's in?"

"Saw him leave a couple of hours ago. He could have come back." He reached for the desk phone. "I can give him a call."

Harper held up a hand. "I'd rather you didn't."

The clerk's eyes got very round. "Oooh." He pointed. "His room's that way if you want to check. It's right next to the back entrance. So he can take the dog out to do its business, you know. We put extra insulation for sound-proofing around the first three rooms on that hall; that's where we put the people with dogs. Or the ones who look like they'll be partying half the night. That way nobody can hear the barks. Or the shouts."

Harper nodded his thanks, put a finger to his lips, and headed for the hallway the clerk had indicated. As he turned the corner, he glanced back and saw the young man elaborately zipping his mouth shut.

I watched Scamp disengage himself from a trio of women whose oohs and aahs sounded like a flock of doves. Usually he was perfectly happy being fawned over. I wondered what was different with this group.

But then I heard his medium-loud *woof* and knew what the problem was. Gilda recognized it, too. She spotted me. Pointed toward Scamp, back at herself, and at the door to the back room. Scamp needed to go out. The alley behind the shop had a convenient grassy verge. I nodded and waved them on their way. I loved the clarity of sign language.

When they returned—Scamp was fast—she waited for me to complete a sale. "I sold another complete kilt set," she said. "Just before you rang up those bookends."

"That's great, Gilda." I really meant it. We sold a lot of ties and scarves and shawls, but someone who bought a complete kilt set—which meant not only the kilt itself, but shirt, jacket, hose with flashes and sgian-dubh, ghillie brogues, belt, and sporran (was I forgetting anything?)—sometimes took less time than a customer trying to decide whether to buy a tie and a scarf or a set of bookends and a pair of earrings. And there was no comparison at all when it came to considering the cash flow. Gilda had gotten very good lately at encouraging the larger sales without being at all pushy about it. "What does that make? Have you sold four so far today?"

She nodded, setting her blond curls to bobbing. Her head wasn't shaking. Her hands looked steady. Her eyes were clear. She narrowed them, her usual response when I studied her. I tried not to do it too often, but I wondered when I'd get to the point where I felt like I didn't have to keep checking. I was glad she'd gone to rehab when she needed it. I wish I hadn't been so blind to the symptoms of her drinking for so long.

Scamp, who had appeared next to us, let out a happy *whiffle*, as if he agreed with my thought. *What a silly idea*, I told myself. *Dogs can't read minds*. He shook himself and headed toward his ottoman in the front window.

"I'm really glad you brought Scamp into the ScotShop, Gilda. He makes a marvelous store mascot, and I think he must be good luck."

She nodded again, but still looked a bit suspicious of my scrutiny.

8

If circumstances lead me, I will find
where truth is hid.
ACT 2, SCENE 2

Harper listened at the door before he knocked. Bowman had to be there. The plastic sign hanging from the doorknob read *Do Not Disturb*. Harper weighed the instructions—he wasn't completely sure Bowman was the suspect. But if Bowman was planning to take a shot at the president, Harper couldn't take that chance. He could always take Bowman in for questioning. If he didn't want to go quietly, Harper was prepared to deal with that possibility.

He knocked. Softly at first and then once more with a resounding thump. Even if Bowman were napping, surely he'd hear the door. Of course, he might be in the bathroom. Harper waited a moment before he ducked out the back entrance, propping the door open behind him, and tried to look in Bowman's window—not easy to do inconspicuously, since sunlight bounced off the large windows. A cloud moved in front of the sun momentarily, though, and Harper could see an empty room. It was almost painfully tidy, as if the person staying there hadn't even opened a suitcase yet. He could see the suitcase, a compact carry-on size, sitting on the luggage rack. There was no other indication of habitation. Except a bright blue dog bed with thick, padded sides. And a bagpipe lying across the bed, its drones carefully splayed out, the decorative cords between the drones stretched tight.

A louvered closet door was closed. What Harper assumed was the door to the bathroom was closed as well. The small entryway appeared empty, what he could see of it. Lamps beside the bed were turned off.

The sun reappeared, but Harper had seen enough. The screened lower half of the window was pushed open. Harper liked open windows, too. He never could understand people who shut themselves inside with no fresh air. Just to be sure, he went back inside, closing the outside door behind him. He ignored the *Do Not Disturb* sign once more and knocked on the door yet again. No response. Harper waited a few minutes; the more he thought about it, the more sure he was that Bowman could be in the bathroom, but if that was the case, why wasn't the dog out in the room? Even if the dog were in the bathroom with Bowman, wouldn't the dog have barked?

He headed for the lobby.

Mac motioned to everyone to be quiet, without noticing that they already were. He was real happy that Fenton had followed his lead when he said he could take them around the back of the old dump. Now, his heart pounded so hard he could almost feel it in his throat. Fenton had already decided that the men who had slipped into position to cover the other three sides of the building would stay in place and stop anyone from leaving. They'd surrounded the house, but they still had to get inside without shooting one another. And without letting the perps get away. Mac loved that word.

His leg ached, kneeling like this in the long grass, but he ignored it.

Beside him, Fenton fingered his earpiece. "Keating? Location?" He listened for a moment and explained to Mac. "They're still checking out the top floor of a big old house with a sight line to the speaker's platform. Doubt they could get here in time."

Mac whispered back, "We have enough men. There're only two doors."

"And about a dozen big windows on the ground floor."

Oh. Mac hadn't thought about that.

Beside him, Fenton conferred briefly. Three of the agents stood and sprinted toward the house, zigzagging as they went. Another trio followed closely behind them. They disappeared inside the house. Mac started to haul himself to his feet, but Fenton reached out a restraining arm. "They have their orders."

A minute or so later, Fairing crept up beside them, and introduced herself to Fenton. "You made it inside okay?"

Fenton nodded. "Six men."

Fairing nodded. "Should be enough."

It seemed to take forever, but they finally heard a shout

from inside, and Mac waited for gunfire. This was exciting. Of course, they could have caught the guys faster if Mac had been in the lead.

Scamp woofed from the front window, and of course everyone in the shop turned to look. I glanced outside. "Just a passing dog," I said. There were a few scattered comments, but fortunately all of it sounded good-natured. I wouldn't want Scamp to disturb their shopping.

Big Willie and Silla were on the other side of the street, passing in front of Sweetie's Jellybean Emporium. Silla's tongue hung from the side of her mouth, and Big Willie stomped along as if his feet hurt.

He'd mentioned an afternoon walk. If so, they hadn't been gone for very long. I hoped he'd gotten somewhere with all that thinking he referred to. I watched them until they turned into the alley beside the hotel. They obviously planned to go in through the back entrance.

Harper reached the hotel lobby just as a group of men pushed their way through the big double doors. The central figure, whom Harper recognized from numerous news reports, was overpowered by a bright red kilt. *Leave it to Leonzini to go for a royal plaid, like he dreams of being a king someday.*

"My secretary called yesterday for a reservation," the congressman said.

Harper knew darn well these rooms booked up a year in advance for the week of the Games. But then, too, he knew a hotel had to keep bigwigs happy, whether they deserved it or not.

"Certainly, Congressman." The young man at the desk fiddled with his computer for a moment. "We're happy to welcome you to the Hamelin Hotel."

Harper wondered briefly where the four aides were staying. Sleeping on the floor outside Leonzini's door perhaps? He waited until a bellhop appeared and led the men away. "One question, please."

"Yes, sir. What can I do for you? Did you reach Mr. Bowman?"

"There was no answer, but I noticed he has a *Do Not Disturb* sign hanging on his door."

"Ayuh. When he checked in, he said he didn't want any housekeeping personnel in his room. I told him to hang the sign on the knob and nobody would go in whether he was there or not. I also sent notice to our housekeeping staff that room 124 was to be left untouched."

"No sheet changes?"

"No nothing. He said he didn't want any of that." The clerk scratched his head, then seemed to remember that he was supposed to act dignified all the time, and dropped his hand precipitately. "I wondered at the time if he was going to be leaving the dog in the room and was afraid somebody might let it out by mistake."

"Did he mention leaving the dog?"

"No. In fact, each time I've seen him leave, he's had the dog with him—although I think they usually go out the back entrance. He can get back in through the rear door with his key card."

"Why do you have all those big brass key rings on the wall?"

"They're just for show. People used to leave their keys here whenever they went out. Not anymore."

Harper nodded. He knew just what the fellow meant.

Once Big Willie and Silla disappeared into the alley, I knew I should stop staring out the window. I had customers to serve, people to keep an eye on, merchandise to tidy up. But I stood there at the window a bit longer, gazing over Scamp's ottoman between two kilt-clad mannequins, thinking about how much I enjoyed living in Hamelin. Sure, there were occasional problems, and a few people in town weren't easy to get along with—Shay came to mind—but for the most part, this was an idyllic place.

So why on earth did I feel like something was ready to explode? For a moment I imagined a Godzilla-like monster rising from the depths of nearby Lake Ness.

But then Scamp knocked his Loch Ness Monster pillow to the floor, and the spell was broken. I had way too vivid an imagination, obviously fueled by Scamp's stuffed toy. I glanced across the street and saw Harper striding past Sweetie's. I found myself touching my cheek, where he'd kissed me that one time. But he obviously wasn't interested. Nothing had happened since then.

I pushed my shoulders back and headed for the other side of the shop. I needed to straighten something or sell something or . . . or something. At the scarf display I saw that Gilda had sold the last green paisley. I spread out the blues a bit to fill in the hole and went on to the clan badges hanging on a rotating rack. Thank goodness we had plenty of those.

Mac couldn't believe it. All six agents strolled out of the house like they were on a beach or something. Two more agents came right behind them. They all looked alike to Mac. Dark suits, white shirts, dark ties, short hair.

He stood. "You lost the perps." He didn't even try to disguise his disgust.

The closest agent scowled. "Those *perps*, as you call them, were Keating and Parks, checking out the place, the way Fenton told them to do. This has been a major waste of time."

Fairing pulled out a copy of the mug shot. "You said to find a guy who matched the mug shot." She pointed to one of the agents. "Well, that's what I did."

The scowling agent leaned closer and did a double take. "She's right, Keating. Maybe you're the one we should be taking in for questioning."

"Maybe I'll take you out back and shut your mouth."

Scowl Face gestured to the abandoned house. "We're already out back."

"Shut up, fellas," Fenton said amiably. "This was as much my mistake as anyone's. If I'd asked where the Sutherland place was on the map—before we stormed out of the station—I would have seen it was the same building." He turned back to Parks. "Did you find anything?"

Parks shook his head. "Place is clean. Doesn't mean he won't show up later."

"Back to the station to regroup. Parks, go tell Eggles and Davis to keep an eye open in case anyone comes back."

"There're four sides to the house," Mac said. "Don't you need to leave four agents?" *Even a ten-year-old could've figured that out. What's my tax money paying for anyway?*

Fenton's hand did a funny little jiggle as he waved Parks away. "Eggles is off the front corner in the woods over there where he can see the front and that side." He gestured with his head and then readjusted the gadget in his ear. "And Davis just situated himself off the opposite back corner so he can see the rear of the house and the other side. Does that make sense?"

Mac led the way back to the cars, but somehow he didn't feel good about it. It was all Fairing's fault. He never should have hired a female.

Fairing caught up with Keating. "Did you check the attic? There's a secret door; it's hard to—"

"Yeah"—he cut her off—"we found it. All clear."

"Are you sure?"

"Yes, ma'am," he said, as if he thought she was a little old lady. "We checked everything."

"That's quite an accomplishment. It's hidden really well."

"We're trained to search thoroughly."

Fairing listened for sarcasm, but all she heard was pride in a job well-done. "Good for you." She quickened her pace. "I'll head back to the meadow. The guy might show up yet."

By the time she crossed paths with Murphy, she'd gotten over her chagrin at having collared a Secret Service agent as a possible assassin. Murphy was okay to tell. He'd razz her about it for months to come, but that just proved she was one of the guys.

Harper reached the station just as the whole group of agents arrived. After some minor jostling at the door, mostly caused by Mac, who too obviously insisted on being the first to enter, they sorted themselves out.

"What did I miss?"

There were general guffaws all around, more in keeping with a high school locker room than with a meeting of Secret Service agents and local law enforcement, or so Harper thought. He decided he was going to have to wait a bit to get the full story.

Mac stomped off to his office, citing a boatload of paperwork. Harper knew the chief kept a stash of candy in his desk, and wondered if that was the sort of *paperwork* Mac had in mind. When Mac closed his door, Harper was sure of it. Either that or he was going to sneak a quick smoke. The windows of Mac's office had a faint yellowish tinge from years of nicotine buildup. And did he really think nobody had ever noticed the smell? He caught the look on Murphy's face and nodded. He wondered if they should clue in Fairing—or did she already know Mac's secret? Probably all three of them knew.

Over in the corner, Moira rolled her eyes. Make that four.

9

Speak to you like an honest man.
ACT 2, SCENE 2

A little after four, my friend Karaline Logg stopped by the ScotShop, and I saw Dirk head her way. He liked Karaline. Her restaurant, the Logg Cabin, served breakfast and lunch and closed at three, even during the Games. She'd steadfastly resisted all requests to serve more or remain open longer. "I have a winning formula," she'd told me recently. "Why should I change it?"

Of course, the fact that she'd had a ruptured appendix last summer and a gunshot wound this past winter might have had something to do with her decision to maintain the status quo. Why take on more work if it wasn't necessary?

Speaking of which, during the rest of the year I closed the ScotShop at five, but during the Games business was always brisk, so I stayed open later. It meant paying overtime to my employees and the temps, but the sales volume more than made up for the added expense.

I was at the cash register, and a line of people waited in front of me, but Karaline topped six feet and was easy to spot. She'd never bothered with the Scottish-themed clothing the rest of us wore during the Games. Karaline favored the most outlandish caftans. If I wore bright orange and black like that, I'd look like a squashed monarch, but on Karaline the color fairly sang. I nodded and went on ringing up sales.

Karaline bent, and I could tell she was scratching Scamp under the chin. She rose and wandered around the store, straightening the displays here and there, waiting until I had a moment free. I could see her trying to disguise her mouth movements as she chatted in a whisper with Dirk. Gilda relieved me a few minutes later, and, once I was sure there weren't any customers who needed help, I joined Karaline by the poet shirts.

"We never decided on when to head down for the opening ceremonies," she said.

"I know. I'd like to keep the store open as long as I possibly can."

"How about if I come back about six fifteen? You know there won't be any customers around that late tonight." *Tonight* being the opening ceremonies. That's what she meant. She spread her arms, and the caftan wings billowed. "I need to change into something warmer than this."

"Your dress is bonny indeed, but ye maun be chilled if ye wear it in the nicht."

Wasn't that the truth? That caftan was a silky material

that wouldn't keep a flea warm, much less a willowy woman like Karaline. Although the early August days were balmy and inviting, the nights—*nichts*, as Dirk would say—had already begun their inexorable creep toward winter. I wore my heaviest wool arisaidh. At six, the top length of plaid would stay tucked into my belt, but by seven or eight, I'd have it wrapped around me. If worse came to worst, I could always ask Dirk for my shawl back. He carried it when we left the house, so he could stray farther than a couple of yards from me, but he was never stingy about sharing it. Ghosts never got cold.

The bell over the front door did its jingle-jangle, and I looked up to see two familiar faces. The woman who seemed entranced with our jewelry counter. Her husband shadowed her footsteps, just as he had this morning. I stepped behind the jewelry case, and sure enough she stopped on the other side of it.

I smiled at her. "Didn't I see you here this morning?"

She nodded. "I can't make up my mind."

"Did you want to try on the necklace again?"

She nodded once more and lifted her long ponytail off her shoulder so it hung down the middle of her back. I unlocked the case and pulled out the black stand. I wasn't sure why I even kept that piece in my inventory. I'd never paid it much attention, because I knew it couldn't be very valuable. I'd bought it for mere pennies at a flea market soon after I opened the ScotShop. And it certainly wasn't particularly Scottish—not a thistle anywhere. Just fat, round, dull dark gray beads strung between some rather dingy plastic leaves. They might have been glass; it was hard to tell. Even though it screamed *cheap*, there was something about it that had made me want it to begin with, and it looked like this woman had the same weird taste as I did. I kept promising myself I'd clean it up, but I continually put that chore at the bottom of my to-do list, afraid that if I did clean it, the whole thing would fall apart. The metallic finish on the beads would certainly flake off. No hurry to clean anything. As it was, it made the other jewelry in the case look much nicer by comparison. Gilda had mentioned cleaning it several times, but I'd always told her not to. There were so many other more important chores.

How could I encourage this woman to buy it, though? Luckily the color of the thing was neutral enough that it would go with just about anything, even the distinctive copper brown plaid skirt she'd obviously changed into for the opening ceremonies. I was pretty sure we had at least one skirt like that in our inventory. She and her husband weren't color-coordinated. His kilt was sort of a dull bluish gray.

I'd put a hefty price tag on the necklace—mostly because of the weight of the thing. Maybe I really should discount it. "I've had this on hand for quite some time," I told the woman. "If you're interested, I could come down on the price. Maybe by twenty-five percent?"

Her husband grunted and walked away. He looked familiar—something about the cheekbones reminded me of someone, but I couldn't place who it was. Or maybe it was just that he'd come in with his wife a couple of times. That was it. He wandered over to the poet shirts, which we'd placed near the window display. He passed perilously close to Dirk, who stepped back out of his way, but then the man's attention seemed to be caught by something going on out-side. I could see yet another crowd gathered around the front window. Scamp must have parked himself there on his tartan-draped ottoman again. Now, if all those folks would just come inside. They must have needed tartan doo-dads to wear or carry, and I was the one to provide the goods.

As I watched him, the man doubled over, coughing heavily. I kept my eye on him. Just as I was getting worried, he pulled a water bottle from somewhere and took a long drink. The cough didn't come back. Thank goodness. The last thing I needed was somebody choking in the ScotShop.

I heard the rattle of the necklace as the woman draped it back over its black velvet stand. When I looked back at her, she shook her head and walked away. I replaced the stand, locked the sliding door, and decided to rope in some paying customers. At least I hoped they'd be paying.

Harper listened as the two agents left in the room joked about what Fairing had done earlier. He watched Mac shuffling papers back in his office—he must have finished his candy and his smoke because he'd opened the door, allowing a draft of noxious fumes to escape—and waited for a lull in the conversation. "Keating *does* look like the mug shot," Harper finally said. "I thought that myself, only I knew he was one of you. The way I see it, Fairing was doing her job. She's spent hours out there, searching. If I'd been in her place, I hope my eyes would have been sharp enough to spot him."

Fenton came out of the restroom and must have heard that last sentence. "You're right, Harper." Turning to the agents, he motioned to the door. "It's time for you two to relieve Eggles and Davis."

"I thought we got to accompany—"

"Not now you don't. Send them back here, and tell them to round up two others on their way."

Harper watched them leave. "Thank you," he said to Fenton.

"It's easy in this job to forget that police officers out in the real world have a tough time—sometimes tougher than our job."

"Mind if I head down to the meadow and tell that to Fairing?"

"Be my guest. She's on her toes. Think she'd like a job in the Service?"

Harper could hear the capital letter in Fenton's tone. "You can always ask her, but we'd hate to lose a good officer."

Fenton glanced over his shoulder at Mac's door. "All of you?"

"Well, the ones of us that know quality when we see it. We're lucky to have her. She's former NYPD, decorated after 9/11."

Fenton raised his eyebrows. "Why is she here, then?"

"In the backwoods?" Harper shrugged and headed toward the door. "Family, I think."

Fenton nodded, but didn't say anything.

Closing time varied each night of the Games. Saturday was always our busiest day, and I kept the shop open until eight. On Sunday we shut down early for the closing ceremonies— everybody in town wanted to see the awards and the bonfire.

Thursday and Friday, my posted hours said we closed at six, but it just didn't make sense to stay open that late on opening night. I should have paid attention to the reason I'd be closing early on Sunday; all the potential customers attended the opening. By five o'clock Thursday, everyone in town would have migrated toward the meadow. The ceremonies never begin officially until seven, but Shay schedules opening acts to keep people entertained. Most folks spread out picnic blankets or wander around the booths.

By five, just as I'd predicted, nobody was in the store. At five fifteen, I started closing procedures. As I ran my eyes down the sales lists, everything looked pretty good. But then I went back and double-checked. The computer said we hadn't sold any bookends. None. Nada. I went over to the display. Four sets of Urquhart Castle bookends. I knew there had been five there earlier in the day.

"Gilda?"

"Yeah?"

"Did you sell any bookends today?"

"No, although I noticed you sold a set."

"But I didn't."

"Sure you did. There were five this morning. The next time I looked there were only four." I shook my head. "Maybe Sam or one of the temps rang one up," she suggested.

"It's not showing on the list here."

She checked with the guys back in the storeroom. "Nope. Nobody sold any." She took a better look at my face. "You think somebody stole a set? No. Those things are big. How could anybody smuggle a set out without our noticing?"

"Darned if I know." I hated the thought.

I looked up. Dirk had his eye on me. As clearly as if he had spoken, I heard his earlier comment. *If I hadna told ye what those twa did, ye wouldna ha' known 'til 'twas too late.*

I needed another two or three ghosts to keep an eye on my merchandise.

Around five thirty, I sent Gilda down to help out at the tie booth, and my two cousins tagged along with her and Scamp.

I locked the door behind them and decided to wander around the shop while I had a few moments, straightening hangers, refolding or restacking items that were only slightly askew. Dirk was uncharacteristically quiet.

I almost ignored the locked jewelry counter, but something made me glance at it. Maybe the stolen bookends and the almost-stolen Green Book were on my subconscious mind, or maybe it was a trick of the light reflecting off the glass. Whatever the reason, I noticed that the big plastic leaf necklace wasn't hanging quite straight on its stand.

I unlocked the cabinet and lifted the stand onto the countertop. It didn't feel right. I adjusted the necklace, picked it up, and examined it more closely.

"Dirk?"

"Aye?" He was closer than I'd thought.

"Have you ever looked closely at this necklace?"

"Aye. That I have. 'Tis bonny indeed."

"Does it look different to you?"

He bent to peer at it. "Did ye clean it somehow? The silver looks more shiny than 'twas."

"Fake silver," I said. "But you're right. This looks shinier. And it doesn't feel as heavy as it did." I held it out to him, but then laughed. Ghosts couldn't pick things up—at least my ghost couldn't.

"None sae heavy? How is that possible?"

"Well, that's the problem. It's not possible. But I'd swear this isn't the same necklace."

We stared blankly at each other and back at the necklace.

"When did ye last hold it? Have ye mayhap forgotten the weight?"

I thought back. "No, it was just this afternoon, I guess, when that woman was here."

"What woman?"

"The one who's been coming in every day to try it on."

He tilted his head. "Oh? Aye? I didna notice her."

"That's right. You were over by the window this afternoon."

He looked at me quizzically. "How would ye remember that?"

"He almost walked into you. The woman's husband."

"Och. Aye. I do recall him. He was the one who coughed so much."

On impulse, I tucked the necklace into the cloth bag that dangled from my belt. I needed to look at it in better light.

I had the cash register closed and the deposit prepared by 6:05, and was ready to leave when Karaline showed up a couple of minutes later, wearing a neon pink caftan over heavy black leggings, topped with an extravagant pink-and-black-plaid shawl that—if I'd been wearing it—would have looked like a horse blanket, but, on her six-foot frame, simply looked magnificent. "And what clan would that pink plaid belong to?"

"Clan Armani," she shot back without hesitation, re-adjusting her enormous shoulder bag. "Don't I wish?"

Dirk looked curious. "I havena heard o' that clan."

"Nor will you ever. She made it up." I held the door for him, and locked the ScotShop behind us. I decided not to say anything to Karaline about the necklace. Not yet. Not until I had a better idea of what was going on. "I met the nicest man this morning," I said.

Karaline raised an eyebrow. "What about Harper?"

"Not that kind."

"What kind?" Poor Dirk. He so often couldn't follow a conversation between us two women.

"He has a little Scottie dog," I said, "and he's a long-time champion here at the Games. Only he hasn't competed for the past three or four years, ever since his wife died. He looks like Santa."

"You mean Big Willie Bowman?"

"You know him?"

"Sure. He's eaten at the Logg Cabin several times."

"I know. I had lunch with him there today. Outside."

"Of course, outside," Karaline said. "Health department rules against dogs in restaurants."

"What would be a *health department*?"

After Karaline explained it to him—I wasn't about to try—she waved her arm in a dismissive gesture. "He's the reason we put those six tables outside. I'm not sure why I never thought of it before. People enjoy eating alfresco."

"'Tis a good thing they dinna have the Games during the winter."

We passed under the flower-bedecked arch, and I veered left toward the tie booth, passing Sam on the way. I could see that business was brisk; Gilda had stepped in to help the two temps, and all three were fully occupied. I motioned for Sam to get in there and help them out. Shoe wasn't anywhere to be seen, but I would have been willing to bet he was at the piper's tent absorbing hints about those toodleloogas or whatever they were called.

Karaline put a hand on my arm. "Stop worrying. They're handling it just fine." Pushing her way past two blue-suited men—hadn't they heard about the dress code? Comfortable or plaid or, preferably, both—she headed for a relatively clear area on the gently sloping land. She whipped a blanket out of her bag and unfolded it on the ground. "Sit."

"How'd you get that thing to fit in your purse?"

"It's some special kind of fabric. Thin, durable, takes up almost no space."

Before I could answer, a set of sword dancers moved into the open area before the stage and we all settled down to watch. Dirk wandered up there, placed his sgian-dubh and his dirk on the ground in an X, and danced. He was magnificent, with his plaid billowing out around him as he spun across weapons only he and Karaline and I could see. The crowd showered the visible dancers with quarters and dollar bills. If they'd been able to see Dirk, I'm sure he would have gotten tens and twenties.

Once I could breathe again, I watched Dirk gather up the two crossed implements. It was funny how nobody tried to walk over that space while he was in it. He headed our way, and once again, people seemed to melt away in front of him.

"I'm hungry," I told Karaline. "If you'll save our place here, I'll go get us some food."

"Not to worry." She pulled out her voluminous purse again and produced two Cornish pasties wrapped in aluminum foil. "Eat before they get cold." She placed a large cloth napkin on my lap.

Dirk eyed her. "Mistress Karaline, your goats give the best milk."

"Huh? She doesn't have any goats." Dirk was silent. Why did everybody always cock an eyebrow at me? Karaline had been raised on a farm in the Midwest, but goats? Where had that come from?

"What I meant to say is she gives verra good value."

"Oh."

Karaline had a silly grin on her face, so I threw my napkin at her. "Sit down, Dirk. You'll block people's view."

"That I will nae do." But he sat between us anyway. Karaline and I scrunched ourselves toward the blanket edges to make room for his massive shoulders. She looked at me—sort of *through* Dirk—and we both laughed.

"Macbeath," I finally said, "I had no idea you could dance like that."

He gave an apologetic shrug.

"No. Really. It was magnificent."

He kept his eyes forward, as if studying the stage, but he inclined his head. "I thank ye for the lofe."

Love? Had he said *love*? I realized in that moment that I did love him—in a special sort of way. Human to ghost. This time to that time. Did that count?

Karaline wasn't afraid to ask. "Loaf? What kind of loaf?"

"Lofe. It means . . ." He groped for the right word. "It means *honor*."

Oh.

10

Run barefoot up and down.
ACT 2, SCENE 2

Silla did not like it when her person's voice got loud.
Except when he laughed. Then it was okay. But now,
it was not fun to listen to. She did not like the other
person's loud voice, either. She grabbed the fabric at the
bottom of that other person's leg and tugged. She barked.
She jumped away from a kick that could have bowled her
over. She snarled. That was when her person grabbed her.

"Get out," he shouted. "I can't prove it yet, but I know
what you did."

Silla added her own voice, although she would have
liked to take a chunk out of that leg first.

Silla reached for her person's face and licked away the
wet. She had never tasted such salty water before. It would
have tasted good except for the sad in it.

"Leave well enough alone, Silla," her person said, and bent to place her on the floor.

When he fell down so fast, right on top of her, she squirmed and wiggled. She tried to dig in her claws and stop when her person's body was dragged across the floor, but her collar was stuck on her person's belt and her person's arm was trapped somehow underneath him, sort of around Silla. As the floor beneath her changed from soft and warm to hard and cold, she tried again to dig in her claws, but her person was too heavy. She could not get away.

She felt her person's head and chest lift, and her own head popped free for a moment. That horrible other person lifted the noisy awful thing off the bed where Silla and her person slept and wound part of it around her person's neck. Silla growled. She barked and struggled and heaved her body as hard as she could. When she managed to almost break free, she grabbed the closest part of that person she could reach— just barely reach—and bit as hard as she could, growling all the time. She heard the shout of anger but it did not matter. She had to stop that person. She had to save her person.

That person, that horrible person, grabbed her neck. Silla could feel the dangle on her collar begin to dig into her throat. She tried to bite harder. The pressure on her neck increased. She didn't know where the dark spots came from, but they filled her eyes. She could not take a breath. But she would not let go. She could not let go. Her person needed her. Her person—

When she woke up, the horrible one was gone. Silla struggled to free herself from the weight of her person. She worked so hard, one of her toenails tore, but she finally squeezed out from under him.

She licked his head and his ear, his hands, his shoes, his neck. She butted her head against his side. She investigated the closed door. She jumped up on the white place where her person sat sometimes. From there she jumped up onto the place where the water came from. She did not know what to do.

Finally, she hopped down and curled beside her person while she licked the blood from her feet. Some of it was her own, but some of it tasted like that horrible other person.

Marti Fairing thought back to her conversation with that Secret Service guy. *Did you check the attic? It has a secret door*, she'd said. And he'd said, *We found it. All clear.* And then he'd called her *ma'am*, like she was decrepit or silly or something. Maybe he was just being polite, but she didn't think so. Patronizing. That's what it was.

She scanned the crowd, spotting dozens of Hamelin residents dotted here and there on blankets or folding chairs. People she knew. Maybe not well, but she knew what hours they were at work, what kind of cars they drove, who their neighbors were, whether or not they decorated their houses for the various holidays. Old Mr. Marley, the guy who had fallen off his roof putting up a big sleigh display last December, sat beside his son and grandchildren in a sturdy folding chair, with his leg propped up on a makeshift stool and his crutch leaning against the chair back. He still had trouble and had to keep his foot elevated as much as possible. She eyed a young man sitting by himself on a nearby blanket. He was within reach of the crutch. The crutch would make a good weapon.

But the president was going to be at least thirty yards away. No chance for the young guy to create a problem. Anyway, he didn't look anything like the fellow in the mug shot. She waited for a group of drummers to pass in front of her.

She spotted Peggy Winn and Karaline Logg moving farther apart on the blanket. Were they mad at each other? No, they were laughing at something.

Her gaze passed over the Sutherland house and back again. The secret door into that second attic room wasn't easy to find. Most of the kids in town knew where it was, but by some unwritten rule, nobody ever told a younger sibling how to get into it. They had to find the secret door for themselves. With the place abandoned, kids had plenty of time to explore every nook and cranny.

The more she thought about it, the more convinced she was that those agents hadn't found it. *There's a secret door. We found it. All clear.* Only, police sergeant Marti Fairing felt fairly sure they'd found only the door to the main attic; it was sort of tucked behind a funny little alcove on the third floor. If they thought that was what she meant by *secret*, no wonder they'd scoffed at her.

No, they hadn't found the secret room off the attic. What the kids called the second attic. It was a corner room that overlooked the meadow. A room with a window. A room that would be a perfect spot for a sniper.

She wasn't sure how Mr. Mug Shot had known the president would be here. But obviously something had been leaked. The more she thought about it, the more sure she was that those agents hadn't been as thorough as they thought they'd been.

She looked around the meadow one more time and happened to notice the line of Porta Potties. They reminded her of the musician guy she'd seen that morning heading for the woods. There could have been a rifle in his violin case. He could have circled around and entered the Sutherland place through the back door. Nobody was watching. Nobody would have noticed. He could have sat there all day, quiet while the Secret Service examined the entire house. Almost the entire house.

The briefing had said the president's helicopter would land on the other side of town and he'd be driven through Hamelin in a closed vehicle. Dallas, this wasn't. No open convertible. No danger to the president. Except when he stepped onto the stage within clear sight of the secret attic room in the old Sutherland house.

She looked around for Murphy or Harper. Even Mac. But nobody was in sight except a few blue-suited guys, and they were all four headed toward the speaker's platform.

Determined not to give herself away, she held her arms closely at her sides and headed diagonally across the meadow, nodding to people as she went, smiling until her cheeks ached. When she reached the woods, she skirted through the undergrowth until she was out of the sight line of the attic room. Overhead, she heard the whir of a helicopter. She called out the agent's name and was surprised when it wasn't Eggles who answered her. *Shift change*, she thought.

"I want you to go with me into the Sutherland house. The assassin is in an upstairs attic room."

He eyed her with what looked like hostility, but Marti couldn't figure out why. She was the one who'd been embarrassed, not him.

"We checked that house top to bottom."

"I tell you there's a secret attic. Come on. There isn't much time."

He waved a hand. "You wanna go in there, go ahead. But I'm staying here where I'm supposed to be."

There wasn't time to argue. *You'll be sorry*, she thought as she moved away from him.

There were always the regular competitions and exhibition events for pipers and drummers, but I loved it when smaller groups of these competitors simply walked around entertaining people—rather like the fiddlers who played at the drop of a hat.

I gazed—probably with my mouth open—as a small cadre of just half a dozen drummers marched past. They were perfectly in step, and conversations ceased along the way as they went by, rat-a-tat-tatting in an intricate rhythm. It was rousing without being too noisy—I could still hear myself think. Anyway, it was fun to watch the tassels bounce on the sides of the drums. The whole group was terribly impressive. Usually Mr. Stone, the Hamelin Pipe and Drum Corps' drum major, led them, with an enormous white tassel on his black fur hat, but I imagined he had plenty of other responsibilities during the Games. I'd never gotten to know him very well, even though his daughter Andrea and I had been friends starting in fourth grade. I'd been in and out of Andrea's house all the time as a kid, when I wasn't playing with my cousins. Mr. Stone was gone a lot, and when he was home, Andrea and I pretty much had to stay out of his way. He didn't like to be disturbed, so it was really Andrea's mother that I'd connected with. Andrea and I used to bake cookies with her. And she loved to read. She introduced me to a bunch of great books and we'd talk about them while we were helping her garden— although I doubt we were much real help with that endeavor. One of the worst things about the debacle with Andrea last year was that I'd lost touch with Mrs. Stone. I missed her.

I saw Harper nearby, outlined against the dark blue of the Farquharson tent. I couldn't be certain, but it sure seemed like he was looking at me. Didn't I wish. He was probably just watching the drum corps.

Andrea, all decked out in a ridiculously short tartan skirt, walked past Harper, and I bridled at the sultry look she regaled him with. Fortunately, he ignored her. At least, I hoped he was ignoring her.

"P? Are you listening to us?"

"Hmmm? What?"

"You'll have to excuse her, Dirk. She gets that way sometimes—lost in a fog."

Dirk nodded, like a Supreme Court justice, filled with import. "I am verra weel acquainted with Mistress Peggy's propensity to listen to words no the one o' us can hear."

"Oh, hush, you two," I said. "You sound like you're paid by the word, Dirk."

"Paid by the . . ."

"Like Dickens," Karaline said. "Nineteenth-century writer. Paid by the word. Very long-winded."

"Aye. I know Master Dickens."

"How?" Karaline asked. "He was after you died."

"Mistress Peggy has *Oliver Twist*, *A Christmas Carol*, and"—his voice took on the breathy tone of an avid fan—"*A Tale o' Twa Cities*." Even after more than a year in the twenty-first century, Dirk was still in awe of the printed word. I had to turn the pages for him, but it was worth it to hear his comments as events unfolded through the ageless stories.

The long winter evenings had been particularly good for Dirk to learn Dickens and for me to refresh my memory. Dirk would read aloud, and I'd knit and turn pages whenever he paused. He really was a very good ghost to have around.

A few minutes later I heard a whirring pulse of sound in the distance. "I sure hope that thing isn't planning to land here."

"What would be making that tumultuary noise?"

"Tumultuary? What a great word. The noise comes from something called a helicopter. It's kind of like an airplane." I'd explained airplanes to Dirk many months ago. "But helicopters can fly straight up and down."

Dirk looked like he didn't believe me. I couldn't blame him. For a ghost from the fourteenth century, the concept of any type of flight in any direction whatsoever must have been hard to digest.

"It's probably some big shot making a grand entrance," Karaline said.

"Ladies and gentlemen!" Archie Ogilvie, our moderator, was at the microphone. I hadn't even noticed the dignitaries filing onto the platform. Sure enough, the governor looked stately, elegant. The congressman looked awkward—maybe he was aware that his knees weren't nearly as good-looking as the governor's. But where was Shay? I didn't see her anywhere. I couldn't think of a single reason why she'd miss the opening ceremonies. Short of death. Or the plague.

But then I remembered that she'd missed the opening four years ago when her sister died. I felt bad—but only for a moment—for having been so flippant. Nobody could have died this time around, though. We would have heard about it.

"Welcome to the sixty-third annual Hamelin Highland Games," Archie bellowed. When the applause died down, he changed to what I always thought of as his radio-announcer voice. "We have a special guest tonight who will be arriving soon. I'm sure you noticed the sound of Air Force One." He turned to face the lane behind the speaker's platform.

As his words sunk in, the murmur of the crowd swelled to a surge of sound. *Air Force One? The president. The president? The president!*

Each voice gave evidence of the feelings of the speaker. Almost without planning it, we were all on our feet, watching along with Archie.

Shay burst onto the field through the archway and ran toward the stage, but a blue-suited man blocked her as efficiently as a linebacker. For half a second, the setting sun glinted off something in her hand, just a bright spark of light. I had one of those insane moments of wondering if Shay had some sort of weapon. But the blue-suited man didn't seem concerned with her hands. He wanted to stop her from getting to the stage. *If she'd just walked in a dignified manner,* I thought, *she probably would have made it.* Andrea was trying to force her way closer, too, but a different agent stopped her. It was good to see our tax money at work. Not that I was gloating.

Fairing didn't dare wait to move quietly. She'd left this too long. She ran up the stairs. She paused just outside the tuck-away door that led to the first attic. She knew the man—or woman—in the second attic would be able to hear her clearly. She poured all the excitement she could muster into her voice: "I'm gonna watch out of that front window! Come on!" With the helicopter already landed, there wouldn't be time for the gunman to leave his post, take her out, and get back up there. He wouldn't dare risk it. She ran loudly toward the front window, trying to make her footsteps sound like two people. She squealed, "Perfect view!" and backtracked as quietly as she could to the attic door.

Thank goodness these old stairs only squeaked in places she was familiar with. She wished she were barefooted; these steel-toed boots could be noisy.

She could easily hear the murmurings of the crowd.

That meant the window above her was open. It had to be. She had to be right. If she wasn't, well—it wouldn't matter much. There wouldn't be anybody here to see her embarrassment. She hoped she was right. She wanted to catch this guy. She hoped she was wrong. She didn't want there to be any sort of assassination attempt. God bless America—what if there were two of them? She crept up the stairs faster, happy now that she had her boots on. He—they?—mustn't hear her, but she couldn't sacrifice speed by trying to be quiet. And she just might need those steel toes.

With very little fanfare, a number of blue-suited men coalesced at the front of the crowd. Half of them faced us, and half had their backs to us. They were so obviously Secret Service agents—or maybe they were FBI—and so intent on their job, I almost laughed. What on earth did they think could happen here in Hamelin, especially when nobody knew ahead of time that the president was coming? But then I remembered Dallas. I looked around the meadow. We didn't have a book depository, but we had the old Sutherland house. What a perfect place for a sniper. I looked back at the derelict building. *It has great bones,* my father always tells me, and I could see his point. But right at this moment it looked positively sinister.

Nonsense, I thought. The Secret Service folks would have checked that place out first thing. I turned back just as a large white car rounded the curve and pulled to a stop behind the platform. From where we were standing

I had a good view of the president as he emerged from the car and raised his arms in a celebratory wave.

He headed up the steps onto the platform, where the governor stood with arm outstretched to shake the president's hand.

Harper spotted Peggy across the field. She had turned away from the stage and seemed to be staring at the old Sutherland place. He looked at it, too, and seemed to see a breath of movement in one of the upstairs windows. No. It couldn't be. Fenton and his men were watching the place. What if it was nothing? What if it was the Secret Service themselves looking out that window, scanning the crowd below? On the other hand, what if it was Bowman, the man with the dog, ready to assassinate the president?

Harper shouted, a sound that had nothing in common with the celebratory calls of the crowd around him. A sound of desperation. A sound that barely competed with the report of a rifle from the house beyond the meadow.

11

The play's the thing,
Wherein I'll catch the conscience of the king.
ACT 2, SCENE 2

To heck with subtlety. Fairing burst through the door and saw him jerk in surprise. The rifle shot in the tiny room deafened her. She prayed she'd ruined his aim. He whipped around, his weapon still in his hands. She knew the Secret Service guys would have already thrown themselves on top of the president. This guy wasn't going to get another chance. Especially not if Marti Fairing had any say in the matter.

She launched herself at him, her ears still ringing from the shot. So much so that, as he turned, she could hardly hear herself say, "Bobby?" before her hands clamped on his wrists. Even with a scraggly blond beard, she recognized him. From fifth grade.

*   *   *

I heard Harper shout. I recognized his voice. But then it only took a moment for the crowd chanting the president's name to morph into a panic-stricken mob. Karaline grabbed my arm and propelled me to the ground. As I landed, my head bounced up and I saw two blue-suited men grab the president, pull him from the platform, and hustle him into the car. It took only seconds, and he was gone. A blur of blue as other agents streaked toward the old Sutherland place.

My next thought was what Shay was going to say about all this.

"Are you okay, P?"

"I would be if you'd roll off me so I could breathe."

Once she complied, I thanked her; but we both knew the danger might not be past. Nearby I saw Don and Brenda Marley cradling their two children between them, shielding their small bodies. Old Mr. Marley, with his leg still in a brace, had overturned his chair and dragged himself to them. He stretched out, forming a barrier with his body between his son's family and the gunman behind us all. A gangly kid, high school age, vaulted over Marley's whole family and tackled a little girl, pulling her to the ground. She wrapped her arms around his waist.

I spotted Leonzini's head peeking over the back of the platform, but the governor lay facedown on the ground where the sword dancers had been such a short time ago. He lifted his head and turned it to his right, probably so he could breathe. I felt a surge of relief—almost of joy, although that emotion didn't seem to fit with what was going on here. He was alive, but the upper arm of his white shirt was red. The red was expanding. Without thinking, I jumped up and ran to him.

Karaline shouted for an ambulance. Dirk handed me the shawl. I stanched the blood as best I could, but it kept pulsing out beneath my hands. *His hand outstretched to greet the president. The bullet that came so close.* Thank God the gunman's aim had been off by—what?—twenty inches? Twelve? Dirk laid a ghostly hand over the exposed half of the governor's forehead. I could hear the helicopter lift off, the sound fading quickly away.

"Governor!" Andrea stood beside me, her camera phone clicking away. "How did it feel to take the bullet meant for the president?"

The governor's aide came pounding up, grabbed Andrea by the shoulders, and spun her out of the way. "I was in back watching the crowd. I couldn't get here—"

"Help me put pressure here. I think he hit an artery."

He leapt over the governor's prostrate legs and wrapped his hands around mine. For such a short guy, he had enormous hands. And—thank goodness—an iron grip. And—double thanks—he'd gotten rid of Andrea. Well before the paramedics arrived, my fingers were numb.

Bobby Turner hadn't been this strong when he was just a sullen fifth grader and they'd wrestled on the school playground. He'd pushed Marti's best friend into the mud, and she'd tackled him. Then it had been a slam dunk to push him in the mud as well.

Now, though, he fought with the desperation of someone who couldn't risk being caught. He tried to slam his forehead into Marti's teeth, but she wrenched her head out of his way. He kicked at her as best he could from such close quarters and she twisted, pulling them both to the hard wooden floor. She hadn't meant to land on the bottom. He grunted as something—probably his shin—slammed into one of her steel-toed boots.

Before she could celebrate, he kneed her in the crotch.

"That's what I'm supposed to do to you," she growled, hanging on for dear life, refusing to let go. Because she knew if she lost hold of him, he'd finish her off, just like he'd probably done to the president. Why couldn't she have gotten here sooner?

He bared his teeth, and Marti had a blinding vision of the time in third grade he'd bitten Georgie Martin's ear. It hadn't been a pretty sight.

"No wonder you knew about this room," she said, and he closed his mouth far enough so he could grin at her. She wrapped her legs around him, yanked his wrists—and the rifle—closer, and threw her head forward hard enough to crash her forehead into his nose.

His blood sprayed across her face just as Davis, Eggles, and the other guy tumbled through the open door.

"Nice of you to show up," she said when they'd hauled a broken-nosed Bobby off her. "Finally," she couldn't help adding, and wiped her face.

Archie Ogilvie's voice boomed out over the meadow. "Let's all settle down now, ladies and gentlemen. Everything is under control."

Under control. Right.

One of our Hamelin police cruisers, followed by a black car so ostentatiously shiny it almost hurt the eyes, sped in back of the now-empty stage and across the far end of the meadow, dodging tents and pickups and travel trailers. Even though I was on my knees, most of the people in the meadow were still lying down, although most of them had their cell phones out, either talking, texting, or taking photos. Over their heads I could easily see the cars as they navigated the gentle slope up to the old Sutherland place, where a group of people was rounding the corner from the back of the building. A man obviously under restraint was herded into the cruiser, and the other people filed into the shiny car. A lone person, a woman, was left behind. She waited until both cars were out of sight and then limped our way. Danny Murphy sprinted past us and, as I watched, skidded to a stop beside the woman, whom I recognized as Marti Fairing, one of our police officers. He dug in his pocket and handed her something. It fluttered in the evening breeze. A handkerchief? "I wish I could hear what she's saying," I muttered, and turned my attention back to the governor.

Karaline held the governor's other hand and kept up a running patter. "You'll be all right. Help is on the way. Just try to breathe evenly. We'll get you to the hospital . . ."

Thank the Lord for paramedics. Surely it had been only seconds we'd held the governor's arm, but I was never so happy as when I heard, "You can let go now. We'll take it from here."

I clambered to my feet, wondering what I was going to do about all the blood on my hands. The good thing about wearing an arisaidh is that you always have a lot of extra fabric around. I lifted one corner of it, but before I could start wiping, Dirk placed his hands over mine.

"I maun be able to help a wee bit." His cool watery touch felt so very different from the urgent hands of the aide.

He rubbed gently, and the blood dissipated. "How did you do that?"

I was whispering, but the aide beside me, busy wiping his own hands with what looked like an entire packet of tissues, must have heard. "Got here so fast, you mean? I think I ran a couple of people down on the way."

"I dinna ken." Dirk looked at his hands, and I was pretty sure he was thinking about when he'd helped Karaline last winter. "It felt the right thing to do."

"Well," I said, knowing full well that I was speaking to both men—man and ghost, that is—at the same time, "thank you."

"Could you make a little room for us, ma'am? Sir?" The paramedics rolled a gurney up beside the governor, lifted him onto it, and strapped him down. One of them handed back my shawl, and the ambulance headed toward Arkane. The hospital there was a good one—I knew from personal experience.

"As you can see" came Archie's voice over the speakers, "the president is safe and the perpetrator has been apprehended." *Perpetrator? Apprehended? Archie's been watching too much TV.* "Our governor sustained a small wound, but he's receiving expert medical care, thanks to our alert and well-trained ambulance crew."

Small wound? I looked down at the bloody shawl in

my hand. Absentmindedly I handed it to Dirk. A woman beside me gasped, and I couldn't say I blamed her. After all, shawls don't usually disappear into thin air.

Dirk laughed. "Ye maun be a wee bit more careful."

I turned to the woman. "I'm an amateur magician," I said, "and I finally got that trick right."

She looked doubtful. "Can you make it appear again?"

Half a minute ago people were terrified, and now I was doing fake magic? I arched an eyebrow at Dirk. "It depends on whether the forces of magic in the air will cooperate." Where on earth did that bit of blather come from? Dirk and I ought to have been in a circus. I held out my hand behind me, Dirk placed the shawl in it, and I produced it, noticing that Dirk had folded it so the blood didn't show. "Ta-da!"

"That was really good! Will you do it again? Let me get my husband over here."

I didn't have to respond because Shay chose that moment to wrest the microphone from Archie's grasp. "Lads and lassies!" The mike squealed and Shay grimaced. "Sorry about that." She pointed to her right. "Porter," she ordered, "bring your pipes up here and give us 'Amazing Grace' in honor of the brave Secret Service agents who averted this possible crisis, and, uh, in honor of our brave governor who, uh, who bravely took the brunt of the attack as he, um, bravely saved the president's life in such, uh, in such a brave way."

Find another adjective, Shay.

People pulled themselves to their feet as Porter Macnaughton mounted the stage and made those preparatory bellows that everyone who's heard a bagpipe knows all

too well. One lone drummer from behind the crowd began
to strike the beat, and we all quieted. A great many people sang along as the time-honored strains of "Amazing
Grace" soared across the crowd. For a moment we had
been at risk. Horribly at risk. And now we felt safe. What
a good reason to sing. Shay's voice at least was in tune.
Now that I was closer to the stage, I could see what had
caused that blink of light from her hand. She turned the
microphone slightly, and an enormous diamond ring
sparkled with sudden fire. I'd never seen her wearing that
monstrosity before. I heard a deep melodious bass voice
just behind me and looked over my shoulder.

Harper.

Beside me, Dirk muttered in Gaelic, and I couldn't
help wincing. I was glad I didn't understand a word.

Harper had been headed toward Peggy and the governor,
but then another man had vaulted into action. Harper
knew better than to overcrowd a crisis scene. He did his
best to calm the people around him, quietly working his
way closer to where she bent over the governor's body.
Paramedics. Ambulance. Exit. Some woman beside her
looking excited. What was all that about? And then he
stood behind her, ready to reach out. He felt glad the
gunman hadn't been Bowman, the Santa with a Scottie.
But he was more glad to be here almost within touching
distance of the woman he loved.

Shay's voice. The shuffling of the crowd. The drum beat.
"Amazing Grace." He could wrap his voice around her.

She turned and looked at him. He was so ready to fold

her in his arms right that moment. But then she grimaced. Maybe he should have left her alone. So much for the ring he'd carried in his pocket for months.

He kept on singing, but more softly now. His heart wasn't in it anymore.

Last winter I'd had a conversation with Harper. He'd told me some things about himself, and I'd been all ready to tell him about Dirk, but somehow the look on his face hadn't been the kind I wanted to dissipate by saying, *By the way, I have a fourteenth-century ghost who follows me around everywhere*. Once that chance was gone, there just hadn't been a right time in the intervening months to introduce the topic.

Now I felt like maybe we were back on track, but then something in his voice shifted—I didn't know why—and he looked away from me, so I turned back to face the piper.

When the song concluded, Shay snatched up the microphone again. "We're going to continue the Games, lads and lassies!"

Continue? Is it safe? I wondered. *What if there's another assassin?*

"I conferred with Archie a moment ago," Shay said, "and he's been assured by the Secret Service that the perpetrator has been arrested. We will not let the actions of a lone criminal stop the Hamelin Highland Games."

A roar of approval went up from the crowd. I could feel the palpable relief overflowing from them. After all, a lot of these people planned their vacation every year around this event. Why would they want to lose their fun? It would have been different, I was sure, if the president had been shot or the governor had died. But both men were safe, the weasel who'd shot at the president had been caught, and Shay was acting in full cheerleader mode as the late-summer sun sank behind the mountain to the west of town. Lights around the meadow came on as Shay called out, "Let the Games begin!"

As soon as Shay's final word faded, the drummers began. Fiddlers dotted around the meadow struck up "Scotland the Brave," something they did every year as if it were spontaneous, even though I'd heard them timing it. Four beats later, the bagpipes were going at full blast. It never failed to thrill me.

Off to my left, I heard a sour note. Several sour notes, in fact. Shoe. I should have known he'd try to join in. Dirk had explained to me that the leumluaths were either three—or was it four? I wasn't sure—trilling notes played very quickly. And the taorluaths were four—or three?— sort of like grace notes, only he hadn't used that term. It hadn't been invented yet when he was alive.

12

'Tis now the very witching time of night.
ACT 3, SCENE 2

Nobody wanted to listen to speeches. Even Congressman Leonzini was smart enough not to try to hold anyone's attention for long. If the governor had been available, I think people might have settled down, but as it was, there was almost a fever pitch of energy flowing through the crowd.

I looked for Harper, but he'd faded back into the throng. Each time I spotted him, it seemed he was farther from me. So much for all the dreams I'd had about us. Finally, I gave up and looked for Big Willie instead. Even with Karaline and Dirk's help, Big Willie remained invisible.

"Mayhap he didna come," Dirk said.

"He wouldn't miss the opening." I think I sounded as indignant as I felt. "Nobody misses the opening."

Karaline wrapped her pink-and-black horse blanket around her. "If he and Silla took those two long walks today, maybe they were both tuckered out. I wouldn't worry if I were you."

I wasn't completely convinced, but I sort of halfway agreed with her.

The dancing competitions were always one of my favorite parts of the Games, but tonight they seemed forced, frantic almost. The sun had set, and the stadiumlike light poles around the meadow blazed with garish intensity. Here and there, campfires sent sparks whooshing up into the night sky. I could hear the cries of babies, the squeals of toddlers awake long past their bedtime, the brash expectancy as groups of men recounted where they had been and what they had thought when the rifle shot was first heard. I saw the gathering in of families as mothers rounded up small children, as fathers made sure their daughters were safe within the fold. Who, I wondered, would make sure I was safe? Who would care if someday I didn't show up when and where I was expected?

I clutched my arisaidh more tightly around me. No Willie. No Harper. No wonder the night already felt cold.

But then Karaline smiled at me, and Dirk said, "I am so verra glad the twa o' ye are safe."

What was I worried about? Karaline and Dirk would care. That was all I needed. Across the meadow, though, I saw Harper pause in front of the piper's tent, and a chill breeze surrounded me.

We left before the first round of Highland dance competition was completed. Tomorrow would be a long day, and I wanted a hot shower and a great deal of sleep. I was glad the failed assassination hadn't put a complete damper on the festivities. At the same time, I was appalled that people seemed able to forget so soon what could have been a total tragedy.

K and I said a brief hello to Mr. P, my neighbor, who stood on the edge of the crowd, but we didn't stop. Karaline and Dirk preceded me through the flower arch. We were about the only ones leaving, except for a couple towing two disgruntled children. As I watched, the father scooped up the shorter child. Far ahead of them, a long-skirted woman passed through the puddled gold of one of the streetlights, but she was traveling faster than we were, so I soon lost sight of her. We didn't talk. I was too tired, and Karaline seemed distracted. Dirk appeared— well—more ghostly than usual. I could see details through him that usually were obscured—not just the streetlights, but the lampposts themselves, the closed blossoms on the daylilies that surrounded the trees along Main Street, the lone bicyclist who passed us.

I always walked during the Games. Parking was ample, but with thousands of extra people—and cars—in town, feet were a better mode of transportation. It wasn't far from the meadow to my house, but we detoured to see Karaline safely home. By the time we circled back to Hickory Lane and passed Mr. Pitcairn's dark house, my feet were dragging.

I sensed Dirk stiffen beside me, and he placed his hand on the hilt of his dagger. "Who would that be?"

I'd forgotten to leave the front porch light on. "Who? What are you talking about?"

"There is a person—nae—a woman sitting on the . . . the moving bench."

To Dirk, *swing* was a verb, not a noun.

As I walked up the wheelchair ramp—installed several years ago after my twin brother fell off the frame around a dinosaur skeleton he was repairing—the dark figure stood. There wasn't enough moonlight to see her. Dirk moved slightly in front of me.

Her voice was a slightly breathy contralto. "It's about time you got home. I'd have brought my sleeping bag if I'd known you'd take this long."

I thought she might be the woman I'd seen walking so quickly up the hill ahead of us. She looked vaguely familiar. Maybe she'd been in the shop? But what on earth was she doing *here*? And why was she so grumpy? "Can I help you somehow?"

She brushed a wispy curl back from her rather prominent forehead. "My name is Paisley Mackenzie. My husband and I built this house right after we married in 1950. I couldn't imagine anyone would take as good care of it as I did."

I took a breath and opened my mouth to thank her.

"And I can see I was right."

I closed my mouth.

She gestured to her right, seeming to indicate the sweep of my bird- and bee-friendly front yard. "Why on earth did you take out our lovely front lawn? No, don't even try to explain yourself. You're probably one of those back-to-nature would-be hippies."

Hippies? That was more my mother's generation than mine, although the thought of my straitlaced mother as a hippie was more than I could imagine. "I'm not—"

"I can see you flitting through all those . . ." She

shuddered. "Those dandelions, probably making daisy chains to wear in your hair. Do you picnic in the clover?"

The night washes away most vestiges of color. There was just enough moonlight—and the stars seemed particularly bright—so the yard looked good, no matter what she said. I loved the texture of it, trees, wildflowers, weeds, and all. The white clover blossoms looked like little stars. "Clover provides nectar for bumblebees and honeybees."

"Ye needna raise your voice, Mistress Peigi. She is mourning what was once hers and isna any the now."

I moderated my tone. "If you saw it in the daylight, Mrs. Mackenzie, I'm sure you'd be able to appreciate all the lovely flowers."

"We'll see about that. When I come back, I'd like a tour through the inside, although from what I've seen out here, you probably painted every wall a different color."

She thought I was going to invite her back? Dirk was uncharacteristically quiet. Why didn't he do something? Like draw his hand across her forehead. Then I could watch her screech before she ran away.

Wind murmured though the branches of the beech tree. My unwelcome visitor pulled her cardigan more tightly around her. She looked old. She looked vulnerable. I felt ashamed of my unkind impulses.

I nodded toward the beech. "Are you the one who planted the trees?"

Even as dark as it was—Hickory Lane doesn't have any streetlights—I couldn't miss the look of horror. "Of course not. Those *people* did that"—she invested the word with so much venom, I took a step backward—"the ones who bought the house when Ken and I had to move to Chicago."

Dirk took a step toward her. "Why did ye have to go?"

As often happened, I halfway expected her to answer Dirk's question.

"This has been a wasted trip." She dusted her hands together, as if ridding herself of unwelcome grime. "At least the hotel is still well run." Dirk moved out of her way, and she paused at the top of the ramp. She seemed to be looking at Mr. P's house next door. "I'll be back tomorrow."

My feet were screaming. "No. I mean, I'm not here during the day. Not until the festival is over. I own the ScotShop, and we have a booth in the meadow."

"The ScotShop?" She touched the paisley scarf at her neck. In the pale moonlight it was nothing but pattern, with no discernible color.

I was pretty sure it came from my store. Of course. She was the woman who'd been in the ScotShop this afternoon, the one who'd been eating the Cornish pasty in the meadow this morning. I wondered if she'd try to return the brown scarf now that she knew the store owner had ruined her precious lawn.

"I'll see you next week, then," she said. "I'm staying for a few weeks, so there's time for me to see everything." She glided down the ramp. Despite her girth, there was nothing even vaguely elderly in her stride. I wondered if she practiced yoga. Halfway down the driveway she turned and looked at the Pitcairn house. Mr. P was still in the meadow watching the dancing, so his house was dark. Almost foreboding. She shook her head and left.

"Ye maun go in, Mistress Peggy. I can tell ye favor your feet."

I unlocked the door. "I'm trying to get them to stop hurting."

"Aye, is that no what I said?"

I slipped out of my shoes and into my softest pair of slippers. Breathing a sigh of relief, I scooped Shorty into my arms and headed upstairs. A long hot shower, followed by enough hot chocolate to fell a horse, and I'd be ready for bed. But first, I removed the plastic necklace from my belt bag and stretched it out on my dresser. It still looked different; I could swear it was newer, shinier somehow.

"I wish I knew what went on in that old house this evening," I said to Dirk about half an hour later.

"Mistress Fairing, the constable, surprised the man with the . . ." His voice trailed off.

"Rifle," I suggested.

"Ryefull. Is that what ye call it? Aye. She made him miss his mark."

"And just how would you know that?"

"I heard her tell the other constable."

"You mean Murphy?"

"Aye. That is his name."

I turned my cup of hot chocolate back and forth on the kitchen table. Dirk had remarkable abilities—although it was a shame he couldn't open doors or turn pages—but I didn't think his hearing was that acute. "Even you couldn't hear that far away."

He tilted his head to one side, just like Big Willie's dog had done earlier today.

"I dinna ken precisely how I did it, but when ye said ye wanted to know what they were saying, I . . . somehow . . . was there, listening to them."

I snorted, not my most ladylike sound. "You never left my side."

"Ye wouldna ha' known. Ye were busy wi' the wee man bleeding on the ground."

"Oh," I said. "Aye. I mean, you're right." But then I thought about it. "You couldn't have left. I was using the shawl on the governor."

His face went blank for a moment, and he spread his hands. "I dinna understand it, but I do ken where I was and what I heard."

A moment of silence ensued. How did I know what sort of natural laws ruled ghostly comings and goings? Once more, I wished I'd known my great-grandmother. But I couldn't think about that right now. "So, what happened? What else did they say?"

When he told me, I decided I wanted to do something really nice for Marti Fairing. The police department would probably give her a certificate or something—or maybe not, what with Mac as the chief—but I could envision that necklace from the ScotShop, the one that was now on my dresser. It would look great on her. Yes. I'd give it to Marti as a little thank-you present. It wasn't much, but hopefully she had a simple black dress to wear it with.

". . . said she misdoubted what the other constable would think about her actions."

"The other? Oh. You mean Mac?"

Dirk looked at me.

He'd gradually gotten used to the way I tended to fade out when I was thinking about something else, but I don't think he liked it. "Mac will probably chew her out for not stopping the guy sooner."

"Chew her out? What would . . ."

Sometimes I felt like a walking dictionary.

Eventually we lapsed into one of those comfortable silences. After a few minutes, I glanced sideways at Dirk. I hadn't asked my grannie all those questions I should have about her mother's ghost. But maybe I could figure out some of this shawl-ghost thing simply by asking the resident expert. "Tell me more about Peigi and the shawl," I said.

He must have been thinking about her because he didn't even seem startled by my question—more like I was voicing a thought of his.

"I had known her all my life," he said. "The last time I saw her . . . she hadna come to me for nigh on a fortnight. We used to meet on the side o' the mountain, in the meadow where I first saw you. After she didna come to me for all that time, I went to her house early one morn to call on her. Her sister tried to turn me away, but I wouldna leave. 'She canna see you,' Gertruda—that's her sister—told me. 'She doesna want to see you.' But I didna believe that for even a moment. I pushed past her into the front room. She came from a wealthy family, ye ken. Their house was the biggest I had ever seen . . ." He paused and glanced around him. "Until I came here."

He was quiet for so long, I almost thought he'd forgotten I was there. "Did you get to see her?"

"Och, aye. She was there, at her loom, weaving. She took one look at me, though, thrust her hand up over her mouth, and ran out of the room. I could hear her retching, but couldna go to her, for Gertruda and five o' her brothers blocked my way. 'Have ye no done enough to her?' Those were Gertruda's very words. I didna understand. I would never have hurt my . . . Peigi." He whispered her name. "How could she think that?"

How indeed, I thought. "So, that was the last time you saw Peigi?"

"Aye. I went back each day for weeks, begging to see her, but Gertruda and her entire family were against me. I found finally that Peigi had been sent awa' to the home of a distant kinswoman, but they wouldna tell me where. Seven months later, they told me she was dead. I think it must ha' been the fever, for that was sweeping through the towns, moving up from the south. There was no avoiding it."

Seven months? I thought over what he'd said. Peigi had been sick—throwing up. And then seven months later she was dead. I was pretty sure what had happened. Having a baby was a risky business in the fourteenth century. A lot of women died if the baby was turned sideways or the mother hemorrhaged. Heck, there were a hundred things that could go wrong. But why hadn't she told Dirk? I had to find out. "Why didn't you marry her?"

He turned his face away and spoke so softly I almost couldn't hear. "She was promised already to another." Well, that answered why they'd sent her away.

"Dirk?" He raised his head and looked in my direction, but I had the distinct feeling he was looking, not at me, but at the ghost of the woman he loved. "Dirk," I said again to get his attention, "did you have any sisters?"

"What? Sisters? Aye, but only the one. Three older brothers and five younger, and the wee lassie who was no more than twelve the last time I saw her. Before I died. But why ask me this?"

He might very well not have known Peigi was expecting his child, if he'd never had older sisters to watch as they got married and bore children.

". . . yon shawl," he said, breaking into my reverie.

"What? What about the shawl?"

"I wanted it. I asked Gertruda for it, but she said me nay. She used it for her wee babe to crawl upon."

"She had a baby?"

"Och, aye. A tiny lassie."

The man was absolutely oblivious. "When was it born?"

"Eh? I didna ken. I was too full of grief to notice. The first I saw it was when I went to ask for the shawl after I learned of the death of . . . of my love."

"Hmm." Were all men that dense, or was Dirk some sort of anomaly? That baby Gertruda raised—I was sure it was Peigi's baby—must have been the first of the great-grandmothers in a chain that had lasted more than six hundred years.

Why, though—why had the shawl come to me? Unless it was through the Winn line, from Wales. And through my great-grandmother, who'd been in Scotland when she died. Had she taken the shawl back to Scotland with her? Had she known Dirk? He claimed never to have known any other life but the one in 1359 and the one now, but maybe he forgot between . . . between visits. It was too much to comprehend.

"Ye look a bit like her, do ye ken?"

"Like Gertruda?"

"No. Like my Peigi."

The mother of that child—*your child*, I thought, but didn't say a word, for I was pretty sure this wee ghostie of mine was my great-grandfather—about forty times great.

No wonder I loved him so much.

Silla did not know what to do. Her person did not smell right. She needed to go outside, but he would not wake up. She scratched at the door, whined, poked her nose against her person's leg. Finally, she jumped onto the side of the hard white box and pushed her way behind the curtain. She scrunched into the farthest corner and took care of her business. Then she went back to her person. She licked his face in apology, turned around three times, curled up beside him, and sighed.

Amy Harper didn't like working two shifts back-to-back in the emergency room, especially on what should have been her "weekend." But a friend needed a favor. And Amy had sure pulled in a few favors herself over the past two or three months, so this was payback time. This afternoon there'd been four people with broken bones, two DOAs from a car wreck, and two men with drug overdoses. This evening, a man with a broken leg and then the governor, no less, with a gunshot in the arm—plus all the usual ER problems. She was so tired, it felt like this ought to be the middle of the night. Oh wait; it *was* the middle of the night. Almost. That was okay. She'd have tomorrow to rest up and then back here the next day. Why had she ever agreed to switch to the ER? She missed her nice quiet ward.

The man in front of her looked—from the blood— like he had a nasty wound under that towel. "Damn dog," he complained through gritted teeth as Amy unwound the plain white bath towel from around his left calf. The man's baggy pants sported a ragged hole. When she looked closer, she could see several smaller holes, too, as if the dog had snapped at him repeatedly. "Stupid beast practically took my leg off."

Not hardly, Amy thought. But she could tell he was in pain; no wonder he exaggerated. Luckily it wasn't too serious a bite. She'd seen bites where the dog's whole mouth was involved. This one had the clear imprint of only the front few teeth—he already had a nasty bruise— but only two teeth had broken through the skin, and he'd need a stitch or two. She was glad he hadn't called 911. Most people in his situation would have. Her blood pressure rose when she thought of the number of people who called 911 when all they needed was some soap and water and a Band-Aid. Someday somebody was going to die of a heart attack while the closest ambulance unit was off attending to a minor wound that elementary first aid could have dealt with.

She took a deep breath. "Who's with you, Mr. Smith?" she asked. "Would you like us to call someone in from the waiting room?"

He hesitated, but then he practically snarled at her. "Drove myself. Don't need anybody else."

Yankee independence in its most irritable manifestation, she thought, trying to suppress a yawn. Fine with her. Amy often ran out of patience as her energy ebbed, but today she was particularly pooped. If he was that independent, why didn't he just keep on whining and see if he enjoyed having to sew up his own leg?

This would, however, make a good story. She didn't usually share hospital events with her cop brother-in-law—privacy rules being the word of the day—but this was one she had to tell him. She wouldn't mention a name, of course, though she doubted it would matter here. *John Smith* sounded like the stereotypical alias. She glanced up at the computer screen beside the examining table. *No picture ID provided—pt. said left drv. license at home. Drove directly to AH.*

Lucky he'd made it to Arkane Hospital, Amy thought. It's a wonder he didn't drive into a ditch somewhere. She knew even minor dog bites hurt like crazy—something in dog saliva was particularly irritating to human tissue. "Did you talk to the owner? Do you know whether the dog has had a recent rabies shot?"

Smith's face went even whiter. "I could get rabies from this?"

The doctor paused, the point of the numbing hypodermic just inches from Smith's leg. "Did the dog have a silver tag on its collar?"

"Yeah," Smith said, and for some reason, he looked at his hands. They were shaking, and Amy could see purple bruises on the pads of some of his fingers. "Yeah, it did."

"That could mean the dog has had a rabies shot, but," the doctor added cheerfully, "there's a possibility the tag could have been expired. You'll need to report to your primary care physician as soon as you can. He or she can keep an eye on the wound and any symptoms you might develop."

As Amy listened to the doctor's instructions, there was a little piece of her mind that wondered what this man had done to the dog to incite the attack. Amy liked dogs. And she knew without a doubt that most dogs wouldn't attack without a reason. Just to be thorough, she added a note to the computer about the bruising on the pads of his middle fingers. "Do you know the owner's name, Mr. Smith? We can contact him for you."

Smith hesitated again. "No." Amy wondered if growling was his preferred method of communication. "Stray dog. No owner."

Then why would the dog have tags and a collar?

She glanced up at a series of boxes on the right side of the computer screen. There was a checkmark next to *will pay cash*. She hoped he had enough with him. Even with only a couple of stitches, it was going to be pricey. She wished, not for the first time, that there was a diagnostic code for royal pain in the rump.

13

O my offense is rank, it smells to heaven.
ACT 3, SCENE 3

Friday morning dawned bright and clear. I stretched and spent a few minutes stroking Shorty's silky back. "Did you know the Games are hardly ever interrupted by rain?" Shorty purred in response. Thus encouraged, I kept going. "There was that one misbegotten tornado in, uh, 1955 maybe? Or thereabouts . . ." *Misbegotten?* I sounded like I'd been hanging out with an ancient ghost. ". . . but nobody was injured. Once they righted the tents, the Games went on."

Shorty yawned, and I took the hint and stopped the history lecture. He hopped down onto the fuzzy area rug, and I slipped on my robe. While I was at it, I detoured into the spare room and rummaged for some wrapping paper. Might as well get that mystery necklace out of my hair. It folded into a surprisingly compact package.

When I walked downstairs in my Winn tartan arisaidh, Dirk smiled. *Great-great-etc.-granddaddy*, I
thought. Nope. I wasn't going to go there. Maybe someday
I'd tell him, but not now.

"Ye look quite bonny," he said. I'd paired it with my
most lightweight chemise and a silk bodice that had almost no heft to it at all. No sense cooking myself in heavy
clothing.

"Thank you." I turned into the kitchen, not to eat but
to feed Shorty. "I'm headed to the Logg Cabin for breakfast. Do you want to come along?"

He thought for a moment. "'Twill be crowded, aye?"

"I think you can bet on that. All these tourists in town."

"I will wander down to the wee meadow and listen in
on conversations."

"Why?"

"For to see what people think o' the happenings
yestreen."

"Yester-what?"

He gave me one of those looks. "E'en."

"Oh. Evening. I get it." I patted Shorty, tucked the end
of my arisaidh more firmly into my belt, and held the
door open so Dirk could pass outside.

At the top of the ramp I stopped and studied the yellow
dandelions and white clover dotting my yard. My dandelions always seemed to bloom from early spring to early
autumn. I was delighted. Poor Mr. P, though, probably
thought I had some sort of weed conspiracy going. But-
terflies flapped lazily in the echinacea blossoms. Even
this early in the morning, I could hear the comfortable
drone of bumblebees investigating nectar sources.

"She didna ken what she was missing," Dirk said. He was a particularly perceptive ghost. Maybe they all were, but he was the only ghost I'd ever known.

"You're right. I felt so angry with her stinking attitude last night. But now, seeing this, I just feel sorry for her."

He inclined his head toward the purple coneflowers. "Let us simply enjoy the day."

I felt like skipping.

I had no idea how soon that feeling would change, but a few hundred feet down Hickory Lane, I began to get those premonitions once more of a monster rising from the lake. It was nonsense. I knew that. But I couldn't help the feeling.

Moira looked up as the station's front door opened. With all the goings-on yesterday, there was no telling what was in store today. Her nephew walked in and grinned at her. She removed her headset and ran to hug him. "What are you doing here? I thought you left with the president yesterday."

He patted her cheek. "You wanted me to leave my favorite aunt without saying good-bye?"

She felt her back stiffen, and didn't realize until that moment how much she'd hoped he was here for at least one more day. "So, it's good-bye?"

"No." His grin widened. "I followed everybody to Burlington last night, but then I thought to myself, I haven't taken a vacation in so long I've forgotten what the word means. All it took was a phone call—a long phone call, what with all the debriefing. But now I'm here for three weeks. If you want me around."

I'm too old to be jumping up and down like this, Moira

thought. "Want you around? You're more welcome than Grandma's pecan pie."

He made a mighty frown. "Think the chief will put me to work?"

"Not if I have anything to say about it. I'm overdue for some vacation myself."

Harper walked in just then. "Hello, Fenton. You have to be kidding, Moira. If you take a vacation, the station will fall apart."

"Well, darlin', just think how happy the chief will be to have me back in a few weeks. Maybe he'll give me a great big raise."

Harper's gesture was dismissive. "Cold day in you-know-where before that'll happen."

"Don't worry. I'll wait until Monday to leave. I do know you can't function without me during the Games."

"That's for sure. When are you going to tell Mac? Right away so he can be mad at you all the rest of the weekend? Or on your way out the door Sunday night so he can take it out on Fairing and Murphy and me on Monday?"

Moira looked Harper up and down like a butcher considering the best cuts of meat. "Don't tempt me, honey child." She turned to her nephew. "Why don't you run down and take a look at some of the competitions? They're a lot of fun."

"Trying to get rid of me already?"

"Never in a million years." Moira noticed Harper looking at her funny. "He's my nephew," she said. "Haven't seen him in umpteen years. We're gonna take some vacation time together."

They slapped a high five, and Mac walked in the door.

*   *   *

"Dirk?"

"Och, aye?"

"Do you really think Big Willie was just too tired to attend the opening ceremonies last night?"

As often happened, Dirk didn't answer my question. He answered the question behind my question. "Ye are worriting about him."

I studied the cracks in the sidewalk. "I know it's silly of me, but what if he's ill?"

"Ye have said he will compete in this day's games?"

"Aye. I mean, yes."

"Could ye no bide a wee bit to see when he appears?"

Even looking at my feet I could see him finger the shawl and pull it more tightly around the hilt of his dagger.

"'Tis nae so verra long 'til the caber toss."

Eventually I looked back up. "I guess you're right." But I didn't really believe it. It felt like time was standing still. And the monster was getting closer.

Mac was in a dour mood. He knew it. But he didn't care. That upstart young agent—well, not so young; maybe in his mid-forties—hadn't said a thing about recruiting Mac for the Service. No. He'd asked about Fairing. Fairing! A female! She was the one who'd sent them all on a wild-goose chase. Didn't Fenton remember that?

He stormed through the station door and found Fenton there, and Harper and Moira acting like it was somebody's birthday or something.

"What are you doing here? I thought you'd be back in D.C. by now."

"Took some vacation time. But first I thought I'd fill you all in on the details from yesterday."

The last thing Mac wanted was to hear Fenton brag about the Secret Service, so he took a pen from his shirt pocket and fiddled with it while the story unfolded. Eventually—not soon enough—Fenton headed for the door. "See you soon," he said.

Harper and Moira did another high five. Stupid. What did they think they were, teenagers? "What are you two doing?"

"We're celebrating," Moira said.

Celebrating what? he wondered. But he wouldn't ask. He wouldn't give her the time of day, much less the pleasure of a question. "Well, keep it quiet," he growled, and slammed his office door. A few seconds later he opened it again. "Harper! Put on a uniform and get out there to the meadow. Do something useful for a change." There. That felt better. Just for good measure, Mac slammed his door. Again.

Before breakfast, I detoured to the tie booth to load the register with plenty of change and be sure my two temps were ready to go. Sam was with them, and I felt confident all would run smoothly.

Unfortunately, I spotted Andrea interviewing her aunt Shay Burns, and the short squat fellow who'd been in the ScotShop yesterday. Shay was acting thoroughly gracious—ha! That meant the rotund fellow in yet another limp polo shirt must have been one of the sponsors Shay was so good at finding. Probably under rotting logs. Why was I suddenly in such a lousy mood?

I said good-bye to Dirk and headed up the hill toward the Cabin. Harper came walking toward me. My heart flip-flopped, and my mood improved considerably. But then I remembered how Harper had looked away from me during the singing of "Amazing Grace." I swallowed and adjusted my shoulders. "What are you doing wearing a uniform? I thought detectives never did. Or are you filling in for someone?"

He shrugged. "Mac wants a show of force. I keep a uniform at the station just in case." He turned to walk beside me.

"Does he do this often? Mac and his power plays?"

"Only when he wants to prove who's in charge." He paused at the flower arch. "Have you heard what happened behind the scenes yesterday?"

How could I answer truthfully? *Dirk told me all about Marti wrestling the gunman to the floor?* "Well," I hedged, "everybody thought somebody tried to shoot the president from the old Sutherland place. Thank goodness he missed. And I'm glad the Secret Service caught him." That wasn't lying. They were the ones who'd driven off with the guy after all.

"You'll never guess who really stopped the guy." Harper had a big grin on his face. I couldn't blame him. Marti had done a spectacular service.

"Looks like you want to tell me." There. Another not-a-lie. "Whoever stopped him deserves a medal." That was the truth.

"Fairing."

"Fairing?" I hated all this prevaricating around Harper. How—when—could I tell him about Macbeath Donlevy Freusach Finlay?—*Stop it, Peggy.* I needed to pay attention. I tried to look surprised. "Marti Fairing?"

"Turns out the fellow lived in Hamelin years ago when he was a kid. Bob Turner. That's how he knew the secret to getting into that hidden room off the attic."

Dirk hadn't told me the name. Maybe Marti hadn't mentioned it in his presence. So at least I could really be surprised about something. "Bobby Turner? I remember him when he was in elementary school. He pushed a friend of his out of a tree." Another truth.

"I wouldn't call him much of a friend."

"But I don't remember him after that."

"They moved away when he was eleven."

"Oh. No wonder." What else could I say?

I heard a commotion off to my right and turned in time to see two men exchanging punches. Real ones. Harper took off running. There weren't usually too many problems like this at the Games; everyone was in too good a mood for the most part. I knew better than to add to the throng of testosterone congregating around the fighters.

Murphy was headed that way, too. And I was hungry. Logg Cabin time.

I surveyed the six full tables, hoping to join Big Willie for breakfast. But of course he must have already eaten. He wouldn't want a full stomach this close to his competition time. So I went inside. Karaline seated me at what I thought of as *my* table. Mine and Harper's. Or at least it *had* been ours.

I hadn't even gone on a date with the guy. We'd solved a couple of murders together—did that count? But despite the distance between us, I had this feeling that if he ever asked me to marry him, I'd say yes. A big *if.* I knew he never would, but I could imagine . . . I felt a blush starting at my toes. Luckily, Dolly walked up then to take my order.

"The usual?"

"Of course," I said. "What else?"

14

O, what a rash and bloody deed is this!

ACT 3, SCENE 4

Dirk was already there when I let myself into the Scot-Shop. "How'd you get in here?"

He shrugged. "I followed Mistress Gilda and the wee dog when they came in."

Gilda poked her head up from behind the cash register. "I let myself in. I have a key, remember?"

Gilda doesn't know the meaning of sarcasm, so I took her comment at face value. Before I could answer, Scamp pushed his way out of the storeroom and bounded up to the front window. "Are you ready, Gilda? Once Scamp gets in the window, we'll have people flocking in, no matter what hours the sign says we're open."

Shoe knocked on the front door. One of the temps I'd hired was with him. Good. I didn't want to be short-staffed today. I could see the customers lining up behind them already.

"Let everybody in," Gilda said. "The only thing I haven't done yet is restock the Loch Ness Monsters."

I looked the shelf over. "We still have two on display. I'll bring out more in a few minutes."

Of course, there was an inrush of people wanting to buy the dog in the window, and all too soon it was time to head to the caber toss. "I'll be back in an hour or so."

She waved me away. "We can handle it."

"I will go wi' ye."

I waited to answer him until we were outside. "You don't need to. I'll be fine. I'm not carrying any money."

"Did ye no think I might wish to see the caber toss for myself?"

I knew that Highland Games began in a formal sense in the early 1300s, chartered by Robert the Bruce, so they would have been a long-standing tradition by the time Dirk was old enough to compete. "You did compete, didn't you?"

"Och, aye. Stone toss and hammer throw, mostly."

"Not the caber toss?"

"Nae. My da was the local champion, but I could never get the caber to flip." He shrugged. "'Twas no great loss. I came near to crashing the caber back on my own noggin more than the once. I decided to quit while I still had a heid to think wi'."

Dirk was in his element. It made me wish we had three or four festivals each year. Of course, that thought only lasted about three seconds. The amount of extra work I put in—I and every shop owner in town—for these four days of brute strength and blatant commercialism would leave me wrung out by Sunday night. Still, he was enjoying it thoroughly.

"I need to swing by the tie booth before I pick up Silla," I said. "Why don't you wander around? I'll meet you in about ten minutes at the caber toss?"

"Aye. I will be there."

I saw Marti Fairing standing in front of the ring where the next round of dancers was scheduled to compete. Forgetting the ties, I headed her way. She wore her full uniform today. I guess Mac wanted obvious police presence. Not that I thought there was any more danger. After all, this was Friday. No politicians around. Just some anxious competitors and a lot of happy spectators. Sunday, though, at the closing ceremonies, with Senator Calais here, that's when I'd be worried if I were Mac.

I was glad I'd brought the necklace with me, I thought. But then I reconsidered. She wouldn't have any place to tuck it away. She practically bristled with accoutrements. No wonder her arms were all akimbo. Well, I could always hold on to it for her if she wasn't able to take it today. "Sergeant Fairing," I said. "I wanted to thank you for what you did yesterday."

"What I did?" She looked genuinely confused. "What do you mean?"

She had a horrible bruise on her forehead. She'd tried to cover it with her bangs, but I wondered if the assassin— the would-be assassin—had hit her with something. "I heard how you stopped that gunman."

"Oh. That. It was . . . well . . . anybody could have done it. I almost didn't make it in time."

"But you did."

She looked beyond me. "I'm not sure I should be talking about this."

"Of course. I'm sorry. I just wanted to say I appreciate you."

The blush went quite nicely with her dark blue uniform.

"And I have a present for you." I dug out the small
package, glad that I hadn't put it in a bulky box, and
handed it to her. "Just a little thank-you gift."

She hesitated. "I don't know if I should . . ."

"It's nothing very valuable—it's just interesting looking, and I thought you'd enjoy it." This was awful. Why
was I giving her a cheap necklace and *telling her* it was
cheap? What on earth was I thinking? I wanted to snatch
it back. "If you don't like it, feel free to pass it on to Goodwill. It's only plastic."

"Well," she said. "Okay. Thanks." She seemed relieved
to know it wasn't anything of value. She tucked it into a
zippered pocket on her leg. "I hope you don't mind if I
don't open it here."

"I understand. You have to stay—"

Someone blew into the stage microphone. "Caber toss
contestants, please report to the field."

Marti and I exchanged a glance. They didn't usually
make such announcements. I was right behind her as she
headed to the designated area. Not that I thought anything
was wrong—I just needed to get Silla so Big Willie could
do his warm-ups. I'd looked at the detailed schedule. He
wouldn't compete until next to last, but I wanted to see
all the competitors.

Marti stopped next to the judge's table. I heard her ask, "Something wrong here?"

A gray-mustached man shook his head. "We're missing one of our contestants, that's all. We like to start with the full slate lined up."

I looked at them and counted—eleven well-muscled men standing in a loose group, some of them stretching, some of them swinging their arms to and fro, all of them wearing kilts and knee-high socks. They all, I knew, wore shorts of some sort under their kilts. In these Games, particularly in the hammer throw, their kilts swung around and up, far enough up that, for their own protection, the men made sure they were well covered. From what I understood, this whole group of men generally went from one Highland game to another, from state to state through most of the summer and, in the Southern states, part of the autumn. They knew one another. They'd know Willie, too.

Willie wasn't there, though. No Silla in sight, either. I scanned the crowd. That announcement should have brought them running. Where was he?

The only one who came running was Dirk.

He followed me over to the contestants. I knew I'd have only a few moments before the contest began. I picked one man at random and approached him. "Excuse me. Have you seen Big Willie around anywhere?"

"Big Willie? No, and he'd better get his tail here in a hurry so I can beat him." He'd spoken loudly enough for all the men to hear, and his braggadocio got the laugh he was expecting.

I saw the man who'd been in the ScotShop with his

necklace-shopping wife. I hadn't realized he was a competitor, although now that I thought about it, maybe that was why he'd looked familiar to me; I'd seen him at prior Games. If I remembered right, he was the reigning champion. Big Willie always used to win, but this fellow—what was his name? Winston or something like that?—had won the last few years in a row. Of course, Big Willie hadn't been here to compete recently. I hoped Big Willie wasn't too out of shape. More than that, I hoped he'd show up. And when Big Willie got here, I hoped this guy would have another coughing fit.

Nobody, it turned out, had seen Willie at all. Not since yesterday afternoon in fact.

But then they called the first contestant, and Dirk and I had to retreat to the sidelines. Well, I had to. Dirk stayed within the roped-off area. I couldn't blame him. Here behind the barrier, people were too crowded together for a ghost to be comfortable.

I looked around, knowing full well I wouldn't see Big Willie. If he were here, he'd be out with the other contestants. I couldn't help hoping, though. Instead, I saw half a dozen Hamelin residents I recognized in among dozens—make that hundreds—of tourists. The woman in the paisley scarf who hated my yard was off to one side. Luckily, she wasn't looking my way. Today she had on a green scarf. I wondered if paisley was her trademark. *Well, of course it is,* I thought. Hadn't she said her first name was Paisley?

The people in front of me stepped aside, and I moved up right next to the rope. Dirk stepped closer so I could talk to him without being overheard by the live people.

* * *

It made sense for them to go ahead with the caber toss without Big Willie. But it hurt to think that he'd traveled all the way to Vermont and was going to miss out on a chance to compete. If he missed this first round, he'd be out of the running.

I watched the first competitor, a brawny man from South Carolina, get the balance of the top-heavy eighteen-foot-long pole and begin his run along the field.

"Where do you think he is, Dirk?"

"I havena any notion. Did ye think I was a soothsayer, forebye?"

The crowd groaned as the caber fell sideways. Luckily the field was wide enough that none of the observers was in danger.

"You're tall—that's what I think. You can see over the heads of this crowd."

"Aye. That I can." He matched his actions to his words. "He isna any the where in sight. Neither he nor the wee doggie."

"Of course you wouldn't see the *wee doggie*." I tried to whisper without moving my lips too much. "Scotties stay with their people."

"What is it ye are saying? Dinna clummest so."

"I'll kloomayst if I want to." A woman standing a couple of yards away stared hard at me. I smiled at her. Best way to disarm suspicion.

The crowd groaned again, and the woman looked back at the second competitor, another brawny fellow—they were all brawny. They had to be to control the 150-pound caber. He appeared to be having trouble keeping the pole upright even before he had his hands under the narrow end of it.

"I can't stand this." I started toward the archway. "Marti Fairing may be looking for him—she probably is—but she's only one person. Let's try to find him."

He caught up with me. "Aye. I think ye maun be correct. If we find him, we can notify the constable. Mayhap Large William has been injured?"

"Hurt, or sick, or . . . or something." An unpleasant vision of my ex-boyfriend's corpse flitted past. Even as I banished that thought firmly from my mind, I walked faster.

"Where d'ye suppose he is?"

"How would I know?"

There was a mighty cheer from the crowd behind us—the caber must have flipped—but I didn't turn around to look. There was another groan, which most likely meant the pole had fallen at a bad angle instead of the straight twelve o'clock position the rules required. At least the man had three tries to get it right and would be judged on the best of his throws.

"Where would ye be going, forebye, if ye dinna ken where he might be?"

I paused and waited until a gaggle of middle-aged women passed by us, on their way to the center of the meadow. "I don't know, but we have to look somewhere." One of the women glanced back at me. I smiled, but I think it was a little forced.

"Mayhap he is still at the inn."

"The inn? Oh, you mean the hotel. You could be right."

I increased my pace. By the time I passed under the flower arch, I was practically running.

Marti Fairing didn't like it when things like this went awry. She didn't believe in dire premonitions, but she couldn't ignore the twist in her gut that said something might be wrong. Was wrong.

She liked the old man. And his dog. Not that he was so very old, not if he could compete in the caber toss. No, not old; but he seemed settled somehow. Sure of himself in a way Marti had never felt. Except when she'd been holding Bobby Turner's wrists. And when she'd broken his nose. Then she'd felt alive. Like something made sense.

She rubbed her forehead and made sure her bangs covered the bruise.

She wanted to hare off like Peggy Winn and go looking for the old man, but Mac had insisted on "plenty of police presence" in the meadow. Like he thought there would be a repeat of yesterday?

She watched the first three competitors. Normally it was an event she enjoyed, but this time she just wasn't interested. With Santa missing, and her with nothing she could do about it, she felt empty.

Silla did not like being this hungry, and she wondered why her person was not eating anything, either. She drank from the bowl her person had put beside the white sitting place, but that did not fill her insides. And it was almost empty now. She licked her paws again and thought about the squirrel she had seen when she and her person—and that awful female person—walked in the woods.

Maybe if Silla could get back there, she could find another squirrel and bring one to her person. Maybe food would wake him up.

She pawed at the door, but it was too hard. She eyed the wall beside the door and began to scratch at it. Bred to pull badgers from holes in the ground. Built with powerful front feet and exceptional strength in their jaws. All the instincts of her Scottie blood came rushing forward, and she began to dig in earnest.

Something recent and civilized, something connected with her person, told her it was wrong to hurt a wall like this, but something deeper and darker, older and more persistent, based on her need to protect her person, told her she needed to get out.

15

These words like daggers enter in my ears.

ACT 3, SCENE 4

The young man at the front desk was helpful. He called the room. When there was no answer, he walked down the corridor with me and knocked on Big Willie's door, where a *Do Not Disturb* sign hung from the knob. There still was no answer.

"He might have overslept," the clerk said.

I thought about how Shorty always insisted on breakfast at a certain time. "No," I said. "He would have had to get up to walk his dog."

"You can go outside and look in his window. I can't leave the front desk unattended."

"Thanks for checking," I said. There was a back door not far from where we stood. "We'll go out that way."

"I can't, ma'am. I just told you, I have to get back up

front." He strode away, barely missing Dirk, who had flattened himself against the wall.

It took me a moment to register that when I'd said *we*, I'd meant Dirk and I. The clerk thought *we* meant . . . Forget it. Life with a ghost tended to get complicated at times.

I—we—headed for the outside door. "Big Willie wouldn't have missed the competition. But where would he have gone?"

Outside, I just barely dodged a Frisbee thrown by a group of teenage boys goofing off. I recognized one of them as the tall, gangly guy I'd seen at the opening. He'd thrown himself across a smaller kid who looked like she might have been a little sister. Let them goof off, then. He deserved some fun. "Sorry," they yelled, and I waved. They made as much noise as the crowds at the Games.

With very little sense of shame, I peeked in the window of Big Willie's room. He sure was messy, but maybe it was hard to be tidy when you're traveling with a dog. Clothes were strewn across the bed. A suitcase gaped open on the floor. I half expected to see Big Willie sprawled on the floor, victim of a heart attack, but the room—other than all the mess strewn around—was bare.

"He isna here," Dirk said, rather unnecessarily. He inspected the wide screened push-out glass panel that stretched beneath the large plate glass window. "Nor could any the one squeeze through such a narrow window."

I glanced at the teenagers, but they were making a great deal of noise and paying no attention to me. I didn't even lower my voice. "Were you thinking robbery?"

"Aye. It looks like it, would ye no say?"

"No. It just looks like he's messy." I felt faintly

disappointed. Big Willie hadn't struck me as the kind of person who'd be such a slob. Not when he'd shown so much pride in the way he packed whatever Silla needed, things like the folding water bowl. At least he hadn't left town. That was pretty clear, with all his stuff still here. He wasn't still in bed. He wasn't on the floor. Where could he be?

Reluctantly, I headed for the ScotShop. I had a store to run. I couldn't run around looking for an elusive Santa. I had a ridiculous mental image of Silla with antlers pulling a sleigh. How silly could I get?

Where the heck was Big Willie?

Silla heard the noisy bell. She heard the knocking, too, but she kept scratching, digging, biting at the wall.

She had a dog's concept of time. Morning was food time, walk time, playtime. Afternoon was rest time, playtime, sit-by-her-person's-leg time. Evening was eat time, walk time, playtime, lie-beside-her-person time. Night was sleep time.

But now? Now had no time. Just the incessant awful-tasting wall. Just the hurt in her paws and her nose and her tongue that she ignored. Just the pulsing need to find a squirrel for her person.

When she finally broke through, she found itchy stuff filling the space behind the wall. The only thing she stopped for was to drink water when she couldn't keep going, but soon the bowl was dry. When she found more wall behind the itchies, she snarled and tore at the obstructions. There was no time. Except the time to dig some more.

*   *   *

A little before three Friday afternoon, Scamp barked from his seat in the front window. I looked up and saw Silla scampering along the sidewalk. She charged across the street, and brakes squealed as drivers tried to avoid her. I ran out and called, knowing full well that a Scottie on a mission, or in a panic, might very well ignore me. But she swerved away from the street, limped to meet me, and sat, shivering, in front of my feet. I grabbed hold of her red collar to keep her from running away.

Where was Big Willie? He ought to have been running behind her—or hollering for her. No responsible dog owner would have deliberately let his dog loose in a town where cars—even though they were going slowly—could be a danger to the dog, and Silla wasn't the type to run away.

I looked down the street, the direction Silla had come from. My hand tingled, and I saw what looked like fiberglass insulation caught on her collar. I knelt and studied her more closely. "What's happened to you, sweetie?" Her nose was badly scratched and her beard was flecked with small pieces of—I pulled one free of the long coarse hair—was it wood? No. Sheetrock. That's what it was. She whimpered and stamped her wide feet in a frenetic Scottie dance. "Gilda! Bring me Scamp's leash!"

As soon as I snapped it onto Silla's collar, she took off running downhill, toward the Hamelin Hotel, the retractable wire unwinding from the blue handle as fast as it could.

16

Thou hast cleft my heart in twain.
ACT 3, SCENE 4

I burst into the lobby and ran for the front desk, scattering a group of kilt-clad men. The clerk, the same red-headed young man I'd dealt with before, looked up in some alarm. "Mr. Bowman's room," I panted. "You have to let me in. I think he's sick. He may have had a heart attack."

"All right, miss. Settle down." He looked around, seeming to wish for a manager to materialize and take care of the crazy woman before him.

His wishes must have worked, because a gray-suited woman with hair as slicked back as a seal's was at my elbow. "May I be of service?" A tag with the hotel logo on it gave her name, but I hardly noticed it. All I saw was her title. *Manager.*

"Yes," I said with some exasperation. "I need to get

into Big Willie Bowman's room right away." Before she could object and cite privacy laws at me, I headed down the hallway, pretty much forcing her to follow. Silla led the parade and clawed at the door.

"Please," I said. "This is very important."

She studied me only for a moment. Something in my face must have convinced her, or maybe it was the sound of Silla whining as she sniffed and pawed at the door-jamb, but she raised her arm. The clerk—I didn't realize he'd followed us so closely—placed a key card in her outstretched palm.

I tightened my hold on the leash and held my breath.

It was just as well, since an unpleasant smell greeted us. He *was* sick. I knew it. He'd probably been lying on the floor for two days. If he was close beside the bed, I wouldn't have seen him from the window. Poor man. Silla tugged on the leash, and I followed her inside. "Willie," I cried. "Willie? Are you here? Where are you?" Pieces of Sheetrock littered the floor once we got past the small entryway.

Silla lunged to her right and tried to squeeze through a gaping hole in the wall, but I held her back and opened what had to be the bathroom door. I tried to close it again, as soon as I saw what was in there—I didn't want to see it—but Silla had forced her way through and stopped with her two front feet on Big Willie's back. His unmoving back. There was no question in my mind—other than the obvious one: Who would do something this awful to someone as sweet as Big Willie Bowman? Strangled with the cords of a bagpipe. Silla whined. When I didn't move, she barked and lay down across his body, her pointy, carrot-shaped tail thumping against the chanter.

Behind me I heard the manager gasp. "Is Mr. Bowman all right? Does he need an ambulance?"

I couldn't blame her for such stupidity. She'd probably never seen a dead body before. "No," I said. "Call the police. Mr. Bowman is dead."

"Are you sure?"

That was when I realized I'd been blocking the bathroom door. She wasn't being stupid. She hadn't a clue. She couldn't see him. Just as well. "I'm sure," I told her. "Just call the police."

Within seconds she was on her cell phone, reporting the death, asking them to send someone right away. And then she was in the hall, ordering the clerk to clear the hallway, telling him—unnecessarily, I thought—to send the police back to the room as soon as they arrived.

I didn't need to feel for a pulse. But I felt an unreasoning impulse to tidy up. Sheetrock and insulation lay scattered around the body. Silla must have worked for hours to escape. How had she known what to do, where to start, how long to dig? I stepped forward, knelt, and laid my hand on her head. She whimpered, but didn't move other than to lick the back of Big Willie's head.

Outside the room I could hear the manager continuing to bark orders. Dirk hovered beside me. "The puir wee doggie maun ha' seen it all," he said. "D'ye think she'd recognize the killer?"

I brushed tears from my face. "Considering the way she ripped apart that wall, I'd say she'd probably tear into him if she had a chance. I wonder how she got out of the room."

Dirk motioned back over his shoulder. "She pushed out the . . . the webbing below the window."

"You mean the screen? The mesh that keeps bugs out?"

"Is that what 'tis called?"

"Aye. I mean, yes." No wonder her nose was bleeding. First the wall, then the screen. Poor brave little dog. What was she going to do now without Willie to care for her? Did he have any relatives who'd take her? He'd mentioned his wife's awful, judgmental sister and brothers, but I had no idea who the next of kin would be.

Thank goodness the police—Harper, I hoped—would be here soon.

I reached for my cell phone. Whatever was—or wasn't—going on between us, I wanted to hear his voice. "Harper," I said without preamble, "can you come to the hotel? It's Big Willie. He's . . . he's dead. It looks like somebody strangled him. Room 124."

"Yes," he said. "I know. I'm on my way."

He knew about the death? Or he knew the room number? I wasn't sure, and I supposed it didn't matter. I reached out and laid my hand on Silla's sturdy back.

Harper wasn't surprised by the messiness of most crime scenes, but he was often taken aback by the difference between what a room had been and what it was after a murder had been committed. He didn't usually see the *before*, except in photographs provided by a victim's family. In this case, though, he'd seen Bowman's room. It was so tidy yesterday when he'd looked in through the sun-drenched window. Now, as he walked into the chaos, careful not to step on anything that might constitute evidence, he wondered how the transformation had occurred. Before or after the death? During the event? The result of Bowman's own actions or strictly the murderer's? He didn't like to form too much of an opinion ahead of time, but he couldn't imagine Bowman having created any of this.

He'd already learned from the hotel manager that Peggy was still in the bathroom with the body. He hoped she was coping with this. He knew from past experience that she'd probably hold all her emotion inside and let it out later, when she was alone, or maybe with Karaline, her friend. He didn't want to leave her alone with the body too long, but he knew he couldn't rush this first view of the crime scene. One step at a time. Murphy was one step ahead of him, taking photos.

"Peggy," he called out and heard a muffled reply. "Don't move out of the room for another couple of minutes. We're taking pictures."

"I know. I can hear the clicking." She sounded calm, but he was sure her calm was superimposed over a deep anguish. He'd heard her concern for Bowman in just those few words she'd spoken to him when she called a few minutes before.

She was talking, but not loud enough for him to hear any words. It sounded like a conversation. Was she talking to the dead body? He strained to listen, all the while taking careful note of the position of the suitcase, the parallel drag marks on the carpet, the scattered clothing, the open dresser drawers, the busted-out screen. If it had been burglary, the screen would have been pushed in from the outside, although he doubted any person could fit through that narrow a space.

He rounded the corner and looked in the bathroom. The dog. She was talking to the dog. He felt a draft of cold air. Or he thought he did. Maybe it was his imagination.

He laid a hand on her shoulder. She nodded, but kept stroking the little dog.

"Can you tell me why you're here? How you got in?" He indicated the Sheetrock mess. "And how this happened?"

"I looked for Big Willie this morning when he didn't show up for the caber toss. In fact, I was so worried, I came here to the hotel. The guy at the front desk wouldn't let me in the room, but I went out the back way and peeked in the window, but he wasn't here. Or"—her voice caught—"if he was, I couldn't see him."

"And what do you know about this mess?"

"It must have been Silla. Her nose is bleeding and I think she's hurt one of her paws, and her fur—see?—is covered with dust and debris. She must have dug her way out of the bathroom. She came to me for help, and I thought Big Willie might have had a heart attack or something, so I came here and talked the manager into letting me in. And then I found . . ." Her voice ran down and she gestured around her. The cords that held the drones of the bagpipe had fallen away from Bowman's throat, but the mark in the flesh on the side of the victim's neck made it fairly clear what must have happened.

One corner of Bowman's plaid was crumpled around one of the drones. It seemed fairly clear to Harper that someone had wiped the drones free of fingerprints using Bowman's own tartan. It seemed particularly heartless.

He studied the hole in the painted Sheetrock. All the way through that, plus a hefty layer of insulation, judging by the amount of it that covered the floor, and then the Sheetrock and wallpaper in the bedroom itself. And the screened window. No wonder the dog looked exhausted, stretched out like that with her hairy chin pressed into her master's back. "We're going to have to move the dog so Dr. Olafson can examine the body."

"Dr. Olafson?"

"He's the new regional medical examiner."

"Is he here yet?"

"No," he told her. "But he's on his way."

"Please leave her alone a little while longer. She'll never get to lay her head against him again."

Peggy broke down then and cried. Sobbed. And, other than pressing his hand more firmly into her shoulder, there wasn't a thing he could do about it. He wanted to scoop her up off that filthy floor and hold her, take her out of this place, give her comfort.

Instead, he crouched there like an automaton, like a robot, like a cop, and let her cry.

After a few minutes that felt like months, the crying eased. "His ring is gone," she said.

"Ring?"

"He had a big dark red ring. I think it was a ruby." She pointed at the arm splayed out on the tile floor. "It's gone."

His other arm, the left one, appeared to be trapped

beneath the body—he hated to think of Bowman like that, but after all, that was what the man now was, only a body. "Are you sure? Could it be on his other hand?"

She cocked her head to one side, and Harper could practically see her whole thought process. She was imagining Bowman standing in front of her, maybe lifting his hand to scratch his cheek. While she went through this process, Harper noted the faint light-colored line around Bowman's ring finger.

"No," she said. "He . . ." She shifted the upper part of her body slightly, almost as if she were putting herself in Bowman's standing position, and raised her own hand to her left shoulder. "He wore it on his right hand."

"We have to wait for the medical examiner to inspect the body before we can move it."

She nodded.

"For now, though, we need to move out of here so Murphy can get some photos. He'll take some of the empty hand, too." He saw Murphy nod. "Let me help you up."

She shook her head. "I can make it, but I have to lift Silla. I don't think she'll move on her own."

"Why don't you stand first? Then it'll be easier to pick up the dog."

She looked confused, as if such a simple procedure were beyond her. Finally, some sort of reasoning took over and she gathered her feet underneath her. When she lifted the dog, it whined and scrabbled its paws a bit, but settled fairly quickly, its hairy chin on Peggy's shoulder. Harper could see a small strand of insulation caught in the dog's splayed eyebrows. He reached out slowly and recovered it.

Harper traded places with Murphy and followed Peggy out of the room. Behind him, Murphy said, "The manager said we could use her office for questioning witnesses."

"Right," said Harper. "Send word when Dr. Olafson arrives, will you?"

I was more aware of Harper's hand on the middle of my back than anything else. Not Silla whimpering softly in my arms, not the other police officers in the hall, not the people milling around in the lobby. Just Harper's hand. And Macbeath walking beside me down the wide hallway. The manager led the way to her office, stepped aside for us to enter, and closed the door behind us as soon as we were inside. When Harper took his hand away, it left, just above my waist, a warm spot that quickly turned cold.

"You're shivering," he said, and removed his dark blue Windbreaker.

"I canna give ye the shawl wi'out the constable wondering how it appeared."

"I know," I said. "That's okay."

Dirk stepped quickly to one side as Harper wrapped the jacket around me, and around Silla as well. I felt very grateful for that small kindness. It held the heat of his body. Silla barely seemed to register it. Poor thing. Could dogs go into shock?

"Are you able to talk about this, or do you want to wait to answer a few questions?"

"I thought you had to get statements right away."

He just looked at me, and his charcoal eyes gave me permission to take all the time I needed.

"I can do this," I said. Silla whimpered again, and Dirk reached out to lay his hand very gently on her head. She sighed and I felt her head go limp against my shoulder. I pulled my head back and studied her. Her eyes were closed.

"The wee doggie has been through enough this day. Her heart is hurting, would ye no say?"

"Poor sweetie," I said.

"Can you tell me what happened?"

"I think she just fell asleep," I said. *My ghost just worked his magic.*

"I mean, what happened with Mr. Bowman."

"Oh."

After I went through the day's events, slowly this time, one step at a time, he asked me when was the last time I'd seen Big Willie, only he referred to him as Mr. Bowman.

I thought back. "I ate lunch with him yesterday at the Logg Cabin."

I could see Harper's involuntary glance at Silla.

"We ate at the outside tables. He asked me if I'd be willing to hold Silla for him while he competed so he wouldn't have to leave her in the room." I felt myself shudder. "That's why I went to the caber field a little before ten this morning."

"So, yesterday around noon was the last time you saw him?"

"I think it was more like one o'clock, but yes. No, wait. He and Silla took a walk after that—he'd told me they were going to."

Harper looked confused. "Are you sure you don't mean yesterday morning?"

"No. I mean yes, I'm sure. He did take a walk in the morning, but he said he wanted one alone—just he and Silla—after lunch. I think the morning walk was the one he took with Shay. Shay Burns. She . . ." Did I want to use the word *confronted*? "They had a conversation in the ScotShop, and then they left together. They headed up Main. That was when I saw you coming out of Sweetie's Jellybeans." I stopped talking. I still didn't know what his favorite candy was.

He seemed to be studying me. "What was it you were going to say?"

I gulped. "That I don't know what your favorite candy is."

"I dinna think that is what he was asking ye about."

Harper opened his mouth, closed it, opened it again. "I meant, what were you going to say about Shay?"

"Oh." Dirk was right, doggone him. "Well, they seemed to be having some sort of an argument. Of course, Shay was the one doing all the talking, the way she usually does."

"Why do you think it was an argument?"

"Later, Gilda told me she'd heard Shay tell Willie—*order* him was the word Gilda used—to leave town. She accused him of something."

"Of what?"

"Gilda didn't say. We had customers, and I told Gilda not to say anything."

"But you didn't hear any of the argument yourself?"

I shook my head, and Silla stirred. I stroked her back beneath the Windbreaker.

"So then, they walked up the hill and the next time you saw him was at lunch? Is that right?"

I thought back to Scamp's *woof* from the window

yesterday afternoon. "Yes, but then I saw him—them—again. I assume they were returning from the afternoon walk, although they weren't gone very long. When I spotted them, they were headed down Main, just past Sweetie's. They turned in at the alley leading to the big grassy area behind the hotel. I think he liked to go to his room that way so he wouldn't have to walk the dog through the lobby."

"Do you know what time that was?"

"Everything's a jumble. I don't . . . Maybe it was . . . about two?"

If I hadn't been looking at Harper's face, I wouldn't have seen the shadow that crossed it. Luckily, Dirk spotted it as well. "Something has bothered our constable. Something about the time of day, forebye."

Hmm. Dirk must have mellowed a bit toward Harper. Before, he always called Harper *the* constable. Now it was *our* constable.

"What's wrong?" I asked.

Harper's eyes narrowed. Not in suspicion, not in doubt. In pain? That's what it looked like. "I must have just missed him," he said.

"What do you mean?"

"It was right around two when I checked Bowman's room. There wasn't an answer to my knock, so I looked in through the outside window."

"I did, too. This morning, like I told you, after he didn't show up at the caber toss."

He nodded, but I wasn't sure he really heard me. "I went back up to the lobby. He must have come in right after that. If only I'd waited another few minutes, he'd still . . ."

He sounded like he was going to say something else, but his voice faded out to nothing.

"He'd still what?"

Harper started, as if he'd forgotten I was there. "He might still be alive."

"Why?"

"I was trying to arrest him."

I raised an eyebrow. "Arrest him?"

"I thought he was the fellow who was trying to assassinate the president."

"You have to be kidding. Big Willie?"

Harper groaned and passed a hand across his face. "I know it sounds crazy now. I'd been tailing him since yesterday morning. He looked like he might be the guy in the mug shot who had eluded the Secret Service."

"Aye," Dirk said. "The man they put in the big carriage"—he meant the car, I thought—"looked a wee bit like our Large William." Dirk had better long-distance eyesight than I had—that was for sure.

"But what does that have to do with Big Willie still being alive?"

"If I'd brought Bowman in for questioning . . ." He took a deep breath. "Bowman and the dog . . . then maybe—" He stopped as if he'd thought of something. "I need to find out what Olafson says about the probable time of death." He looked at his watch. "He should be here by now. Will you be okay if I leave you in the lobby?"

"Can I go back to the ScotShop? Gilda's good, but I shouldn't leave her on her own this long during our busiest season." How could I be talking about store sales while Big Willie was still lying facedown in a bathroom?

With bagpipe cords around his neck. I swallowed the lump I felt forming at the back of my throat.

"Yes. Just don't talk about this to anyone." He looked like he was going to add something, but he just shook his head.

"Right." I unwrapped myself from his Windbreaker and handed it back to him. I could feel the tears beginning down by my toes, now that this was almost over. "Thanks."

"One more question."

"Umm?" I could barely talk.

"What did his room look like when you peeked in the window this morning?"

I didn't have to think about it. "Messy." I gulped back my tears. "I remember feeling kind of disappointed that he wasn't . . . tidier somehow."

"As messy as it is now?"

"Yes. Why?"

"When I looked in his window yesterday, it was one of the tidiest rooms I've ever seen. The dog bed was set up, and the suitcase was on the luggage rack." He looked like he was about to say something else, but all he added was "That was about all." I wondered what else he'd seen.

It was funny how relieved I felt, though, to know that Big Willie had truly been a tidy person. Silla whined in my arms, as if she were agreeing with me.

"And you didn't see him at all after he walked down the street around two o'clock yesterday? Thursday."

I shook my head. "No. He didn't make it to the opening ceremonies last night. I looked around for him, but he wasn't there. I'm pretty sure I would have seen him." And if I'd missed him, Dirk would have spotted him.

"If ye hadna seen him, I would ha'."

I smiled at Dirk, and saw Harper looking a question at me.

"I'm glad Silla feels comfortable with me," I said. "I'll take her home until you can find out—" I stopped because I wasn't sure what I wanted to say. Silla whimpered again, and I knew I wanted to help her through this. I hugged her closer and stepped toward the door.

"Peggy?"

My name sounded golden in his mouth. I gulped. Even with the image of Big Willie before me, I was totally aware of Harper. Here. Now. "Yes?"

"It's chocolate. Dark chocolate."

"What is?"

"My favorite candy."

I left the hotel in something of a daze, narrowly avoiding running into a man carrying a large black case of some sort.

17

Is now most still, most secret, and most grave.

ACT 3, SCENE 4

Harper hated to send her away like that, but he didn't have a choice. Dr. Olafson walked into the lobby just as Peggy was leaving, and Harper had to shift gears back to cop mode. Nothing but a cop.

He knew Olafson had been mentored by Dr. Gunn, the state ME. Both men liked to see the scene by themselves at first. Harper was relieved to find that Murphy, after having taken pictures of everything, had cleared out and was waiting in the hallway.

White male, deceased was all that Harper had said to Olafson. Olafson nodded and studied the entryway of the room before he stepped in, just one step, and appeared to study everything one more time from this different perspective. After the third step, followed by the third stop, Harper gave up and turned to Murphy. "Any surprises?"

"How closely did you look at the body?"

"Not very. I was more interested—" If he were being truthful, he'd have to admit he was more interested in comforting Peggy, but he couldn't very well say that. He cleared his throat. "I was more interested in getting the witness statement."

Murphy studied him.

Harper was determined not to squirm. "So, what did you see?"

"Back of the neck. Deep depression."

"From the bagpipe cords?" Harper didn't think so. The cords were only long enough to wrap around the front and sides of the neck. Particularly a neck as massive as Bowman's.

"No," Murphy said. "More like the victim had been chopped with a judo or karate move. The head's at a funny angle. I'd say his neck's broken."

"Think it comes through well enough on the photos?"

"Ayuh. Sure do."

Harper waited a long time and then walked into the room, still careful not to disturb anything lying on the floor. The crime scene technicians would have conniptions if anyone disturbed possible evidence. Somebody had been looking for something—that seemed fairly clear, although he tried never to make assumptions this early in a case. All the zippers on the suitcase were unzipped, and the main compartment of it gaped open. The drawers of the ward-robe hung open. The ruffled skirt around the bottom of the bed was all messed up, as if someone had thrust an arm in as far as he could reach, sweeping back and forth to see if anything was secreted between mattress and box spring. He was surprised the mattress hadn't been upended onto

the floor. The bedspread itself was thrown back, the sheets
all awry. The bagpipes that had been so carefully spread
out on the bed when he'd first looked in . . . Harper did not
want to complete that thought.

He paused outside the bathroom door. Olafson was
still crouched over the body, but now he looked up. "I
want to turn him over. Come help, please."

At least he'd said *please*, which was a big improvement
over the brusque orders Dr. Gunn always had given at the
crime scenes Harper and Gunn had been at together. Olafson was a lot more pleasant, but Harper sure hoped he was
as competent as Gunn. Harper stepped carefully into place,
judging the best angle to lift from so he wouldn't throw his
back out.

Olafson had already positioned a body bag, opened to its
full extent. Even though Harper didn't require an explanation,
Olafson said, "I want to move the body as little as possible.
If we try to lift it onto the bag or slide the bag onto the
body, we could lose vital evidence. I have the feeling there's
a bigger story here, and I want to see what's underneath."

Big Willie was built like a linebacker. Even with decom-
position well under way, Harper knew the body would be
heavy. Olafson had placed a soft brace on Bowman's neck,
and it held the head steady in relation to the body.

Harper knew better than to ask if Olafson had made
any preliminary deductions. When the medical examiner
was ready, he'd give out information. Before that, Harper
might as well save his breath.

So he was surprised when Olafson paused and said,
"You might want to look for someone with knowledge of
jujitsu, karate, or one of the other martial arts."

Just what Murphy had suggested, but of course Harper didn't say anything about that. "Was a karate blow the cause of death?"

Olafson took in a long breath. Harper wondered how he could do that this close to a day-old dead body. "The neck appears to be broken, but that may have resulted only in partial paralysis. Let's get this man turned over."

Together they hefted the bulk, lifting as carefully as possible on his shoulder and hip. Once Bowman's body was faceup on the body bag, Harper could see the wisdom of Olafson's decision. A clump of long black hair protruded from Bowman's belt buckle.

Olafson photographed it and then, using tweezers, pulled on one hair. The entire clump dislodged and fell to the side.

Olafson placed the hair in an evidence bag, labeled it, and stood. Indicating the hole in the wall, he said, "Any preliminary information on what caused that?"

"The victim owned a dog," Harper said. "A Scottie."

Once he'd finished telling what he knew so far, Olafson asked, "Was that the dog I saw a woman carrying out the door when I came in?"

Harper nodded.

"Do you have easy access to the dog?"

This time when he nodded, Harper hoped Olafson wasn't a mind reader, wasn't able to see Harper's mental image of Peggy clutching the dog in her arms.

"I'll need a hair," Olafson said.

Harper nodded for the third time.

"The autopsy will give me the final answers. Death may have resulted from strangulation with the bagpipe cords."

Harper held his breath. It was so unlike Olafson to give out information prior to an autopsy, he was afraid to move for fear of stopping the flow.

"My dad had a bagpipe a lot like this one," Olafson said, gesturing to the object under discussion. "Only he loved it and cared for it. He never would have put it to such use."

"As far as I know," Harper ventured, "this belonged to the victim."

"Ah," said Olafson. "That would make more sense, then." And with that, he snapped back into his usual demeanor. "Thank you, Captain. You may wait outside. I'll call you when I'm ready to have the body transported."

My first impulse, of course, was to close the shop for the rest of today—not that there was that much time left till our normal closing hour—and maybe even close it tomorrow, too. Close the store, call Karaline, call my twin, call my dad. But as I crossed the street, I knew I couldn't do that. I'd been very fortunate; the ScotShop was doing well. But I had to face facts. Sales during all four days of the Hamelin Highland Games represented a major chunk of my yearly gross income. If I cut out even one afternoon, much less one whole day, people would find other places to spend their money, and there was no guarantee they'd come back when I reopened.

But what was I going to do with Silla? What had Big Willie called her? *My brave little trooper.* She'd certainly proven that by digging her way out of the room and coming for help. Well, she was going to have to be even braver now. I pasted what I hoped was a pleasant look on my face—I couldn't create a smile to save my soul—and opened the door of my ScotShop.

I should have known. Scamp was there, almost as if he'd been waiting for me. For us. I kept Silla in my arms, but when Scamp let out one of his commanding *woof*s, she wiggled and I let her down. The two dogs disappeared under the Fair Isle sweater rack, and within moments I saw four front paws peeking out from beneath the natural wool. I reached in between two sweaters and unhooked the leash—Scamp's blue-handled leash—from her red collar. Scamp's black nose appeared. His tongue shot out and licked Silla's paw, the one she'd been favoring. *What natural healers dogs are,* I thought. Just in case, though, I asked Dirk to keep an eye on her. "I don't want her running out into traffic if someone leaves the door open too long."

"Nae. That she willna do. Can ye no see she is mourning? She knows Large William is gone."

Large William. Taking more care than the task required, I wound the leash into a small circle and placed it in the cloth drawstring bag at my waist. The handle made an awkward lump, but I didn't care.

"She may nae ken the how or the why, and she may hope he will come again someday, but for now, can ye no see her sadness?"

"Aye. I mean yes. I guess I can."

"Can what? What's wrong with Silla? Where's Big Willie?" Gilda was full of questions, but I had to put her off until closing time.

It was probably best all around that we stayed incredibly busy right up until eight. I didn't have time to think, much less to cry.

Still, at the back of my mind, while I advised customers about the best way to wrap an arisaidh, helped people find the perfect tie or the right scarf, straightened those poet shirts that insisted on slipping askew on their hangers, and rang up plenty of sales, there was one corner of my mind that wondered, *Why did Shay confront Big Willie here in the ScotShop? Why was she late showing up for the opening ceremonies? And where is Big Willie's ruby ring?*

About seven, I sent Shoe and Sam down to the tie booth to take over from the temps. My two cousins worked long hours during every single Highland Festival. So did we all, only Sam, Shoe, and Gilda got paid for their overtime, and I didn't. By the time I closed the door behind the last customer of the day, I felt completely drained. I never attended the Friday night ceilidh at the hotel. Most of the townspeople—the ones who had stores at least—chose not to. We were too pooped by the end of the day to do all that dancing. Anyway, today, after Big Willie, it didn't seem like a good time to dance. It took every ounce of self-control to count up the sales for the day, empty the register, put tomorrow's cash in the safe, and tally the bank deposit. I placed cash and checks in my bank bag and tucked it safely into my arisaidh.

I should have known Gilda wouldn't let me off so easily. She planted herself in front of me and demanded to know what was going on. "Why is Silla here? Where's Big Willie? Why were you gone so long this afternoon?"

"Ye canna answer her."

"I know."

"Know what?"

"I'm sorry, Gilda. I meant, I don't know. I don't have any answers for you."

"You're lying."

I stared at her. The alcohol rehab program she'd gone through had taught her a great deal about speaking her truth, or some such thing. I didn't want to hear it right now. "I'm not lying. I have no answers to your questions. Or, at least, none that I'm allowed to talk about."

"So, what happened to Big Willie? Is he hurt?"

I shook my head.

"Sick?"

"No."

Her wide eyes clouded over with a film of tears, and she whispered her question. "Is he dead?"

Scamp woofed and Silla howled a mournful sound. *A-roooo.* The timing was coincidental of course, but shivers ran up and down my back and wouldn't go away. Dirk handed me the shawl. Luckily Gilda had turned away from me, so she didn't see it magically appear. I could have wrapped my arisaidh around me, but right at that moment, the shawl felt better. By the time I had it around my shoulders, relishing the warmth of it, she was on her knees beside the two dogs.

"Poor little girl," she crooned. "Do you want to come home with Scamp and me?"

"No!" I held up my hand. "I mean, I don't mind taking care of her."

Gilda's curls shivered as much as my back was doing. "You're a cat person. What would Shorty say if you brought a dog into your house?"

I wrapped the shawl more tightly around myself and pulled the leash out of my waist bag. "He gets along just fine with Tessa, and she's a dog." Tessa was my twin brother's service dog, and while Shorty tolerated her, I couldn't in all honesty say the two were friends. But at least they weren't enemies, either.

I bent and snapped the leash on Silla's collar, but Gilda reached out and took hold of it. "That's Scamp's leash. And Silla needs to stay with Scamp."

Doggone it, she was probably right. I didn't answer her. I just stood and walked to the front door.

Gilda clipped a green leash onto Scamp's collar. Thank goodness we'd had an extra one in the storeroom. The two dogs led the way to the door. When we went outside, I locked the door and then turned to the right, knowing Gilda would turn to the left. I heard the whine of Silla's leash unwinding. I didn't even want to watch her walking away from me, so I kept my eyes resolutely on the courtyard between the ScotShop and the Logg Cabin. A low *woof* emanated from somewhere near my left Achilles tendon. Silla had planted herself as inexorably as Gilda had done only a few minutes earlier. *Woof*, she said again when the blue leash had stretched out to its maximum point. It pulled at her collar. "Come, Silla," Gilda called from the other end of the leash, but Silla didn't move.

Neither did I.

Moira turned over her little kingdom to Mary Beth Armstrong, the part-time night dispatcher Mac had hired a few months earlier. He'd grumped about it, but he eventually was convinced when Moira had mentioned how great it was that now he'd be the chief of a twenty-four/seven department. Sounded childish, she thought, but then again, Mac was nothing but a big baby half the time. Moira saw through all his posturing. He was irritating as all get-out some of the time, most of the time. But every so often she'd glimpse the little kid who never seemed to get what he really needed. An unfortunate attitude to have in a chief of police.

It had taken a while to find the right person for the night dispatcher's job. They'd gone through, what? Three now? But Mary Beth was by far the pick of the litter.

They didn't get that many calls late at night, so Mary Beth had a lot of time to study for her part-time college courses. When the girl slept was anybody's guess, but Moira had checked on her often enough at odd hours and always found her alert and ready to do her job right. Not like that last one, who'd fallen asleep so deeply nothing could wake her up. Alert and competent. That kind of combination could be hard to find. The Hamelin force was lucky to have Mary Beth.

"You're liable to get more calls than usual tonight," Moira warned her. "And the team will be checking in off and on all night long, what with this murder on our hands. We've tried to keep it quiet, but with this many people in town, the word can leak out."

"Has it? Leaked out already, I mean."

"Good question. Not that I know of. The people who were at the hotel know something was wrong, but when they wheeled the body out, they cleared the lobby first."

Mary Beth looked dubious. *As well she might,* thought Moira.

"The ceilidh's going on this evening, so there may be some drunk and disorderlies from that."

Mary Beth nodded and adjusted the green plaid scarf around her ponytail.

"But we have extra officers there just in case."

"Plainclothes?"

"Yes." Of course, Moira knew most of them would stand out like sore thumbs, but at least they'd be there.

Moira's nephew walked in, took a look at the officers still writing reports, looking up things on their computers, doing the normal stuff cops do—only they do more of it when there's been a murder in town—and threaded his way between the desks. He nodded a hello to Mary Beth and turned to his aunt. "You ready to go?"

Moira grinned and turned on her Southern charm. "Honey chile, yew got heah jest in the nick of time. I was about wore out waitin' fer yew."

Mary Beth laughed and waved them away.

On the way home, Silla stopped to take care of her dog business, so I pulled out my phone. "I have to call Karaline and let her know what happened."

"Aye," Dirk said. "That ye do for certes."

"I'm not looking forward to this. She really liked Big Willie."

"Aye," he said again. "He was a good man."

"Karaline," I said when she answered.

"What's wrong?"

How like a friend to know, after hearing only three syllables, that something was wrong.

"Do you need me to come over? I can leave right now. Where are you?"

"No. No, it's just that . . . there's been a murder."

She breathed something that sounded like *not another one* but all she said was, "Are you okay?"

"Yes. No. I don't know. It was . . ." I hated to be the one to tell her it was Big Willie. I couldn't tell her on the phone. "I know you have to get up early tomorrow," I said, "but could you come by for a little while?"

"Be right there. On my way. I'll bring food." And she hung up. How had she known I'd be hungry?

Silla bumped her head against my leg. I was going to have to figure out all her dog language so I'd know when she had to go out and when she needed to eat. Oh shoot— I didn't have any dog food. Poor Silla, she probably hadn't had anything to eat since yesterday morning. Maybe longer. I knew some people believed it was good for dogs to fast one day a week—I'd read that somewhere—but this was no time to starve her. Dirk and I would have to drive to that all-night grocery store in Arkane to get her something.

But I took off running as soon as I turned the corner onto Hickory Lane and saw my brother's van parked in my driveway. Silla ran along beside me, obviously not understanding what was going on, but happy—or at least hopeful—with a dog's sweet acceptance of whatever was happening, that something good was in process.

"What are you doing here?" I called as I rounded the back of his vehicle. "I thought you'd be out of town another week."

"Finished the job early." He clasped his hands in the

air above his head. "Didn't want to miss the Games, and now I don't have to. Who's this?"

Silla had bounded up the ramp ahead of me, and came to a screeching halt in front of my twin's wheelchair. She ignored Tess, who had risen, stretching her rear end skyward as her front legs reached out before her in blissful ease. She reminded me of that yoga pose I hadn't been practicing lately, the one whose name always made me smile. Downward-Facing Dog.

"Hello, sweet Tessa," I said, ruffling her soft black fur. She licked my hand, dipped her head in Dirk's direction—she knew better than to try to lick him—and turned to investigate the interesting end of the new dog on the porch.

"This is Silla," I said. "Silla, meet Andrew, my twin, better known as Drew, even better known as primary drive-me-nuts guy because he travels around the country on his job and I never know where he is."

Drew took a swing at my arm, which I didn't quite manage to avoid. "I go wherever the dinosaurs are."

"And this," I continued with my introductions, "is Tessa, Drew's all-around good dog, better known as the best dog in the world."

Silla sat down.

"Change that to *tied for first place* as best dog with Silla, the other best dog."

Silla stood and bobbed her head. Darn, it looked like she'd understood my silliness.

"Ye didna introduce me."

"You've already met," I said.

"Huh?" said my brother. "Met who?"

Dirk laughed.

"Me," I said.

Ignoring my apparent inanity, Drew said, "You sure took long enough to get home tonight. I've been waiting forever."

"Let me guess. Twenty minutes?"

He grinned. "More like ten. Where'd you pick up this sweet little Scottie?"

When I didn't answer immediately, he looked at me. "Let's get you inside, sis. You need a cup of tea, or something a little stronger, and maybe a good long cry on your big brother's shoulder."

"Whaddya mean *big*? You're five minutes older than I am."

"Isn't that what I just said?"

"You're right. That might help." I unlocked my front door. "Do you have any dog food in your van?"

"Yep. Do you have any people food in your house?"

"Not enough for a chowhound like you, but Karaline will be here in a few minutes."

His eyes lit up with more anticipation than the thought of a free meal deserved. I could only wonder why he hadn't swung by her house first. But then, I *knew* why he'd come here. He was my twin. He knew when I needed him. Just as I'd known he needed me that day he broke his back falling off the dinosaur frame. That was when he'd lost the use of his legs.

Silla woofed. It sure sounded like *feed me*. Drew laughed and headed back out to his van.

Dirk waited for the door to close. "What would be a 'tchow hown'?"

18

Alas, how shall this bloody deed be answer'd?
ACT 4, SCENE 1

Marti Fairing couldn't say she loved murder investigations; the reasons that drove that part of her work were just too horrible to contemplate. But she couldn't help loving the connection she felt with everybody at the station when they were actively working a case. She glanced over at Mac's closed door. He was probably taking a nap in there. Okay, so the connection with *almost* everybody. She wondered why they hadn't roped in Fenton, the Secret Service fellow, as some sort of consultant. Seemed to her he might have been a good resource. But Mac was awfully touchy about his territory. Mac made a lousy alpha dog. She wasn't sure about town politics or the details of who was related to whom, but she was fairly sure the only reason he'd gotten appointed chief was that he was related to a couple of town big shots.

Murphy, at the desk beside hers, was looking something up on the Internet. Harper was studying the huge wall map of Hamelin, tracing an imaginary line from here to there and back again. Mary Beth, the relatively new night dispatcher, was hunched over a big book, her headset lending her the air of a studious Dumbo. Outside, the dark night seemed to beat against the station windows. Fairing knew it was just the wind, and she spared a moment to pity the people in tents on the far side of the meadow; it sounded like it would create havoc once it made its way inside.

"We need a name for our murderer." Harper's voice seemed to float over the desks.

"Duh," said Murphy. "Once we have a name we arrest the guy, right?"

"No," Harper said. "I mean we need something we can call this guy instead of saying 'the murderer' each time we refer to him."

"Or her," Fairing pointed out.

"Gotta be fair to the opposite sex," Murphy said.

Fairing threw a pencil at him. "Opposite to what? Maybe you're the opposite one."

Murphy threw the pencil back at her, and she caught it with a deft movement. "How about Piper?" he suggested. "Name for the murderer."

"No," Fairing said. "Piping isn't easy. Somebody who worked hard to learn to play the pipes would never risk damaging a set that way." She thought a moment. "How about *Cord*?"

Harper made a little humming sound. "I like it."

"Sounds good to me," Murphy agreed. "Kills with cords, hits hard enough to break a spinal cord."

Ewww. Marti hadn't thought of that angle.

Cord it was.

Fairing pushed aside the yellow legal pad she'd been scribbling notes on and started to stand, but something poked her in the leg. The little package from Peggy Winn.

The blue wrapping paper matched her uniform. The silver ribbon matched her badge. She smiled to herself and untied the ribbon. She smoothed out the paper and laid the necklace, a rather pretty concoction of big silver-toned beads and faded white plastic leaves, across it. She didn't have a thing in the world to wear it with, except that little black dress she never had reason to put on.

"What's that?" Murphy jostled her elbow. "You been shoplifting again?"

"Cretin," she said with a totally fake frown.

"Oh, forgive me. I forgot. You don't shoplift. All you do is chase innocent Secret Service agents."

Fairing grinned.

"You two planning on getting any work done?"

"Nope," said Murphy. "Now that we have a name for our perp, we plan to goof around all night."

"Come look at this."

Fairing led the way to the map. "What have you found?"

"Bowman was last seen alive around two, here." He pointed. "After that, to the best of our knowledge, he stayed in his room."

"Doing what?" Fairing knew there was no answer to that, but she sure wished she knew. It might have had something to do with why he was murdered.

"Right." Harper had obviously read her mind. "If we

knew the answer to that, we might be a lot further along."
He moved his pointing finger to the meadow. "How long
would it take . . . Cord . . . to get from the hotel to the stage?"

Fairing couldn't figure out where he was headed. Murphy saw the reasoning first. "Shay Burns? You want her
as the suspect?"

"Shay? Why Shay?" Marti couldn't see a connection.

"That's right," said Murphy. "You were busy wasting
time in the attic with Turner. Shay—who I might remind
you has never once been late to her opening ceremony, except the year her sister died, when she missed it altogether—
came running onto the field just moments before the president
arrived. The agents wouldn't let her on the stage until the
action was all over with."

"Which direction did she come from?"

Harper laid a finger on the map.

The flowered arch. At the end of Main. Where the
hotel stood only a few blocks up the street.

Fairing couldn't see Shay as Cord, though. First of all,
she didn't move like somebody who'd studied martial arts
long enough to know how to give a killing—or at least a
paralyzing—blow to the back of someone's neck. She
voiced her concern, and Murphy snorted.

"Secondly," she said, "doesn't Shay live farther up Main?"

Harper nodded. "Third house above the hardware
store."

How would he know that? Fairing stared at him.

"Moira told me."

Moira ought to know. She knew everything about
everybody in town. Except who had a reason to kill Big

Willie Bowman. "So, why couldn't she have been coming from her house?"

"You on her side?"

"I'm on the side of reason, Murph." Even as she said it, she knew it sounded corny.

Murphy saluted. "Truth, justice, and the American way?"

"You got it." She stood her ground. She *was* on the side of justice. Justice represented by the statue of the blindfolded woman with the scales. Not because justice was blind, but because justice should be dispensed equally for everyone. And she couldn't think of a single reason why they should concentrate solely on Shay Burns.

"You're right." Harper lifted his finger from where it hovered over what Fairing assumed was the location of Shay's house. "And we don't have a motive for her."

Murphy made that disgusting sound again. "We don't have a motive for anybody. Why kill Santa Claus?"

Fairing fiddled with her pencil. Murphy and Harper both had a point. They needed a motive.

"There is one thing," Harper said, and Fairing could feel her ears perk up. Something about his tone of voice. "We have a witness, Gilda Buchanan, assistant manager at the ScotShop, who heard Ms. Burns accuse William Bowman of letting her sister die."

Murphy looked confused. "Whose sister?"

"Burns said, 'You let my sister die.' That appears to be why she ordered him to get out of town."

"Bingo," said Murphy. "Motive."

"Did you ask Ms. Burns about it, sir?"

"Not yet, Fairing. I saw Ms. Buchanan in the street

just this evening. She approached me and told me about the argument she'd overheard."

Murphy asked, "So, why aren't we talking to Ms. Burns about this?"

"She's not home and not answering her phone."

Fairing still couldn't see Shay as Cord. "What happened to the dog?"

Harper's hand, roving over the map again, paused. "Peggy Winn took her home." He got a funny look on his face that Fairing couldn't interpret. "I'll be right back," he said, and left the station.

I placed one of the chairs against the side wall to make room for Drew's wheelchair and settled at the kitchen table across from him. Tessa crawled under the table. Dirk leaned against the counter beside the sink. Silla curled into a ball at my feet. Shorty was nowhere to be seen. I missed her usual greeting, but couldn't blame her, what with a strange dog in the house. Was this even going to work out? *Nonsense*, I told myself. Big Willie probably had a will directing who would get Silla if . . . if anything happened. I reached for a tissue.

Dirk stepped forward, but I waved my hand. "I'm okay."

"No, you're not. Okay, sis, give. Tell me what's wrong."

I couldn't talk coherently for a minute or two. By the time I had myself under control, Karaline was at the door. Drew wheeled out of the kitchen to let her in. It took the two of them a few minutes to get back to me. I spent the time stroking Silla's head. She didn't even move.

Karaline came in, hugged me, and dished up meat loaf, while I sat there like a lump.

The first bit tasted like cardboard, but I gradually thawed out a bit as Karaline and Drew prompted me with gentle questions. Dirk, naturally, added his comments, which Karaline could hear but Drew couldn't. "Harper told me not to talk about it," I said, "but I can't just hold it all inside."

After I told them everything I could remember, we stared at one another for a few minutes. "It sure would be good," Karaline said, "if we could solve the case, sort of like we did the other ones. Well"—she looked at me— "like *you* solved them."

"I want part of the action this time," Drew said.

"Fine with me. Any ideas where to start?" But none of us had any ideas at all. Any worth following up on, that is.

"I liked Big Willie so much," Karaline said. "He reminds me—reminded me—of my uncle Arnold. He's in his eighties, but still farms. He always has a dog or two following at his footsteps. Always has a big genuine smile for everybody." She glanced at Drew. "You'll love him when we—" She clamped her mouth shut.

I looked from her to my brother and back again. "When you what?" Drew shook his head, but he looked guilty and, somehow, pleased at the same time. "What's going on?"

They stared at each other and I saw some sort of silent signal pass between them, but I couldn't for the life of me figure out what they were saying. I glanced at Dirk and he raised both hands, palm up in that *don't ask me* gesture.

"Cat's out of the bag," Drew said.

"Well, *now* it certainly is." Karaline smiled at him. She reached out and took his hand, then splayed her other hand, her left hand, flat on the table so I could see the sparkly diamond on her fourth finger.

I jumped to my feet, narrowly avoiding a collision with Silla, and grabbed both of them in the biggest bear hug I could manage.

"I am most pleased for ye, Mistress Karaline. I have great respect for your intended."

"Thank you. We're planning a trip next month, so Drew can meet my family." She looked from me to Dirk. "The rest of my family." She smiled.

I burst into tears.

"I thought you'd be happy for us," Drew said. "I'm sorry we didn't tell you sooner."

"She is happy," Karaline explained. "It's just that, coming so fast on Big Willie's murder, this feels like it's too much to take in." She turned to me. "Is that right, my friend?"

I couldn't do anything except nod. I felt like a war was waging inside me. I felt so angry over Big Willie's murder—with his own bagpipe cords. How could anybody have been so cruel? And to lock little Silla in there with the body of her master, somebody she loved with all her little doggie heart? I couldn't think of a punishment harsh enough for somebody who would do that. And now here I had to shift gears. The love I'd seen developing for a long time between Drew and Karaline, the love I felt for both of them separately and now, soon to be, as a unit—how could I ever express my happiness for them?

I thought of Justice, blindfolded and stately, holding her scales in an outstretched arm.

Hate balanced by love.

Anger balanced by joy.

Which way would the scales tilt?

The doorbell rang.

Harper wasn't surprised when Karaline answered the door. After all, her car was in the driveway. Next to Peggy's brother's van. "It looks like there's a party going on," he said. "Do you mind if I come in for a couple of minutes?"

Karaline reached for his arm and drew him in. "It's not a party, as I'm sure you've already figured out."

But Harper could sense something—something not related to murder and despair, something buoyant—underneath her words. "I have some things to get out of my car first."

"Do you need help?"

He shook his head. "Be right back."

Karaline waited for him to load up with dog bed, red retractable leash, water bowl, and food.

"I had to sign my life away to remove these from the crime scene," he told her.

"Thanks," she said. "Peggy's going to be so grateful." She paused. "It may take her a while to thank you, though."

"I understand." He followed Karaline to the kitchen.

Peggy sat with a supersized box of tissues next to her plate. She looked up—her eyes were red and swollen—but she said nothing as Harper placed his armload of stuff on the counter. "Where do you want this?" He held out the dog bed. Drew took it from him and set it down beside Peggy's feet. Harper shifted position a bit so he could see Silla's reaction.

She perked her ears, looked around, and dropped her head. Peggy reached down and lifted the little dog, setting her gently inside the bed. Silla didn't even bother to do the doggie-turn-around-three-times thing. Harper thought they always did that. But all she did was sink down and rest her head over her curled-up feet. The perky eyebrows that normally stuck up, giving most Scotties an aura of faint surprise, seemed droopy somehow.

"You want something to eat?" Karaline didn't even wait for an answer. She pushed him into a chair, the one next to Peggy, whipped out a plate, and piled it with food. "Here. You need your strength for what's ahead of you."

"Thanks." Before he took a bite, he looked at Peggy. "You told them?"

She didn't meet his eyes. "I know you told me not to talk to anybody about it, but this is my twin."

"I know. You and he tell each other everything."

"Not quite everything." She looked at her brother, and Harper thought the stare was a bit pointed. What was going on?

"And what about me," Karaline said, taking her place beside Drew. "Don't I count?"

"Well, of course I'd tell *you*. Harper knows that."

The funny thing was, he *did* know that. He'd known a few hours ago that she was going to tell Karaline everything. And Drew as well, only Harper had thought he was out of town.

The meat loaf was delicious; everything Karaline ever

cooked was delicious. But the good food wasn't enough to stop him from being a cop. "I assume you haven't solved the case yet," he said. "Otherwise you would have called me, right?"

He hadn't meant to be funny, and he was pretty sure he hadn't been, but for some reason, all three of them burst out laughing. Even Peggy. It didn't last long, but it lit her face. Harper had to restrain himself from reaching out to her. Hadn't she made it clear enough she wasn't interested?

Silla did not want to leave her bed when this new person tried to coax her out of it. Her bed still smelled like her person. She could not find his smell anywhere else except, just a little, on the floor by the soft cave in that other place. Where the other dog licked her foot.

When the new person picked up the bed, with Silla still in it, Silla simply buried her head deeper into the soft pillowy side and waited to see what would happen. Waited to see if her person would come back.

She barely registered the new room, the gray cat who hissed at her and jumped up on the big person-bed. None of it mattered. Silla would wait as long as she needed to for her person. When he came back for her, she would be ready.

19

O, this is the poison of deep grief.
ACT 4, SCENE 5

Saturday morning, Moira knew she'd be late for work, for the first time ever, but she hoped Mary Beth wouldn't mind staying a little longer than usual. She didn't really care, though. Not even with a murder to solve. It seemed like she'd practically lived at the station for, what?—twenty-two years? Had it really been that long? Was she getting burned out? Was that what this attitude—or lack of one—was called? All she wanted to do was stay home today with Russ. She wasn't even tempted to walk down to the meadow to see any of the exhibits or events.

She had this little one-bedroom house, tucked into a corner lot where Hickory intersected with Maple. Her fridge was ten cubic feet. Her stove had only two burners. Her bathroom was minuscule. She loved it. She really did. And she'd always thought if she ever retired, she'd like spending time here. But now she kind of wondered if maybe she should have bought a bigger place. A house with a guest room.

Yesterday, Russell had insisted he'd get a hotel room, but once he'd made the rounds and found every place booked solid, he'd called her and admitted as how her living room couch sounded mighty fine. When he'd knocked on her front door, he carried a grocery bag full of food. She liked the idea of a man who could cook his own breakfast—and one for her at the same time. He'd make some woman a great husband someday. Maybe they'd settle down right here in Hamelin.

"So, did you sleep okay, Russ? That couch isn't nearly long enough."

He plopped some scrambled eggs onto her plate. "Grab yourself some bacon. The couch was fine. Once the Games are over, I'll get a hotel room and get out of your hair."

Moira surveyed her full plate, picked up her fork, and said, "You can stay in my hair as long as you want to, sonny, and as long as you can stand that couch. I ain't complaining."

He laughed and joined her at the tiny table. "Too bad you have to work. I'll walk you to the station and then check out the town."

She scoffed. "Walk me to the station? Ha! You just want a chance to get in on the investigation. Am I right?"

He sure looked cute when he was shamefaced. Just like when he was a little kid.

The early-morning sunlight poured through my bedroom window. I was already dressed and ready to go, but Silla hadn't moved. Not even when Shorty investigated her soon after dawn, sniffing almost every hair, one at a time, poking at her tail (what she could see of it) and her ears, and finally placing one gray kitty paw on top of Silla's head as if to say, *I the conquering hero-cat, you the subservient dog.* I had a feeling that once Silla got to feeling better, that dynamic might change. If she ever got to feeling better. Maybe she was sick. "Do you think I should take Silla to the vet, Dirk?"

"What would be the vet?"

"You know, a doctor for animals."

When he didn't respond, I stopped patting the unresponsive Silla and looked up at my ghost. "What?"

"A doctor? For animals?"

I couldn't see why the concept should be so alien to him. "Didn't you have doctors—healers—who helped animals when you were alive?"

"I spent many a sleepless night wi' the does when 'twas time for kidding."

Kidding—that meant the birthing of the baby goats. And a doe was a mama goat. I'd learned that much at least over the past year, but there was still a boatload of goat lore I had no clue about.

"Although," he added, "to be perfectly honest, our family's goats didna have many the problems."

"But it sounds like you worried about them."

"Nae. No so much about the goats as about the wildies who would come around when the sounds o' the new kids attracted them. Only on occasion did I ha' to pull on a wee one."

"Well, I don't have those sorts of skills, and I've never

to the best of my knowledge even seen a wildie," I said,
"but I do know when somebody's drooping." Before he
could question the word, I asked, "Don't you think Silla
should get a checkup?"

"Ye ha' told me she was naught but a tiny pup when
Large William found her in the puppy grinder."

"Puppy mill," I said automatically.

"Aye, is that not what I said?"

"Not quite. But never mind that. What was your point?"

"She is a grown dog the now, is she no?"

"Aye. Yes."

"So-o-o"—he drew the word out until it was several
heartbeats long—"he is the only master she has known
for the most o' her life—is that nae true?"

"Uh-huh." I thought I could see where this was headed.

"When a woman loses a child, does she no grieve?
When a man loses his wife or a wife her husband, do they
no mourn?"

I nodded. Dirk was getting downright poetic in his old
age—not that he'd ever be anything other than thirty years
old, but he seemed to have learned a lot in the past 654
years.

"Why can ye no bear to let the wee doggie grieve in
her own way?"

When he put it like that, I had to agree. I gathered up
Silla's red leash, snapped it onto her collar, and picked
her up. She hung limp in my arms, and I tucked the end
of my arisaidh around her. Maybe she'd get a little comfort from the warmth of it.

I looked back at Dirk. When I was seventy years old,

he'd still be thirty. The thought unnerved me, and I hugged Silla a little bit closer.

Gilda was once again at the ScotShop ahead of me. We seemed to be starting a new trend.

"Are you ready for our extra-long day?"

She nodded. "I slept pretty well last night, so I think I'm up to it."

Sam knocked on the glass. I could see Shoe right behind him. I let Gilda open the door for them. My arms were still full of Silla. I halfway wished I'd brought her dog bed.

"Shoe," I said, "will you count on spending most of the day at the tie booth?"

He shrugged. "Sure. I could take my pipes and lure people into the tent that way."

"You can leave your bagpipe behind," I said pointedly, "and help with matching people to their clan ties. Understood?"

"Grump," he said, but his voice was quiet enough that I could pretend not to have heard him. I couldn't risk his alienating people with the squawks and wheezings of his inexpert playing.

"Where *is* your bagpipe, by the way?"

He looked hopeful, but only for a moment. Then his eyes strayed back toward the storeroom.

"You didn't," I said. "That room is for ScotShop's excess merchandise—"

"And for the coffeepot," Gilda added helpfully as she headed that way, presumably to get said pot a-brewing.

I ignored the interruption, other than to say, "Bring the cash box for the tent while you're back there." I turned back to Shoe. "It's not your own private storage unit."

"They don't take up much room."

It took me a second to register what he'd said. "They? They, as in *plural*? You have two bagpipes now?" *Bagpipes* was one of those strange words that was sort of singular and sort of not. It was one bagpipe or one set of bagpipes. People referred to their *bagpipes* if they'd collected fifty of them. But sometimes they used the same word if they had only one of the blasted things.

He wrinkled his forehead and looked down at his feet, as if they'd suddenly become the most interesting objects in the room. "I . . . uh . . . bought another one. This one's more portable than my big one. It doesn't take up as much room. The drones aren't as long, and it comes with its own carrying case." He held his hands out to indicate something about the size of a boot box.

"I don't care," I said. "You are not to leave them—no matter how many—in the storeroom."

Gilda handed him the cash drawer, tucked into a box with *SCARVES & TIES* written on the side. She let him out the front door and locked it behind him. So far we didn't have a line outside, but I knew from past experience that would soon change.

I looked around the store. What to do with Silla. Dirk must have read my mind. "Why d'ye no put her beneath the rack where she and the wee Scamp like to stay? Will she not be more at peace there than any the where otherwise?"

Why did Middle English use so many words? His language—translated somehow into twenty-first-century

American English—must have lost something, or gained something, during the translation. And how could I possibly know how Chaucer had really spoken? Poetry was one thing; everyday speech was another.

"Under the sweaters," I said. "Right."

I spent a good deal of the morning and half the afternoon trying not to think about Big Willie's body as I'd last seen it, but events conspired against me to keep the image fresh in my mind. A pipe band marched up Main Street, preceded by Mr. Stone and his drummers. The sound brought to mind a funeral dirge. Several people with Scotties came into the store, reminding me of my little Silla. No, not *mine*. And I didn't know if she ever would be. Scamp emerged to investigate each one of the visiting dogs, but quickly returned to Silla after each foray out from under the Fair Isle rack. The weather was warm enough that not many people even looked at the sweaters, so the dogs remained relatively undisturbed all day.

Around four my cell phone vibrated, and I excused myself to answer it. "We have a problem," Shoe said without an introduction. "Josh cut his hand. It's pretty bad. We're at the first aid tent and they say he needs stitches."

I judged the relative merits of what was open to me. Should I send Shoe to the hospital with Josh, or take him myself, leaving Shoe to supervise the newer temp in the tie booth and Gilda to oversee the store? Neither option was particularly inviting, but the second seemed easier to deal with. "Can he walk, or is he in danger of passing out?"

"He made it here to the first aid tent just fine."

"Okay. You two head back to the booth and sit him down somewhere at the back of it. Be sure he drinks some water. He didn't bleed on any of the ties or scarves, did he?" Without giving him time to answer, I added, "Give me ten minutes to get my car. I'll call you when I get close to the arch and you can walk with him. From then on, it'll just be you and—" I couldn't remember her name. "Uh, just you and her on your own. Can you handle it?"

"Does a bear . . ."

"Shoe, do *not* finish that sentence," I interrupted, "especially if there's anyone within earshot. I'll call you as soon as I can."

Gilda rolled her eyes yet again when I told her what was going on, but she stepped up to the challenge. "I'll get back as quickly as I possibly can," I promised.

"Drive safely," she said. "I can't handle any more labor shortages."

On the way to the front door I asked Dirk to stay behind and watch after Silla. He'd heard me explain the problem to Gilda, so I didn't need to fill him in.

"Of course I will," he said, the *r* in *course* sounding like five of them strung together.

Amy Harper took a quick break to use the restroom. She stopped a moment to call her husband. "It's crazy around this place . . . Oh, you know, the usual: a knifing, a drug overdose, an underweight baby born in the car on the way here. As I left to take a break, some guy came in who'd slammed his hand in a cash register drawer and split it wide open . . . No, he wasn't trying to steal anything; he worked there. Just careless, I guess . . . Yeah, love you bunches. Speaking of *love you*"—she let her voice drop to what she hoped was a sultry tone—"I'll see you tonight."

With a smile in her heart, she passed the double doors that opened from the waiting room. They swung apart and she glanced out. She recognized a woman sitting there and took a brief detour. "Ms. Winn? I don't know if you remember me—"

"Sure, I do," Peggy Winn said. "You were my nurse when I had that car accident last year." Amy was intrigued to see Peggy blush. What was that about? "You're Amy, Harper's sister-in-law." Her voice caught when she said *Harper*.

Oh, so that's what the blush was about. Amy wondered how she could encourage Harper to do something about this. Speaking of her brother-in-law, he still hadn't called her back about the surprise party. Maybe she could suggest he bring Peggy along.

Speaking of Peggy, Amy couldn't see any outward sign of injury. "Has someone helped you yet?"

"Oh, I'm fine. I brought in one of my temps. He needed stitches."

"The cash register guy?"

Peggy nodded with a woeful grimace.

Two nurse's aides wearing blue scrubs walked past, one of them chattering nonstop. "Did you hear about the dog bite that came in Thursday night?"

Amy excused herself and pulled the two to one side of the public area. "You don't ever, ever say a single word about any patient when you're in a public place." Her tone was quiet, but forceful. "Do you understand? You have no idea who might be sitting in that waiting room or how they might use—or twist—that information."

The aide blanched. "I didn't mean anything by it, and anyway nobody was listening."

"I wasn't *listening*, but I heard you loud and clear. Don't let it happen again." She sent them on their way, hoping there wouldn't be a lawsuit of some sort from someone else who might have heard. She loved her work, except for hassles like this.

"Sorry about that," she said when she returned to Peggy. "I can't stay long. I just wanted to see how you were doing."

Peggy seemed distracted. "I'm all healed up. Doing well, I guess."

She guessed? Didn't she know? "How are the Games going?"

"I haven't seen many of the events. In fact, I haven't seen any of them. I've been . . . uh . . ." She lowered her voice. "Did you know there was a murder?"

Amy nodded. "It was on the news this morning, but here at the hospital we find out things early. I'd already heard about it yesterday."

"I . . . uh . . . I'm the one who found the body."

Amy reached out and touched Peggy's arm. "Oh, I'm so sorry. That must have been awful for you."

Peggy nodded. "I'm just wondering. That nurse said something about a dog bite?"

Oh crap, Amy thought. "They weren't nurses, and they had no business talking about patients like that in a waiting room."

"But there was a dog bite?"

"I really can't talk about it, Ms. Winn. Hospital policy. Privacy issues. I'm sure you understand."

Peggy nodded, but she said, "Thursday night," as if she was planning to use the information.

20

One woe doth tread upon another's heel.

ACT 4, SCENE 7

Luckily, the stitches didn't take too long. Of course, I ended up with a temp sporting a fat bandage, but maybe it would engender sympathy buying.

I returned Josh to the meadow, dropping him off as close to the arch as I could. I watched him until one of the traffic cops motioned me to move on. By the time I went home, parked my car in my garage, and walked back to the ScotShop, I'd lost a total of two and a half hours. Considering we'd gone to an emergency room, I thought that was a fairly quick turnaround. And I'd had a lot of time to think about that dog bite.

"How's it been going, Gilda?"

She looked a little stressed out, but not too bad, all things considered. Dirk wandered over close by and gave me a hello nod. "The wee doggies havena stirred from where ye left them, but Mistress Gilda seems to be in something o' a dither."

"Sales are good," Gilda said calmly enough, although Dirk was right. I seemed to hear some strain in her voice. "The dogs have been quiet."

I bent to peek under the sweater rack. As Dirk had predicted, Silla still lay in a tight curl. Scamp had draped his head across her shoulders. It didn't look at all comfortable for either of them, but what did I know about how dogs relaxed?

I motioned to Sam to cover the store and asked Gilda to follow me into the back room. Dirk slipped through the door after her.

"All right, Gilda. What are you not telling me?"

"There's been a theft."

"Oh, no. What did they take? Did you see it? Did you call Har—call the police?" Not that I thought that would do any good, what with all of the cops working on either the Games or the murder. A theft here would be the lowest priority imaginable.

Gilda's voice sounded strained. "The necklace," she said. "The really expensive one. It's gone. I have no idea when it happened, either. I don't think I looked in the case at all yesterday. I certainly would have noticed if it had been gone."

"You mean the plastic one with the fake silver beads?" What a relief. "It hasn't been stolen, Gilda. I gave it to Marti Fairing."

Gilda's face drained of its color. "You didn't. Tell me you didn't."

"Whyever not?"

"She can't accept anything that valuable. It would look like a bribe."

"Valuable? You're kidding, right?"

"Don't you know what that was?" Gilda sounded incredulous. What had gotten into her?

"It was a cheap necklace," I said. "It was cute, but it was just something I bought at a flea market."

"What would be a 'flea market'? Why would any the one choose to buy a flea?"

I shot Dirk a quelling glance, but he just looked a bit bewildered. It had been an honest question. He scratched idly at his shoulder, as if imagining a fourteenth-century fleabite.

"You never told me that."

"Told you what?"

"That you got it at a flea market."

"Why should I?"

She examined my face, as if looking for someone who wasn't Speaking Her Truth. "If you thought it was so worthless, why were you charging so much for it?"

I shrugged. I needed to get back to the customers. "It was hefty. It felt substantial. I thought somebody might pay a lot for it. But I should have cut the price three or four years ago when it didn't sell. I would have let it go for half of the tagged price. Or even a tenth of it, and I still would have made a healthy profit."

Her face went even more pale. "You wouldn't."

"What on earth is wrong with you, Gilda? It was a cheap plastic necklace, and I only paid a few dollars for it. It couldn't be worth very much." How often did I have to repeat myself?

She shook her head back and forth, like a ponderous buffalo contemplating a yipping prairie dog. "It was old ivory and solid silver, Peggy. Probably worth ten times the price you put on it. Or more. Maybe a lot more."

I pulled out one of the wooden straight-backed chairs at the worktable and sat down rather suddenly. "Tell me you're kidding. Please."

Her face was grim as she shook her head.

"I . . . uh . . ." I took a strangled breath, only that reminded me of the bagpipe cords. I hunched my shoulders up to my ears and let them fall. "I told Marti if she didn't like it she could give it to Goodwill."

Gilda sat down and buried her face in her hands.

Fairing hated sitting around staring at her list. She'd been interviewing possible witnesses for what felt like forever. Nobody had seen anything. Or heard anything. She and Murph, and Harper, too, were just running around in circles, talking to anyone who'd ever spoken with Big Willie Bowman, trying the whole time to avoid talking about *murder*. With the reputation Bowman had—a good one, earned over many years of Games competition—that meant just about everybody in town knew him, as did half the people who were visitors. And, of course, everybody knew *of* him. Many of the people she'd talked with had expressed their surprise that Bowman had left town before competing, and she hadn't enlightened them. Mac had been absolutely insistent that they keep quiet on the M-word—that was what he'd called it. Still, people knew. Many of them.

Harper and Murphy kept coming back to Shay Burns. They kept drawing that narrow triangle on the map. Shay's house to the Hamelin Hotel—the murder site—to the meadow—late for the opening ceremony—and back again. If the streets hadn't meandered a bit, it would have been a straight line, right down Main Street.

But Fairing still didn't buy it. She was willing to admit that someone could strike out in anger with a force they never would have been able to command otherwise, but Shay? No. Fairing couldn't see her as Cord. Even though when Fairing and Harper had told Shay of Bowman's death, she hadn't seemed all that put out. "Can you keep it quiet," was all she'd asked, "so it won't disrupt my Games?" Like she owned them.

Marti had to be fair, though. Shay put more effort into the Games than anyone else. She had a committee, supposedly, but seemed unable to delegate anything. Four years ago, when her sister had died and she'd left before the Games even opened, things had been in something of an uproar for the first day or two.

Mac walked through the room. "Anything yet?"

"We're working on it."

He stared at her.

"Sir," she said.

"Well, get busy." And he disappeared once more into his lair. She had to stop thinking of it like that. Not his lair. His office.

There was a commotion at the door. Shay walked in, followed closely by Harper. Fairing pushed the wrapping paper with the necklace on it to the back of her desk and laid a blank yellow legal pad over her list of people still to be interviewed. It wasn't too long a list. Only half the town to go. She stifled a sigh.

"Just for a few questions," Harper was saying.

"I don't see why you couldn't ask me in my office, or even my house, but for heaven's sake, hauling me in here like some common criminal or something?" She tugged irritably at her wide belt. "What will people think?"

Fairing could see Harper take a deep breath. "If you'd agreed to come in and talk to us when we first requested it, this whole process would have been easier." Fairing had to strain to hear Harper's well-controlled voice.

"In case you hadn't noticed, Captain"—Shay invested the title with particular venom—"I've been busy. I have the town's biggest moneymaking event of the year to oversee. Do you think I want to be pulled away from real work just so I can mollify you on this fishing expedition of yours?"

Whoo-ee. Fairing saw Moira, headphones over only one ear, whip around in her swivel chair and give Shay the evil eye. Not that Shay noticed it.

"If you'll follow me back this way, we can have some privacy while—"

"While you grill me?"

Fairing thought this might be a good time to clear her throat. Loudly.

When she did, Shay whipped her head around, almost as fast as Moira's chair had turned. "Did you have something to add?"

"No, ma'am," Fairing said across the length of the room, happy to see that the few other officers in the room all seemed to be following the conversation. "I was just listening. It was hard not to hear."

That stopped Shay in her tracks. "All right, Captain. Let's go see this interrogation room of yours."

"The interview room is back this way." Harper led the way past Fairing's desk, without looking to see if Shay followed. He didn't have to. Her footsteps in those clunky high-fashion shoes of hers tracked her like a homing beacon.

She sailed past Fairing without acknowledging her. Her steps faltered and she backtracked. She pointed a hand weighted down by an enormous diamond ring. "Where'd you get my mother's necklace?"

"Sergeant Fairing, would you please join us?" Harper didn't want to be alone with Shay Burns even for a moment. Not only because it was police department policy, but because he felt for just an instant that he might need protection.

Fairing, professional as could be, nodded slightly and said, "Yes, sir." But Harper thought he detected a gleam in those brown eyes of hers.

Once Shay was seated at the oblong table, Harper sat across from her. Fairing took a chair against the wall and pulled out an unobtrusive notebook.

Harper made sure his face was perfectly neutral. "Do you have something you'd like to tell me, Ms. Burns?"

"That necklace out there was my mother's."

"How do you know that?"

"How do I—what a stupid question." Shay flipped her hair back away from her face. "It's an absolutely unique art piece. Ming dynasty ivory leaves strung on silk cords with solid beads of silver between the leaves. It's worth tens of thousands. Hundreds of thousands. There's not another piece like it. Ming jewelry was usually made of gold. The fact that this was silver makes it practically priceless."

Harper didn't dare look at Fairing, but he had a feeling her expression would have been a sight to see, even though he knew she'd probably been practicing keeping a straight face. He was having trouble keeping his own face straight. The necklace had been casually pushed to the back of her desk like a trinket, a bit of carnival detritus. How had Fairing come up with something that valuable? And why had she left it lying around like that?

"You said it was your mother's?"

"Yes. But it was stolen one night and nobody's seen it since."

"Tell me about the theft of the necklace."

"It wasn't just the necklace." Shay leaned back and crossed one leg over the other. "Mother and Father had quite a lot of jewelry, silver, vases, most of it quite good. Whoever planned the theft knew just what to look for. Luckily, Mother was wearing her diamond." Shay spread her left hand and gazed at it. Harper wondered if the garish stone on her finger was the diamond in question. "And Father had his ruby ring on, so those two pieces were safe."

Harper waited a moment, but Shay kept her eyes on her ring. She recrossed her legs, but she didn't lift her eyes.

"What happened to the ruby?"

"Don't you believe me?" She reached into the bottom

of the sturdy leather bag she wore hanging from the heavy belt around her red plaid arisaidh and pulled out a small zippered pouch.

Silk, Harper thought. He could feel the ring he kept in his pocket. The one he intended for Peggy. The one he'd never given to her. And maybe never would. But he could always hope. Maybe instead of the small blue box it was in, he should get a silk pouch like the one Shay held. Shay Burns. The person he should be concentrating on instead of letting his mind wander.

Shay pulled an enormous dark red ruby ring from the small bag. Harper studied it. Peggy, kneeling next to Bowman's body, had told him, *He had a big dark red ring*. A ruby. "How long have you had this?" He kept his voice casual. He wasn't surprised when Shay paused before answering.

"Father died shortly after the burglary, not quite ten years ago."

He didn't want to give her time to concoct an elaborate cover story. "Did you inherit it at that time?"

She stared at him. "No, of course not. Mother got it."

That much sounded like the truth. "Is your mother still alive?"

"No. She died within a few months of Father."

"Did you inherit both rings at that time?"

Shay twisted the diamond around her finger three or four times. "No," she finally said. "They went to Lorena, the oldest of the four of us. Windsor, as the second oldest, was supposed to get the sterling silver tea set, but of course, it had been stolen, and Father and Mother hadn't thought to change their wills after the burglary. Robert's share was to have been all the silverware . . ." She waved her hand as if *all the silverware* hadn't been very impressive. "And I was supposed to get the necklace. Mother believed jewelry should always go to daughters."

"Did you?"

"Did I what?"

"Get the necklace."

"Of course not," she snapped. "I told you. Everything was stolen, except for these two rings."

"Wasn't your mother wearing any other jewelry that night?"

Shay made a derisive sound. "It wasn't that important an event. Everything else she had on was paste." She looked over at Fairing, as if judging whether the policewoman would know what that term meant. Apparently Fairing failed Shay's test. "Imitations," she said in a voice like a rasp. "So the good items wouldn't be at risk of damage."

Harper remained quiet.

So did Fairing. Harper was impressed. Some cops didn't know when to keep their mouths shut, especially if they were being taunted by an uncooperative suspect. Harper hadn't really considered Shay to be a viable suspect. Other than the ease with which she could have gone from her house to the hotel to the meadow. That had convinced Murphy, but Harper had to admit he'd never been truly serious about believing in Shay's guilt. But now? Now that he'd seen the woman's vitriol—and that ruby ring—firsthand. That should have been a lesson to him. Never assume.

He wondered what Shay would say if she knew Marti

Fairing was the only one on the team who believed Shay Burns was innocent. He wondered if Fairing still believed it. He wouldn't blame her if she'd changed her mind.

Shay heaved a theatrical sigh. "She should have worn the good stuff."

"You said Lorena inherited the rings."

Shay nodded. "She always flaunted the diamond. And Big Willie, that husband of hers, wore the ruby like it had been made for him."

Harper waited, absolutely still.

"The rest of us thought they should have sold the rings. It would have been much more fair if we could have split the money four ways, but Lorena refused."

"Do you know why?"

"Because she was selfish. What else?"

"If Lorena wouldn't sell the rings, how did you get them?"

"She died. Four years ago. That was the year I had to leave the Games. Because she went and died . . ."

She didn't say *at such an inconvenient time*, but Harper could feel the words hanging in the air above the table. He noticed, too, that she hadn't answered his question.

"Did she leave them to you in her will?"

"Of course not. She left them to that husband of hers."

If she'd just tell the truth, the whole truth, and nothing but the truth—and tell it quickly, Harper thought, *I wouldn't have to sit here playing games to try to get it out of her.*

"And?"

"And what?" She shifted in her seat, as if her rear end was going to sleep.

"You said she left the rings to her husband. Would you like to explain how you have them now?"

"He . . . he gave them to me."

Harper continued to look at her, wondering if she'd explain what she was obviously leaving out. "When?"

She uncrossed her legs yet again. "When what?"

Harper was barely able to keep from rolling his eyes. "When did he give them to you?"

She paused. Was she simply trying to remember? Or was she calculating what would be the best answer? He couldn't tell. Maybe she was just trying to decide whether or not to cross her legs one more time.

"It was Thursday morning. We took a walk up through the woods."

"Which path did you follow?"

She looked surprised at his question, but she answered without hesitation. "The one that heads uphill from the empty lot next to my house."

"Which fork did you take?"

At that, she raised an eyebrow. "Does it matter? We took the one to the right."

"Were both rings in the little silk bag?"

Shay seemed to appraise him for a moment. A man who recognized silk when he saw it. Or so it seemed to Harper.

"No. The diamond was in the bag. In his sporran. He took the ruby off his finger before he gave it to me."

"And why did he give them to you?"

Shay looked amused. "Because I asked him for them."

Harper heard a faint snort from Fairing.

"When I informed you that there had been a murder

at the hotel, why didn't you tell me William Bowman was your brother-in-law?"

"He wasn't."

Harper raised an eyebrow.

"Not for the past four years." She crossed her arms. "He stopped being my brother-in-law as soon as Lorena died. And as soon as he . . ."

Harper watched her grind her teeth together. He could hear the grating sound of it even from here, across the table. "As soon as he what?"

"Do I need a lawyer?"

"You're certainly entitled to call a lawyer if you feel you need to."

"I want to see the necklace first."

Harper took his time strolling to the door—he could play games, too—and motioned across the room to Murphy. "Would you retrieve the necklace that's lying on Fairing's desk?"

Murphy nodded and turned.

"Be careful with it, would you, Lieutenant? And don't smudge any fingerprints," he added. "Wait. On second thought, I'll get it." Harper stepped back into the room. "Sergeant Fairing, could I speak with you privately? You'll excuse us for a moment, Ms. Burns?"

"So you can turn the thumbscrews?" She waved him away. "Be my guest."

Harper waited for Fairing to step out and close the door. She didn't wait for his question. "It was a gift from Peggy Winn. She gave it to me yesterday as a thank-you present. She said she'd heard about how I stopped Turner, although how she knew it was me, I have no idea. I didn't tell anybody except you and Murphy." Fairing motioned toward her desk. "I brought it here—I hadn't even unwrapped it yet—because I thought I'd better check first to be sure it was okay to keep it. I didn't want anyone thinking it was a bribe. But then, with the homicide in the hotel, I didn't think to mention it. In fact, I forgot about it altogether."

"Why would Peg—Ms. Winn—give you a necklace worth thousands of dollars?"

"She didn't. I mean, she did; she gave it to me, but she said it wasn't worth a lot. In fact she said it didn't have much value at all, but she thought it was pretty and thought I might like it. She said it was plastic."

Harper mulled that over.

"She said if I didn't like it . . ."

"She wanted it back?"

"No." Fairing tilted her head to one side. "She said to give it to Goodwill."

Harper couldn't believe how bizarre all this was. "Murphy," he said, "would you and Sergeant Fairing keep Ms. Burns company for a few minutes?"

Murphy hadn't been very far away. "I gotta protect our sergeant from the public?"

"Just from Ms. Burns."

Murphy grinned.

Fairing didn't.

Harper headed for Fairing's desk.

Sam stuck his head in the door. "We really need you two out here. It's pretty busy."

Gilda was the first to recover. No wonder; she wasn't the one who'd given away a necklace worth thousands of dollars. How could I have been so dense?

I followed her through the door. Sam hadn't been kidding. We were inundated. The next hour hardly left me any time to draw a deep breath, much less to think about my own stupidity. Eventually, though, as usually happens, there was a lull. Scamp left the sweater shelter long enough to sit in front of Gilda and give one of his woofy commands.

"He's thirsty," she said. "I think." She looked over at the door to the back room. Sam had installed a small dog door last summer so Scamp could get to his water bowl and his food anytime he wanted without interrupting us. But there Scamp sat. "What do you want, boy?"

"Mayhap the other wee doggie"—Dirk sketched a brief wave back over his shoulder—"is in need o' some water as weel."

"That's right, of course," I said.

Gilda looked at me. "Do you talk dog talk now? What's he right about?"

"Silla needs some water." I parted the sweaters and picked her up. How long was it going to take for her to come back from this dark depression? Because that's truly what it looked like. "Let's go get you something to drink, you brave little girl."

Silla lifted her head, as if the whisper of an echo had bounced around the shop. I took her through the staff door and set her next to the water bowl.

After she lapped a few unenthusiastic mouthfuls, she turned aside. I hooked on her red leash and led both dogs outside, where they dutifully took care of their business—Scamp with enthusiasm and Silla almost as an after-thought. Inside again, she went right back to the sweater cave.

"The puir wee doggie," Dirk said.

I agreed. The phone rang and Sam went to answer it.

"When my grandda died, his dog lay upon his grave for the next five years."

"Big Willie doesn't have a grave yet," I said.

"Of course not," Gilda said. "How long do you think it will be before they release the body?"

I just shook my head.

"Peggy, this is for you," Sam called. "Harper," he added as he handed me the phone.

I took it warily. "Yes? This is Peggy."

"I know you're probably busy at the shop, but I need to ask you a few questions."

"Okay. There's nobody here at the moment." Dirk stood right beside me, trying to listen. Nobody here except for two employees and a ghost. "I mean, no customers."

"Could you take a few minutes to come down to the station?"

"I guess so. What's this about?"

"I'd rather wait to tell you until you get here."

"Okay. I'll be right down." I hung up the phone and whispered, "I don't know whether to ask you to watch the dogs or come with me to the police station."

"Mistress Gilda can watch the wee dogs. I will go wi' ye to the constable's office."

Why did that not surprise me? I knew he'd want to be in on the action. Whatever it was. I hadn't a clue.

*   *   *

Harper clicked off his cell and picked up a blank sheet of legal paper off the top of Fairing's paperwork. He slid it carefully underneath the necklace, along with the blue wrapping paper and silver ribbon upon which it sat.

Murphy eyed the collection with a raised eyebrow.

"When Peggy Winn arrives, ask her to wait a few minutes. I'll be out as soon as I can."

Murphy nodded and surrendered his position just inside the door of the interview room.

Harper set everything on the table, keeping his hands close to it. When Shay reached for the necklace, he stopped her. "I can't let you touch it," he said. "We haven't checked it for fingerprints yet."

Shay's eyes widened. "Where did you—I mean where did *she*—find it?"

"The real question we have to consider is whether this is the necklace you claim was your mother's." He knew he was going to have a long conversation with Fairing, but not while Shay Stone Burns was around.

"Of course it was my mother's." Shay was awfully good at this snapping routine of hers. Harper didn't say anything. "You can see the leaf veins carved into the—" She stopped and bent closer. "Could we have a little more light in here?"

Harper nodded, and Fairing stepped to a bank of switches. The intense spotlight made the room look like the interrogation chamber Shay had accused him of taking her to in the first place, but she didn't seem to notice. She focused all her attention on the necklace. After far less than a minute, her shoulders drooped and her leg went back to jiggling up and down.

"It's the fake," she said. "The one my father ordered right after he bought the original."

"How can you tell?"

"In the real necklace, each leaf was individual. Every vein was carved by hand. Some of the leaves had four veins on each side of the central one. Some had five, some three. Each leaf had a slightly different shape, too. But these are all alike. It's the same leaf stamped out over and over again." She sank back into the chair and drummed her fingers on the table. "And these are plastic."

"Wouldn't people at those events you mentioned have noticed that your mother was wearing an imitation?"

Shay shrugged. "Mother never sat still long enough for anyone to take a closer look."

Rather like yourself, Harper thought. He studied Shay's face. She'd withdrawn from the room. Her hands still drummed and her leg still jiggled, but she'd gone somewhere else. He'd give almost anything to know where.

"May I leave now?"

He had no reason to keep her. Except that he now thought there was a good possibility she'd killed for those two rings. He had no proof, though. Nothing even close to it. Motive. Opportunity. It wasn't enough.

But as she stood to leave, he mentioned one more thing. "Ms. Burns? What did you argue with William Bowman about in the ScotShop on Thursday?"

Her lips pursed. "Who said we argued?"

"The shop was crowded. There were a number of witnesses."

"He . . . he told me four years ago he wouldn't be coming back to the Games."

Why didn't she just tell the truth and get it over with? "Why not?"

"Because his wife died."

"And?"

"And what? I just wanted to know why he changed his mind."

"Then why did you tell him he had to leave?"

"Leave? I didn't say anything like that. Whoever told you I said that . . . simply misinterpreted." She smiled, but her smile didn't reach her eyes. "Is that all, Officer?"

"Not quite. I've been wondering why you accused him of having let your sister die."

Her inner pirate peeked out in one raised eyebrow and one narrowed eye. "I never said that. I said I was sorry she died before I had a chance to talk with her. She was in a coma toward the end, you know. Whatever your *witnesses* heard, it was just a misinterpretation. 'You . . . you let her die before I got there to talk to her.' That was what I said. Something like that. I can't remember the exact words I used."

And she refused to alter this version of her story.

Harper knew she'd lied. The part about the coma sounded true enough, but he wasn't sure whether any of the rest of it was. Maybe none. Maybe only half. She *was* lying, though.

21

There is a willow grows aslant a brook.
ACT 4, SCENE 7

I was surprised to see Shay come out of the police station as I approached the door. She had one of her storm cloud expressions on, and I was just as happy when she turned downhill, away from me.

"Does she no look as if her milk had gone and curdled afore she had her churn prepared?"

"If you say so. I thought she looked like a hurricane a-brewing."

"What would be a 'herrikehna bruing'?"

"I've shown you the weather channel. You know, those big storms out over the Atlantic?"

"Och, aye. The large circles and . . ." He spread his plaid and gave it a quick sideways shake. It looked surprisingly like the swirling clouds of a major hurricane.

"Swirls," I said, and made the movement with my hand.

"Swir-rels," he said, using two syllables for the word, the same way he said *squirrels*. Poor Dirk. He'd never seen the ocean, and no matter how many pictures I showed him, he simply didn't seem able to grasp the enormity of that much water. Or that big a storm.

I stopped at the desk inside the front door, but heard Harper speaking my name before I could say anything. He walked toward me, and opened the little swinging door between the two major sections of the room. I slowed to let Dirk go through ahead of me.

"It shouldn't take too long," he said, obviously misinterpreting my pause, and led the way to a back room.

Dirk walked in ahead of me and nodded pleasantly to Marti Fairing. "Good day, Mistress, uh, Constable." Of course, she didn't respond.

I said good afternoon, too, but she stood there as stiff as a store mannequin.

The necklace lay on the table beside her.

Behind me, Harper closed the door.

"You probably think I'm an idiot," I said, "to give away such an expensive necklace, but believe me I didn't know what it was until just a little while ago when Gilda told me."

"Told you what?" He sounded genuinely curious. That was good. He didn't sound angry.

"That it was worth a lot of money. She said she's known right from the start when I first put it up for sale, but I'd never let her polish it up because I thought it was fake and thought the silver paint might flake off and thought the plastic might discolor, only she thought I just wanted to keep it looking old, so she never mentioned its value and I never mentioned what I'd paid for it."

I wound down my spiel and turned to Marti. I hated to ask for a gift back, but I was fairly sure the police department wouldn't let her accept such a valuable present anyway. "Do you want me to take it back? I have several other necklaces that you could choose from instead. I guess you can't keep it. Not with its being worth as much as it is."

Marti Fairing didn't answer me.

Harper just kept looking at me, as if he were trying to piece together a puzzle. "Just out of curiosity, what *did* you pay for it?"

"About three dollars if I remember right. I bought it at a flea market in Montpelier, beside the river, where all those willow trees are, shortly after I opened the Scot-Shop. Only then, yesterday—or was it the day before? I can't remember—I picked it up and thought it didn't look right and it didn't feel as heavy, and I couldn't figure out what had happened to it, so I just decided to take it out of my inventory. Nobody had even tried it on in about five years except for that one woman who's been coming in every day for the past week and asking us—well, asking Gilda—to let her try it on, only she never bought it, and I couldn't see hanging on to something that wouldn't sell. I told her I'd mark it down by twenty-five percent, but even that didn't entice her into buying it, so I thought I'd rather give it away and be done with it."

Why was I chattering like a magpie? Marti Fairing stood there like a statue, and Harper examined me like I was a fresh corpse—I shuddered at that thought—and Dirk hadn't said anything at all.

"You mentioned Gilda—that would be Ms. Buchanan, your store manager?"

I nodded. He knew that perfectly well. Why was he asking me?

"You said she thought it was valuable?"

"She did. I didn't agree. It looked kind of, well, dowdy, just hanging there on its stand. I thought it made all the rest of the necklaces in the case look better by comparison, though, which may be one reason I kept it. Then, just a little while ago, she told me it had been stolen and she was all upset to lose such a valuable item even though she said I wasn't charging nearly enough for it, that it was worth ten times as much."

"How much were you trying to sell it for?"

When I told him, he glanced at Fairing, and she shook her head. What was that about?

"And why did Ms. Buchanan think it had been stolen?"

"She didn't know I'd taken it to give to Marti—to Sergeant Fairing."

"But you said it felt different to you?"

I nodded and thought back, trying to remember when I'd gotten that impression.

"'Twas just before you left the wee shop to go to the ceremony o' the opening," Dirk informed me helpfully.

"That's right. It was Thursday just after I'd closed the wee—the shop. I walked past the counter and it looked . . . I don't know . . . different somehow. And when I picked it up, it felt lighter. Or something. It's hard to explain."

"The necklace was heavy?"

Why did Harper keep asking me all these questions about the stupid necklace? Didn't he have a murder to solve? "Yes. I've told you that. It always felt, uh, like it *mattered* somehow, if you know what I mean. But now, it . . . doesn't." I turned to Marti. "I don't want you to think I was giving you junk. It's still a really cute necklace, especially if there isn't a better necklace right next to it. I mean, I . . . I don't know what I'm trying to say."

"I think I'm beginning to understand," Harper said. "Tell me more about the woman who came in to try on the necklace."

I thought back. "Gilda usually handles the jewelry. I noticed the woman come in several times, but I didn't pay much attention to her. I know she was there Thursday morning, but Gilda waited on her. I saw the woman try it on and then she left, only I wasn't paying a whole lot of attention. But then she came back later to look at it again."

"On Thursday?"

"That's right. Gilda was busy with another customer, so I opened the case and let the woman try it on."

"And then," Dirk said, "dinna forget about how her man began to cough."

"That's right. I'd forgotten that."

"Forgotten what?"

Oh dear. "Her husband choked or something. He was coughing so hard he doubled all the way over. I was about ready to run and help him when he pulled out his water bottle and drank something, and then he seemed to be okay."

"Where was he when he started coughing?"

"Over by Dir—uh, by the poet shirts. He was looking at them. Next to the front display window."

"What was his wife doing during all this?"

"I didna notice the wife."

I nodded. "She was finished trying it on, I guess, and she draped it on the stand—it's one of those black velvet things for displaying necklaces—and I put it back in the case because she said she couldn't make up her mind. And then they left without even looking at anything else. I thought he'd at least want to buy a poet shirt."

Harper looked back up at Fairing and she nodded.

"And you're sure Ms. Buchanan was convinced of the value of the necklace before that?"

"Absolutely. When I told her I'd given it away, she about bit my head off."

"When was that?"

I looked at my watch. "An hour or two ago."

"Can you describe the woman? And her husband?"

Marti Fairing sat down and pulled out a notebook.

It was the same old song. Distract the storeowner; switch the merchandise. Only Marti Fairing couldn't figure out how such an elaborate necklace played into this. Shay Burns must have been right. The real necklace, her mother's necklace, was worth a minor fortune. But how had it ended up in a flea market? And how had the couple with the fake necklace known it was at the ScotShop? For that matter, how had they gotten the fake necklace in the first place?

She knew thieves didn't get a fraction of the value of

stolen goods when they tried to resell them, but surely even a fence would have recognized the value of that ivory-and-silver piece. Especially a fence. Wasn't it illegal to sell ivory? Or, if not completely illegal, at least there were a lot of restrictions. And now someone, this anonymous couple who had their switch routine down pat—all they'd had to do was wait until they were dealing with someone who was easily distracted—had a necklace worth thousands and the cops had a necklace worth a few dollars, and nobody had proof of anything. This was, truly, all speculation at this point. And how had the couple gotten their hands on the fake necklace to begin with, unless it had been part of the original heist?

Harper had asked all the right questions, but it hadn't seemed to get them any closer to an answer.

Even the description Peggy gave them seemed generic. The man had had on a gray-blue kilt. The woman had long hair and a brown tartan skirt. That would describe, let's see, maybe 45 percent of the strangers in town and 55 percent of the residents.

When Harper told Peggy this necklace was a fake one, she'd seemed almost relieved, and then she said she didn't believe it, and then he'd shown her what Shay had pointed out. Why was he giving a possible suspect so many details? Marti knew why. Peggy wasn't a suspect. It was all there in the way Harper was so careful about not saying Peggy's name, or taking a deep breath before he said it, how he avoided touching her, how he tried to school his face when he looked at her. Marti liked Harper like a big brother. She knew he was a great police officer. But she knew he was a man, too. And she could practically see the waves of love pouring off him when Peggy Winn entered a room. Why on earth was Peggy so oblivious?

Fairing had never been interested in dating or in all those silly games teenage girls seemed to thrive on. Who was going out with whom, who had a date to the prom. But just for a moment, Fairing wondered if Peggy might benefit from a little hint. On the other hand, she and Peggy weren't really friends. Not the kind that could say something like that to each other.

Fairing watched Harper open the swinging door for Peggy. Peggy stopped for a second, almost as if she wasn't ready to leave, but then she walked to the front door, held it open and—this was crazy, but Fairing halfway imagined she saw somebody walk out through the door. It was obviously a trick of the sunlight being at a funny angle or something, but for a split second, it had looked so real. Like a man in a kilt. Then Peggy left and Harper turned back around.

"We need to talk," he said to Fairing, and called Murphy into the conference room.

Gilda didn't believe me when I told her the necklace was a fake, just plastic and silver-colored beads. "That can't be true," she said. "I know what it felt like. I handled it almost every day."

"No, you didn't. It's only been the last few days that anyone's wanted to try it on."

Gilda lowered her eyes. "I used to try it on myself whenever you weren't in the store. I really loved that necklace. The ivory was so, so soft almost, and the leaves had those delicate veins carved into them. Each leaf was a tiny work of art. Didn't you ever notice?"

"It just looked like plastic to me."

She rolled her eyes at me. "I hate to be the one to tell you, Peggy, but your artistic sense is sorely lacking."

"And you're wrong about the leaves, Gilda. Harper showed me how all the leaves were the same, and the design was stamped on."

Gilda got very still. "Are you sure about that?"

"Of course I'm sure. He showed me under a very bright light."

"Then somebody," she said with great precision, "stole the real one and replaced it with the cheap imitation."

"That's impossible."

"You don't know what you're talking about, Peggy Winn. I studied that necklace. Really studied it. Each leaf had its own . . . personality."

"Mayhap that is why our constable asked so many questions?"

"Yeah. Mayhap."

"Huh?"

"Nothing, Gilda. Just thinking."

Of course, there was a huge inrush of customers right then—not that I wasn't grateful for paying customers, but it left me with very little time to think about what Gilda had said or whether I should call Harper about it.

Nonsense. There was no reason to call him. He needed to concentrate on the murder investigation. Why had he even taken the time to ask about the necklace when he needed to be finding out who'd killed Big Willie? Why were his priorities so skewed?

That was easy to answer. The police department had to be careful about officers accepting bribes.

As if I'd try to bribe Marti Fairing?

A mental image of our illustrious chief of police came to mind. He'd probably like nothing better than to find an excuse to fire Marti. It looked like Harper's priorities were right where they needed to be. Protecting his fellow officers.

I wished for one brief, useless moment that he wanted to protect me.

Not that I needed any protection. I was fine. I was a successful businesswoman. I had everything I needed.

Then why did I feel sad?

It was because of Big Willie's death. And Silla's malaise. That was why.

I bent to help a customer try on some ghillie brogues. Two hours till closing time. I couldn't wait to take my dog home and put my feet up.

Harper listened to all the arguments, frustrated that it was all speculation. Here it was late evening already and they weren't getting anywhere.

"Somebody," Fairing said, "stole the real one and replaced it with this cheap imitation."

Murphy ran the beads and leaves around and around through his fingers, pausing each time he reached the simple clasp. Harper knew it still felt like there was a fine layer of fingerprint powder on it, although if Murphy kept handling it like that, the grit would be gone soon enough.

"And," Murphy said, "whoever did it—probably that

guy and his wife who kept trying on the necklace, waiting for a time when nobody was watching—must have had this planned for a long time."

"But how," said Harper, "did they know the real necklace was in the ScotShop?"

"Or did they just happen to notice it one day and say, 'Oh, look'?" Murphy's voice went into a silly falsetto. "'There's the necklace we've been waiting to steal all these years.'"

Fairing grimaced. "It does sound pretty stupid when you put it that way, but how else could anyone have had an exact fake available unless they'd stolen the fake from the Burns family to begin with?"

"If they stole the fake," Harper asked, "why did they let the real one, worth so much money, sell for three dollars in a flea market?"

Fairing shifted in her chair. "If what Ms. Burns says is true, anyone who saw the two necklaces together could tell the difference." She used both palms to push her hair back off her forehead, and the big bruise showed purplish and greenish. Harper was fairly sure she'd forgotten about it. "I can't believe this whole thing happened. And it has to be connected to Big Willie's death. With everybody related—Big Willie to Lorena, and Lorena to Shay—it's just too much coincidence to think there's not a connection."

Murphy laid his palms flat on the table. "It keeps coming back to Shay." He looked at Harper and Fairing. "Do you think she's our Cord?"

Fairing cleared her throat—*for real this time,* Harper thought. Not like that fake throat clearing she'd used to get Shay to calm down. "I agree she's part of the necklace mess," she said, "but that doesn't necessarily mean she killed William Bowman."

Harper couldn't believe she was still defending the woman, not after the way Burns had tried to lord it over Fairing. And not after that *let my sister die* thing.

"Let's say your fake necklace there got stolen along with the real one," Fairing said. "Maybe by the husband-wife team. And then maybe they get robbed by somebody else and lose the real necklace."

Murphy started to make a rude gesture, but Harper quelled him with a look. Murphy settled for "Are you in fairy-tale land, Fairing? What are the chances of that happening?"

"Snowball in you-know-where?"

Murphy went into falsetto again. "You got that right, Secret Service Catcher."

Fairing grinned, as if she thought the jibe was funny. But Murphy was right, Harper thought. What were the chances?

"She had the rings," Murphy insisted. "And all we have is her word that he gave them to her. Not a single witness."

"We also don't have anything that says he didn't give them to her."

He laid the necklace on the table, none too gently. "Why are you defending her?"

"Why are you so ready to indict her?"

"That's enough, you two." Harper leaned back in his chair. "Are we agreed that the necklace is somehow connected to the murder?"

"Yes," said Fairing.

"No," said Murphy. "Maybe," he added reluctantly.

"But not necessarily connected to Burns," Fairing said.

They were back at square one. Cord—one. Cops—zero.

"Murphy, I want you to look into the death of Bowman's wife. Find out if it was natural. Or otherwise. How long she was in a coma, too."

Murphy headed for his computer. Harper got up stiffly, stretched, and walked to the window. The glass reflected his face. The twilight outside reflected only the dismal state of this investigation. Tomorrow, Sunday, was the final day of the Games. After that, people would leave. Was Cord one of the visitors to Hamelin? Or was Cord a local who would stay? Harper had no idea.

I glanced at my watch. It was time for me to head down to the meadow, as I tried to do each evening of the Games. Before Dirk and I left, I pulled Gilda aside. "I don't want either of the temps back in the storeroom at any time. If stocks get low, just make a note of it and wait to replenish them until we have a lull, and then only one of you goes back there at a time. I want all of you, unless you're at the cash register, circulating around the store as much as possible, keeping an eye on everything."

She nodded. "I get it, boss. We have to keep the merchandise from flying out the door."

"That's right. Unless it's been paid for, in which case it can fly as far as it wants to and as fast as it can."

Dirk waited until we were partway down Main Street before he commented, "Ye appear to be worrited indeed."

"I guess I am. It seems like there's been more shoplifting this year than ever before. Don't people realize when they steal, eventually the prices of everything will have to go up so the retailers can pay their overhead costs?" I felt like I was on the verge of tears. It all seemed so unfair, and then with Big Willie's murder . . .

"Aye. I ken that weel. And so do ye. And so does Mistress Gilda."

"Now if we could just get the rest of the world informed."

He stepped in front of me and I ground to a halt. "What?"

"Mistress Peggy, there are a great many things I see that appear to me to be wrong in this world o' . . . o' now . . ."

I nodded, but before I could say anything, he went on.

"But I have also seen a great many good people here, now, who care about ither folk, who ken what needs to be done and who do it weel, people who treat their friends wi' love and their acquaintances wi' respect."

"Where are you headed with this, Macbeath?"

"I do believe ye need to take adequate care to make sure your wee shop is safe, but I dinna like to see ye in such a dither. 'Tis nae good for your health whan that ye are all a-flutter so much o' the time. And more than a' that, ye canna tend the goats in the next valley."

"Goats?"

"Ye willna make much headway against the flood if ye try to stop it w' a wee spoon."

"Spoon?"

He let out an exasperated breath. "Ye canna change the whole world, Mistress Peggy."

"Oh. I see what you're getting at. Who made you a psychiatrist?"

"What would be—"

"Never mind." I walked a few steps. "Thank you."

"Ye are most welcome."

Fairing had to take her turn in the meadow for an evening rotation of about two hours. Even with officers and security guards from neighboring towns borrowed for the duration of the Games, the Hamelin police were too spread out to handle all the crowd control, traffic, and general police presence needed during the four-day period. Harper and Murphy were still poring over reports and throwing ideas around, reading and rereading the autopsy findings—broken neck, with death caused by strangulation, which, of course, they'd already guessed.

She left the station and turned to her right. Peggy Winn stood on the sidewalk across from the station, talking to herself. Fairing wondered what that was about. She liked Peggy. Cops didn't usually have too many noncop friends, though. They just wouldn't understand.

Fairing walked down the street and through the arch. She headed for the piper's tent, feeling a wave of nostalgia for her assassin patrol, as she'd begun to think of it. Crazy thing to feel nostalgic about.

She began to notice couples, some of them walking hand in hand, some of them chatting busily, some of them barely seeming to acknowledge each other's presence. She wondered which of these couples might be the necklace woman and her coughing husband. Even discounting the women with short hair, there were still a lot of possibilities. And the woman might have cut her hair as a way of disguising herself. Now there was a happy thought.

She heard some mighty groans and cheers, so she migrated to the hammer throw area. It looked like it had been going for quite some time; there were deep divots of dirt torn up by the sixteen-pound hammer slamming into the soil time and time again. Soon they'd start the next round, where the hammers weighed twenty-two pounds. By then it would be full dark, but the Games must go on until each contestant had had his three tries at each event scheduled for today.

The lights that ringed the athletic field on this end of the meadow were worthy of a college football stadium. Hamelin, Marti's hometown, had a tremendous investment in these games, and Marti wouldn't let a couple of crooks—and a murderer, she reminded herself—scare everybody into leaving.

She watched as the most recent throw was measured. From the trig, the board that marked the line behind which the contestant planted his feet, they stretched a ruled line to the hole in the grass where the hammer landed. Pretty straightforward. She looked at the people of all ages cheering and calling encouragement. Fairing couldn't imagine why anyone would want a son playing around with hammer throwing. She could imagine all the broken windows and a few broken arms that must result when young boys and men began to learn the sport. It took a lot of control to let the handle of the hammer go at just the right moment so it went *that* way down the field, instead of *this* way, right into a spectator, or a neighbor's brand-new car.

Still, her mind kept bringing her back to the question of which couple. At the far end of the meadow was the Tartan Tie booth. Maybe she'd circle that way and see if Peggy Winn had made it to the booth after her weird street-side monologue. She might have recalled some more details about the two people. Fairing was convinced that if she found the woman with the necklace, she'd find Cord.

The crowd watching the hammer throw seemed to surge forward and backward, almost like the sea. *Mother never sat still enough for anyone to look closely.* Shay's words were just an echo, just a memory, but Marti heard it clearly. Shay never sat still, either. Was her restlessness caused by guilt?

She calculated. The bonfire would begin at eight tomorrow night. People would start leaving by ten. That left her a little more than a day to find this murderous couple before they left town. If they were even still here. And Marti Fairing couldn't believe anyone would be stupid enough to stick around after they'd stolen something that valuable. Or after they'd murdered someone.

Still, it would make sense that the cops would look for somebody who'd left unexpectedly. She knew for a fact that Harper had asked one of the junior officers—one of the *other* junior officers, she corrected herself—to look into that. So far, he hadn't found anybody who'd left, except for one woman who'd found out her daughter had gone into labor two weeks early.

Hardly a good candidate for their murderer. For Cord.

22

I prithee, take thy fingers from my throat.
ACT 5, SCENE 1

I'd become something of a scarf-tying expert in the seven years I'd owned the ScotShop. With the number of tartan scarves we sold, there were always women wanting to know how to wear them in something more interesting than a square knot or a simple bow.

Every time I did a little demonstration, it resulted in a hefty number of sales. This time was no exception, but all the while I was talking about loops and whorls and twisty roses, I kept an eye on the couples passing by. Surely that woman who had stolen my necklace—I was sure she was the one—wouldn't have the nerve to show her face anywhere in Hamelin. But I couldn't stop looking. The more I looked in vain, the more certain I was that they'd taken the necklace and skipped town.

After all, who'd have been dumb enough to stick around?

Dirk could tell what I was doing, of course. He stayed out on the periphery of the crowd around the tent, not wanting to collide with anyone. It wasn't a pleasant feeling for him, and it tended to make the collidee pass out. I spotted him gazing around the meadow, and I knew he was looking, too.

In the back of my mind, I couldn't erase the picture of Big Willie on the bathroom floor. The necklace was one problem, but the death of that sweet man was an even bigger one. I'd felt sure Harper could locate the murderer, but now he seemed sidetracked by that stupid necklace. It made no sense to me. Until I remembered that he had to clear Fairing's reputation. And it was my fault that Mac might single her out for a reprimand. If it weren't for me and my impulsive gift, Harper would have been able to concentrate on the murder.

Well, that just meant I'd have to find the necklace stealer so he could work on the other problem.

And then I saw her. Her husband wasn't with her. She was walking alone, heading in the general direction of the piper's tent, skirting around the raised platform where the dance competitions were held. I excused myself, wished everyone there a happy scarf-tying experience, and headed after her, dodging around people as best I could, trying to keep the woman in sight. Her long hair, coupled with her distinctive tartan skirt, set her apart from the countless women thronging the meadow. By the time she reached the pipers, I was almost on her. I could hear Dirk behind me, calling my name. Within seconds, I skidded to a stop beside her. "I need to talk to you," I said, unsure what precisely I'd say to her.

She spun around to face me.

"Mistress Peggy," Dirk was saying. "Stop! She isna the one."

He was right, doggone him. It was the wrong woman. This one was too young, too wide-eyed, too . . . too wrong.

"Did you need me for something?"

"I, uh, I was just wondering what clan your tartan skirt represents." How lame was that?

"I don't have the slightest idea," she said, "but I bought it at a cute little store up the road. Something like the Scottish Shop or whatever it's called."

I cringed.

"The guy who sold it to me looked absolutely dreamy in that kilt of his"—*Sam*, I thought—"and he had this sweet little dog."

"You must have bought it on Thursday," I said, for want of anything better to say. "Or maybe early on Friday."

"That's right. I bought it yesterday morning. How did you know?"

"Just a lucky guess." A little luck, and the fact that starting Friday afternoon, I'd had two dogs that hid under the sweater rack, out of sight the entire time.

I thanked her and suggested that she might want to head to that tent over there and buy a scarf to match her skirt. "There are a couple of cute guys in kilts to help you find the right one." Was that blatant commercialism? I didn't care. Her eyes widened and she headed off toward the ScotShop booth. I headed for the arch. It was past time for me to go back to the ScotShop. *Or whatever it's called.* I felt thoroughly discouraged. And thoroughly fed up with myself.

Of course, even if Dirk had called out to me sooner, I most likely wouldn't have stopped, but I didn't have to admit that out loud. And I still didn't know the name of that tartan. It might have been a clue.

I was about halfway across the meadow when a group of pipers struck up a rousing blast of sound—I couldn't recall the name of the tune. Ahead of me, I saw Shay pull out her cell phone and punch in a number. She was—still— in storm cloud mode. As I walked past, she turned her back to the pipers, clapped her free hand over her free ear, and said, "It's about time you got back to your room. Why don't you carry a cell so I can reach you when I need to?"

Her stiffening back didn't look happy with the answer she must have been hearing, although how anyone could hear anything over the sound of the bagpipes, I had no idea. I edged a little closer to her. Dirk got even closer. I saw him tighten the shawl around the hilt of his dagger.

The pipers marched nearer still, and the sound swirled around us. I'd have to depend on Dirk to tell me what was going on.

When Shay snapped her phone back into the holder on her belt, he turned to me and raised his voice to such a bellow I could imagine the sound pouring from the throats of ancient Scots charging down a hill to repel invaders. "I will follow her. Something is awry, and I dinna want to—"

With bagpipes braying right beside me, I missed the last part of his sentence. "I will see ye at the wee shop anon," he shouted as the pipers moved away from me. He turned to follow Shay, and they both were soon lost to my sight among the crowd.

Anon. That meant *soon.* Good.

Mistress Burns pounded on the hotel room door. When the long-haired woman opened it, Mistress Burns pushed her way in and Dirk slipped through just before the door slammed. "Where did you get it, Dolores?"

"What are you talking about?"

"Don't play games with me. You're in this up to your scrawny neck, and I want some answers. I know you're involved."

The woman pushed back her tangled brown hair. "Involved in what?"

"I said, don't try your games on me. Where's that worthless brother of mine? He's part of it, too."

"It's hammer throw time. You know he can't miss any of the events."

"So why aren't you there, cheering him on the way you usually do?"

"He said I should . . . uh . . . stay here."

"Stay out of sight, you mean? So the cops won't see you?"

"What do the cops have to do with this?"

"Little Miss Innocent, is that the way you're going to play it? Then please explain to me how that cop got hold of the imitation necklace."

"Cop? What cop? What do you mean?"

"Like you don't know?" Mistress Burns strode around

the room. Dirk had to jump onto the bed to keep her from running into him. "This is too much coincidence. You come to town and a necklace that's been missing for ten years just happens to show up? I saw it in the police station."

"The cops have it? That shopkeeper must have realized it was a fake."

"What shopkeeper?" Mistress Burns pulled out a chair and sat at the small round table by the curtained window. Dirk stepped off the bed and inspected the rest of the room. The more Mistress Dolores stammered, the less Mistress Burns seemed to believe her.

"I mean, uh, somebody must have thought it was fake and, like, turned it in."

Mistress Burns narrowed her eyes. Dirk wouldna ha' wanted to be the object of such scrutiny. "And just how did it get here, to Hamelin, in the first place?"

"Maybe Robert sold it to her," Mistress Dolores said.

Dirk did not recognize the name, but it looked as if it was well-known to Mistress Burns, considering the way she pursed her lips, as tight as the drawstring bag at her waist.

"Did that ever occur to you? It could have been Robert. After all, he lives here." Mistress Dolores sank down onto the chair on the other side of the small table.

"I know he lives here, but how could someone as inept as Robert have gotten his hands on the imitation to begin with? It was stolen along with the original."

The long-haired woman massaged one hand, as if it pained her. Mayhap it did. Her knuckles were swollen, just like the aulde grannies in his village.

Mistress Burns snaked her arm out so fast Dirk hardly saw it happen. "You're lying, Dodie." She tightened her hold on Mistress Dolores's arm, so much so that her knuckles went white. As white as her bloodless lips. "Tell me the truth. Now."

Dirk moved closer and studied the faces of the two women. One was red and angry. One was white and angry. He couldna tell which one was the worse.

"All right. I'll tell you. But let me go."

Mistress Burns opened her hand slowly, as if her fingers didna want to cooperate. She left her hand lying there on the table within striking distance.

"I didn't know anything about the necklace for a long time. Windsor told me—only a couple of years ago—that he found it in the bushes after the burglary. We all went out looking, remember, as soon as we noticed the silver tea service was gone. Windsor said that when he found it, he knew it was just the fake and nobody would be interested in that. He thought maybe the thieves had dropped it on their way out. He . . . saved it. He was going to give it to me for our twentieth anniversary next February but I found where he'd hidden it, so he gave it to me for our eighteenth instead. That's when he told me how he'd gotten it."

"You've known about this for two years?"

"Not two." She looked down at her fingers and seemed to be counting on them. "One and a half."

"Why didn't you tell anyone? Why didn't you tell me? That necklace was supposed to be mine."

"This one was just the fake. You never would have worn it."

Dirk could believe that for certes.

Mistress Burns leaned forward. "You said *a shop-keeper*. What shopkeeper?"

"That Scottish store. The one up the street on the other side."

"What does the ScotStore have to do with the necklace?"

Mistress Dolores began to rub her hand again.

"Tell me." Mistress Burns lowered her voice 'til 'twas almost a growl. "You don't want to know what I'll do to you if you don't."

"She had the real one." Mistress Dolores squeaked like a wee mousie. "It had to be the real one. There couldn't be another one like it. Last week we walked into that shop and saw it on sale for practically nothing, and . . . and Windsor thought we ought to make a trade."

"A trade? A *trade*?" Mistress Shay's upper lip curled back like a wildie about to jump a goat. "It's called stealing, Dodie. But no matter what you call it, you stole my necklace. Did you honestly think nobody would notice?"

"The price she was asking wasn't even a fraction of what it's worth. Everybody knows shopkeepers jack the prices up really high, so she probably didn't pay more than a couple of hundred for it."

"Did you think *I* wouldn't notice?"

Mistress Dolores raised her chin. "I never wore it when the family was around. The only time we ever see you is here at the festival. And at Lorena's funeral, but I didn't have the necklace then. Windsor hadn't given it to me yet."

"And this time, here, even though you weren't going to be wearing it, you just happened to have it with you?"

"I wear it a lot. And I always keep it with me."

Dirk didna think a voice could go any deeper than where Mistress Burns had already gone wi' her voice, but it could indeed. Like the angry grunting of a boar. Like the snarl of a wolf. Like the rumble of thunder no sae far away. Only this storm was here in this room. A room Dirk couldna get out of. "And now, dear wife of my thieving brother, you are going to tell me where my necklace is. The real one."

"I don't know," Mistress Dolores wailed, and Dirk could tell she wasna being a breugadair this time. Nay. She was telling the truth this time for certes. "He hid it somewhere and wouldn't tell me where. All he said was it's not here in the room. He knows I'm really good at finding things, and he said he didn't want me to be tempted."

Mistress Burns leaned back in her chair. "That story he told you, about finding the fake. It sounds a little bit too pat for me to swallow." She tapped one finger on the table. "I think he stole everything."

"No." Mistress Burns sounded sullen now. "Windsor said he always thought you or Lorena, or even Robert, had staged the burglary."

Shay stood up so suddenly, Dirk had to jump back out of her way. "That stiff-necked, self-righteous Lorena wouldn't; I certainly didn't; and Robert couldn't find his way out of a five-by-ten storage unit, much less plan a burglary. And you can tell my brother he's an idiot if he thinks any of us did it." She slapped Mistress Dolores wi' the back of her hand, and her big ring left a trail o' blood across the red-blotched cheek. "There's one more thing you can tell that husband of yours. On second thought, I'll tell him myself. If I don't get my necklace, I'll strip him of every trophy he ever won at any of the Games here, and he'll never compete again."

"You can't do that! He *lives* for these Games. He'd kill to win them." Her eyes got verra wide, as if she couldna believe she'd said that.

"Did he?" Mistress Burns asked. "Did he kill, just to win?"

She smiled. It reminded Dirk of a picture of a monstrous sea dragon he had seen on a map in Brother Marcus's cell once, back when he was alive. The dragon had had steam curling from its mouth, and ferocious teeth. Before he could blot the picture from his mind, Mistress Burns stormed to the door and left, slamming it behind her seconds before Dirk reached it. He drew his dagger and pounded on the door, but of course, nothing happened except that Mistress Dolores sat down on the side of the bed, cupped her bloody cheek in her hand, and began to cry.

Dirk was left with plenty of time to contemplate what might be a *fyveby ten storge younit*, but he couldna decipher the strange words.

I waited the rest of the evening, well past the eight o'clock closing time, but Dirk didn't reappear. The temps cleared out right away. No Dirk. Shoe delivered the cash box from the tie booth. No Dirk. Gilda and Sam left soon after that, taking Scamp with them, and I could tell they were happy to be headed for some well-deserved rest. They'd worked their tails off all day long. Silla crawled out from under the sweaters and seemed to attach herself to the bottom of my skirt.

Finally, about nine, I called Karaline.

"He's gone, K," I said. "Dirk's gone, and he said he'd

meet me here at the shop and he hasn't come and I'm worried. What if he's . . ."

"Lying dead in a ditch somewhere?" Karaline wasn't usually that sarcastic. "Don't be silly, P. What could possibly happen to a ghost?"

Silla bumped her head against my leg. "But I don't even know where he went."

"Are you still at the shop?"

"Yes." I bent over and scratched Silla's head.

"Stay put and I'll be right there."

"Maybe he went home," I said, not sure whether I meant home to Hickory Lane or . . . or home to his Peigi, although how he could possibly have gotten there, I had no idea. He did have the shawl, though.

"Did you hear me? Stay where you are. I'm on my way."

I put Silla's red leash on her so I'd be ready to go, but Karaline wouldn't let me leave until I explained what had happened.

"Okay," she said when I finished. "The first thing we do is go to your house and see if he's there."

Shorty greeted me at the front door, took a whack at Silla's poor nose, and jumped onto the couch.

Dirk wasn't anywhere in the house.

I thought about it. "Wait! He couldn't have gotten inside. The door was locked."

"He couldn't have gotten inside even if the door was unlocked," Karaline said.

So we looked outside.

When that turned up nothing—no ghost at least—Karaline sank onto a chair at my kitchen table. "The next thing we do is think about this."

We thought.

"He's never stayed away this long," I said. "This is the last time I ever let him take the shawl. What if he got lost—"

"I'm pretty sure ghosts can't get lost, P."

"How on earth would you know?"

Finally Karaline said, "Tell me again exactly what Shay said on the phone."

I thought about it for a moment. "She complained that whoever it was didn't have a cell phone."

"Who doesn't carry a cell?"

I shrugged.

"Did she say anything else? Anything about where she was going?"

I tried to envision the scene before the bagpipers began their joyous wailing. "She said something like 'It's about time you got back to your room.'"

Karaline stood so fast the chair knocked over. "Let's go."

"Where?"

"The hotel, of course."

Oh. Of course. But then I wondered, "What if it's not a room at the hotel? What if it's in a B and B or one of the motels, or—"

"Shut up, P. We'll deal with one step at a time."

Fine for her to say. She wasn't the one missing a ghost. I hadn't told her yet how Dirk—Macbeath—was my great-multiple-times-grandfather. I'd do that later. After we found him.

23

You will lose this wager, my lord.
ACT 5, SCENE 2

Karaline and I roamed the hotel lobby, hoping our ghost would appear. The clerk at the desk wouldn't let us back in the hallways, since we weren't registered guests. He gave us some cock-and-bull story about security being tighter, and maybe that was true, considering there'd been a murder, but it was darned inconvenient.

Finally, we left.

I got up four times during the night to open the front door and peer out onto the porch, hoping to see my ghost sitting in the swing.

The first three times, Shorty accompanied me downstairs while Silla stayed curled in her bed.

The fourth time I got up, Shorty wasn't with me on the bed. I couldn't see him in the dark bedroom, and I finally turned on a light. Shorty lay splayed across Silla's back.

I couldn't tell if he was comforting the wee doggie simply soaking up Silla's warmth. By the time I checked the porch—no Dirk—and returned to my bedroom, Shorty had moved to one side and was curled between the plush side of the dog bed and Silla's tummy. Silla had a paw resting on Shorty's shoulder.

Early Sunday morning, Dirk still hadn't shown up. I finally get a grandfather and he disappears.

I called Karaline to make sure he hadn't somehow found his way to her house, and then I called Harper and begged him to stop by my house. "I need your help," I said. And he didn't even ask what it was about. He simply came.

Living room or kitchen, I wondered while I waited for him to arrive. Kitchen. I could serve coffee. I started it brewing, made sure Silla had taken care of her business, and opened the front door before Harper was even halfway out of his car. "Let him believe me," I breathed, even though I wasn't sure whom I was talking to.

I took one more look at the swing, just in case. Nothing. "Come on back to the kitchen. I have coffee ready."

Once we were seated, I stared at him for a moment. His dark eyes were tired-looking—no wonder, he'd probably been working the murder investigation nonstop—but they were curious as well.

"I have something to tell you. And I know you're not going to want to believe it at first, but could you just give me some time to explain the whole story before you try to leave?"

His eyes got that wary expression that's hard to describe but impossible to miss. "Okay." He lifted his coffee cup to his lips. I tried not to think about that one time he'd kissed my cheek.

I took as deep a breath as I could. "When I went to Scotland last year and bought that shawl, it . . . it had . . . it had a ghost attached to it."

Once we'd cleaned up the coffee he'd spluttered all over the table, I told him the rest of it.

"And now," I finished, "he's gone. He hasn't been back since he went running off after Shay yesterday, and they wouldn't let Karaline and me in the hotel to search for him last night."

"Karaline? You took Karaline with you?"

"Of course. She's the only other person in town who can see Dirk."

He pressed his palms over his eyes. "You and Karaline can see this ghost, but nobody else can?"

"That's right, and I need you to get me into the hotel so I can find him."

"Why doesn't he just . . . walk through a wall or something?"

"That's the problem. He can't. He can't get through a door unless somebody opens it for him. He can't turn the pages of a book—"

"What book?"

"Any book. He likes to read. *A Tale of Two Cities* is his current favorite."

Harper let out his breath, like he'd reached the end of his limit. "I thought you said he can't turn the pages."

"He can't. He reads out loud to me while I knit, and I turn the pages for him. Quit laughing. This is most definitely not funny. My ghost may be trapped somewhere and I have to find him and I need your help to do it and you're laughing at me?"

"Peggy, Peggy, Peggy." His voice sounded softer with each iteration of my name. "It's so outrageous, I almost have to believe you. And you obviously believe it, so even if it's an unexplainable hallucination—"

"It is *not*!"

"I still have to go along with it, just to see how it's going to turn out."

"You're patronizing me."

He reached out and touched the tips of my fingers where they lay pressed against the table. I was tempted to jerk my hand away, but I didn't want to miss the soothing calm of even that slight touch. "I'm trying to understand you," he said. He pushed his chair back. "Let's go find ourselves a ghost. I'm betting we won't, but maybe I'll be wrong."

I still thought he was laughing at me, but at least he was on his feet.

I held Silla in my lap as we drove into the center of Hamelin.

As Harper parked curbside—illegally—in front of the hotel, a man opened the door and I spotted Dirk behind him, trying to slip out.

"There he is," I yelled, and Silla barked. "Stay here, and I'll get him in the car."

Harper grabbed Silla's collar. I jumped out and opened first the hotel door, and then the back door of the cruiser. Dirk climbed in as I leaned forward and said, "Of all the ghosts in the world, I get stuck with one who doesn't know how to walk through a wall! Didn't you ever read *A Christmas Carol*? Didn't you ever see *The Ghost and Mrs. Muir*? How dare you worry me like that?"

"Ye needna beceorest so. Ye know verra weel I have read

about the ghost of Jacob Marley, but as ye can see, I ha' no chains to clankity around. Any the way, that particular ghost was nae a real ghost. And ye probably are aware that I havena met either Mistress Muir or her ghost, because ye have never thought to introduce us. I seem to remember me that ye said ye didna ken any ither ghosts. Perhaps ye would oblige next time they come into our wee shop."

He said *our*. He said *our shop*. He could accuse me of baykoraysting all he wanted to. "Oh, Macbeath, I'm so glad you're safe and alive—uh—well—you know what I mean. I'm glad you're here."

"I accept your apology, for I assume that is what ye intend by all this dithering about. For the now, ye maun quit talking. The folk walking past are beginning to wonder about ye." He turned his head to peer over the back of the front seat. "And so is our constable."

"Let's go. There's a lot we have to discuss."

I closed the car door, careful to be sure his dagger was out of the way, and got back in the front. "I think it will be easier to talk at my house. Can we go back there?"

Harper studied me for quite a while before he eased the car into gear.

Silla whined and tried to jump over the seat, even though that barrier was in the way.

Harper was wasting a lot of energy, I thought, shaking his head so much. I called Gilda and told her I'd be a little late.

I opened two more doors for Dirk—police car and house. Harper followed me, shaking his head slowly.

"Ye did tell him about me?" It wasn't so much a question as an observation on the part of Dirk as Harper and I seated ourselves.

"Yeah. I told him." I reached out a foot and pushed a chair away from the table. "Have a seat, Macbeath. I think this is going to take a while."

"Ye needna rush. Our wee murderer isna going anywhere soon."

"He isn't? Who is he? How do you know?"

Harper held up a hand. "Would you please explain to me what's happening?"

It took quite a while, of course, but once Dirk explained the whole story—or what he knew of it from his sojourn in Dolores and Windsor's room—Harper no longer sounded quite so skeptical. In fact, he ended up asking, "If your ghost can't walk through walls, how did he get out of the room this morning?"

"I tried for to leave, but the man near filled the door with his shoulders so brawnish when he did come home yestreen."

"I think he means brawny," I told Harper as I translated from ghost to present-day. "And 'yestreen' means last night—yesterday evening." I had the feeling I'd left something out. Some vital piece of information, but I couldn't think what it might be.

"Whan that he threatened for to kill ye, Mistress Peggy—"

"He threatened to *kill me*?"

"Kill you? Who?" Harper was almost on his feet.

"Why did he say he wanted to kill me?"

"He is afeared ye will identify Mistress Dolores for the stealing o' the necklace."

"He should have thought about his wife before he came up with the idea in the first place. What did you do when he threatened me?"

"I struck his head w' my hand and he fair passed out."

"Good thinking." I explained it all to Harper.

"Why would that make him pass out?"

"You know, this would be a whole lot easier if you could just hear him. And see him," I added. "Remember that time you were here last year and all of a sudden you got very dizzy and fell down and couldn't walk very steadily for a while?"

He nodded.

"What happened was, you ran into Dirk."

"I—I—"

"Right. You did. That's what happened."

Apparently Dirk wasn't interested in all that explaining. "I waited until the wee woman called for help," he said. "Whan that the . . . the . . ."

"Paramedics," I suggested.

"Aye. Whan that they came, they left the wee door wide open, and I walked out, but then I couldna get all the way outside until . . ."

"Until Harper and I showed up," I finished for him.

Dirk stood and paced between the table and the fridge. There wasn't a lot of room, and each time he changed direction, his kilt swirled out.

Harper cleared his throat. "Until we showed up where?"

Once I'd transmitted Dirk's explanation, I asked, "So, what do we do now?"

"*We* don't do anything." Harper's voice had turned steely. "*I* will handle it from here. My team and I. The problem is that—if your ghost is to be believed—" He indicated the chair where Dirk had been. I didn't want to interrupt him to tell him Dirk wasn't there anymore. Anyway, it didn't seem relevant.

"I now know the motive," Harper continued. "I can plot the opportunity, and of course, I already knew how it was done with the karate chop and the bagpipe . . . cord." His voice took on a funny tone when he said that last word, but I couldn't interpret it.

Dirk sat back down. "He didna quite admit to the murder o' Large William. He said only that he was glad he had no more competition for the caber toss and hammer throw."

"That's a terrible reason to kill someone."

"Aye. I agree wi' ye. He told his wife that he had the necklace in his sporran but he had taken it off during the hammer throw, and somebody took it."

"Took the necklace?"

"Took the entire contents of the sporran along wi' the necklace."

"That's crazy."

"Upended it. 'Tis what he said."

Harper didn't like it when I told him all of that. "So now I'm looking for a completely unknown thief?"

"Maybe he was lying to her," I suggested.

"Why would he do that?"

"For why would he?" They sounded like slightly skewed echoes of each other.

Harper shrugged off the necklace situation. "If somebody did steal it, it'll show up soon enough in the pawnshops. And if he's lying, then when I arrest him it'll show up in his sporran. I'm more concerned now with proving the murder."

"I would like to know how Large William ended up in the water room."

"Bathroom."

"What about it?" When I told Harper what Dirk had said, he told me that didn't matter. "We already knew he was dragged. There were parallel marks on the carpet." He drummed his fingers against the table for a few seconds. "The problem will be to convince the rest of my team—and the district attorney—that I was able to get all this information through good solid police investigative techniques. Somehow I doubt the DA would believe"—he looked at the (to his eyes) empty chair—"that I learned it from a chatty ghost."

Chatty. The nurse's aide. That was what I'd forgotten. "You might talk to your sister-in-law," I said. "I think a dog bite might make a good starting point."

When Harper left soon after I explained what I was talking about, I turned to Dirk. "Don't you ever leave me like that again. Never."

For some reason, Dirk looked at the door through which Harper had just passed. "I willna say *never*, but I do promise to stay as long as 'tis possible."

Of course. He was thinking about going home to his Peigi. Someday.

I hoped it wouldn't be too soon.

Harper held the phone away from his ear while his sislaw vented.

"I knew that aide should have had her mouth taped shut."

"Amy?"

"As many times as I've told her not to talk about the patients—"

"Amy?"

"And she goes ahead and does it anyway. First it was—"

"Amy!" This time his voice seemed to penetrate her rant. "It's a good thing, believe it or not. I needed to know about the man who was bitten."

She stopped. "Why do you need to know?"

He crossed his fingers, a CYA habit left over from the childhood he and his brother and Amy had spent getting into and, sometimes, out of scrapes. "I can get a subpoena easily." Not without better cause than *a ghost told me.* "But for now what I really need is just to know the location of the bite. And your best guess as to when it happened. And maybe the severity of it."

"That's three questions, brolaw. You're going to owe me."

"Steaks, grilled the way you like them, once we get this guy in jail?"

"You got it. Lower part of his calf. Only a couple of stitches. He came in late Thursday night, but the bruising was already fairly severe. I'd say he waited a while before coming to the hospital—maybe four or five hours."

"Thanks, Amy."

"Wait. One more thing. I don't know if it has anything to do with the murder—"

"I didn't say anything about a murder."

Amy scoffed. "I wasn't born yesterday. Why else would you be asking with that *I could get a subpoena* fiction? Smith had bruises on the pads of a couple of his fingers. I've never seen anything like that, except once on a guy who just barely hung onto the gutter of a roof for about ten minutes before they could get a ladder to him."

"Smith?"

"That's what he said his name was."

If Smith had a dog bite from Silla, that pretty much cleared Shay Burns. Unless she'd been an accessory.

"Thanks again, Amy. One more question?"

"This is your last one."

"Promise. If I show you a picture, would you be able to identify this Smith guy? Or maybe pick him out of a lineup?"

"Piece of cake." She giggled. "For a piece of steak. Medium rare. Don't forget."

Harper couldn't think of anything else to ask. For now. "Keep an eye out for a text," he said.

"You never answered me about the date of the surprise party. Are you going to make it?"

Harper's mind had already leapt ahead. "What? Oh, yeah. I'll be there."

"Why don't you bring Peggy along?"

"Peggy?" His mind stopped churning.

"You know, Peggy Winn?"

Why did his sislaw sound like she was laughing at him?

"Yeah. I just may do that." If she'd agree to go with him.

The churning began again. How was he going to get a photo of—he smiled to think of what Peggy had said the ghost had called this guy—the wee murderer?

As Dirk and I walked down the hill toward the meadow after closing the ScotShop Sunday evening, I resolutely refused to talk about what was going to happen. The truth was, I didn't know what was going to happen, but since everybody would be leaving town the next day, I sure hoped Harper and his team had managed to get some proof. I turned my thoughts—or tried to turn them—toward the evening ahead of us.

One of the fun things about Highland Games is that each one is unique. Oh, they all have a great many of the same elements. You'll always have bagpipers and drummers galore and dance exhibitions and the hefty competitors throwing big heavy things around as if they were so many matchsticks. There's usually a tug-of-war, and there frequently is a bonfire of some sort, although I firmly believe Hamelin's is the best of the best. But the opening and closing ceremonies are seldom the same from one Highland Festival to another, even though the two may be geographically close, say, in neighboring states.

Hamelin has always given out the winners' awards early on in the final ceremonies. I guess the idea was to get all that folderol out of the way so people could enjoy the bonfire, which really was the high point of the entire long weekend. Even before the award part began, a lot of the people would stake out their chosen seating in relation to the huge pile of firewood.

Karaline and Drew had arranged to get there early and set up the blanket. I, of course, had to wait until I could close the shop. I veered to my right inside the flowered arch—the wilted flowers from yesterday had been replaced—and looked around until I saw the red foot-wide hibiscus flowers on Karaline's caftan billowing in the breeze her arms created as she waved to me.

They'd spread the blanket fairly close to the stage. I didn't like to have my head tilted back at such an acute angle like that, but it looked like there weren't many other places available. I also would have preferred to find a place a little closer to the bonfire site so we wouldn't have to move after the awards were completed, but maybe everybody had shown up early and there hadn't been much choice. I shortened Silla's leash and headed that way. Andrea Stone and her mother sat in the middle of my planned route, so I steeled myself.

Ahead of me I could see Sergeant Murphy in civilian clothes, with an Irish plaid sash thrown across one shoulder, taking pictures, as if he were a tourist. He asked several groups of the people congregated behind the stage to pose with arms linked. It looked like a class reunion. It looked like a Scottish festival. But why was Murphy collecting photos? He snapped several of the Highland Dance teams, the drum major with two of the drummers, some of the caber toss contestants. After a very short time—it's no fun watching someone else take pictures— I headed toward Karaline, but I had to pass Andrea and her mom first.

Andrea for once wasn't roaming the crowd with her reporter's paraphernalia. She sat with her mom near the right front corner of the stage. I could see the empty chair they were obviously saving for Andrea's dad. I smiled at Mrs. Stone as we walked past them, and I even would have nodded at Andrea if she'd deigned to look at me. Instead she took a long drink from her Pepsi bottle and placed it with some deliberation in the cup holder on the arm of the well-padded folding chair. Silla and I kept walking. I doubted the Stones knew why Andrea and I had stopped being friends.

Karaline hardly said anything, other than to smile at Dirk and mutter *hello* at me. She seldom showed nerves like this. In fact, she looked like I felt. Dirk scanned the crowd and said, "I willna sit w' ye. 'Tis more important, d'ye not ken, that I find our wee murderer."

Since he and Karaline and I had already agreed on this plan, I couldn't see why he was repeating it. Maybe he was as nervous as Karaline. I was nervous, too. Not having anything concrete to do was my least favorite way of approaching a problem. But this really did have to be in Harper's hands.

Dirk craned his neck and headed off to the right of the stage, past Mrs. Stone and Andrea. I noticed that they both unconsciously folded their legs back out of the way as Dirk drew near. He stepped over a rope boundary of some sort and hovered near the necklace husband, who kept clenching and unclenching his fist. Part of me wished I didn't have such a clear view of him. I swiveled around, looking for Dolores, the necklace-thieving woman, but couldn't spot her. Surely she'd show up for the awards. I didn't know what I'd do when I saw her.

Silla curled between Karaline and me, her head resting on my lap. I stroked her with one hand and kept the leash wrapped around my other. Tessa watched Dirk, but then folded herself into a tight circle on a corner of the blanket next to Drew's feet.

A minute or two after I was settled, Shay and her entire committee trooped out onto the stage. I was fairly sure she hadn't managed to get her necklace from Windsor. I knew if she'd gotten it out of his grasp, she would have been wearing it in triumph. She and the other committee members did the usual self-congratulatory stuff, and then Shay introduced Vermont senator Josie Calais. Everyone was attentive, although the people had their eyes on the stage and the police officers had their eyes on the crowd. Except for Lieutenant Murphy. He seemed to be texting somebody. If he didn't pay attention to his job, he was going to get a reprimand of some sort. I couldn't decide if he was off work for the day—that was ludicrous; all the cops worked during the Games—or if he was undercover, so to speak. Probably the latter. But taking pictures? Made no sense.

Senator Calais looked stunning in her blue-and-black Clark plaid as she handed out the medals and trophies to winner after winner. The *Traveled the Farthest* award went to a couple from Australia, who cracked everyone up with their obviously exaggerated accents as they accepted. It took a long time to get through the list, but the audience was unusually subdued. I did wonder if they were remembering the earlier ceremony—the opening on Thursday night—and wondering if there might be another sniper somewhere out of sight. But there were an inordinate number of police officers and security guards roaming through the crowd and ringing the stage.

I picked Harper out of the crowd behind the stage. He, too, was texting someone. The bluish glow on his face was unmistakable, and his thumbs were going so fast they almost looked blurry.

As the presentations wore on and on, folks relaxed, lay back on their blankets, stretched out in their folding chairs, or simply sat on the grass, and absorbed the soft evening air. Karaline and Drew held hands. I stroked Silla and watched Dirk watching Windsor.

I had no idea what was going to happen, how Harper would handle this. I had barely heard a word from him. There had just been two texts, about an hour ago. Amy helped. Thanks. Big lot of info that was. And Bring Silla to closing. Keep her close to you on leash. What on earth was that about? Anyway, I'd never had any intention of leaving her alone.

As I stroked her, my fingers felt an area where her fur seemed to be thinner. I pulled out my phone and used the flashlight app to inspect the area. She was definitely missing a patch on her side. Poor thing. She'd probably scraped it while she was digging through that wall.

I looked up to see Mr. Stone watching me from where he stood near the top of the stage steps. I drew in my breath. As drum major, he had on a tall bearskin hat, with his sashes and badges all shiny and his plaid elegantly pleated and arrayed. He'd tucked his silver-headed mace close against his chest, the pointed end of it resting on the stage beside his booted left foot, the head reaching almost to his shoulder. He looked so magnificent in that stunning outfit, all I could do was shake my head in wonder.

Silla stirred in her sleep, and I bent to murmur some gentle nonsense. When I looked back, Mr. Stone still seemed to be watching me. Probably wondering why I wasn't talking to his daughter anymore. I wondered briefly what she'd told him.

Shay droned on and on. There sure were a lot of awards to hand out.

It took me a while to discern what was different about the ceremony this year. Always before, the winners had been called up from the audience, and they wove through the chairs and blankets to reach the stage. But this year, all the winners seemed to have been asked to gather in that roped-off area in back of the stage, and as Shay Burns announced each name, the winner walked up the same steps the president had used, to receive their medals from Senator Calais before they headed out into the audience to rejoin their friends or family. One of the drummers beat the drum along with each winner's footsteps. Everybody laughed when some of the winners walked either very fast or very slowly, and some obviously tried to flummox the drummer by skipping or dancing. The drummer—I wished I knew his name—never missed a beat, though.

The sound of the drum made me think of a steady rainfall—why, I'm not sure—and that made me think about Big Willie's funeral. I didn't know when it was going to be, or where, but I wanted to attend it. I tightened my hold on Silla's leash.

The final awards on the agenda were always the heavy games—the weight toss, stone put, hammer throw, and caber toss—followed by the People's Choice award, the one event festival attendees had enjoyed the most. As people voted on Sunday afternoon at the People's Choice tent, they had their hand stamped with an indelible-ink thistle. Once stamped, a person couldn't vote a second time. Just a little safeguard.

I hadn't voted. I hadn't seen enough of the Games to have a preference. Still, when I thought about it, I realized

I did have one. A preference. I looked back at Mr. Stone. I would have voted for him and his group of drummers. They were fun to watch and fun to listen to, and to hear off in the distance, and even up close.

Karaline leaned across Silla and whispered, "What are you so pensive about?"

"I just figured something out."

"About the murder?"

"Don't I wish. No, I decided I should have voted for Mr. Stone and his drummers."

She looked up at him and nodded her head. "He sure does look great in that hat, doesn't he?"

I nodded. It felt like we were at a bobblehead convention. "I wonder why he isn't in place on the far side of the meadow. He's supposed to walk in front of the lone piper."

Karaline shrugged. "Beats me."

She turned to say something to Drew, and I puzzled over the logistics for another few seconds. Oh well, Shay had probably figured out how it was all going to work. I supposed they'd take a few minutes after the awards for all the parade participants to quietly disappear and convene at the starting point on the Perth Trail.

"And now," Shay effused into the microphone, "the awards for the Highland athletic competitions!"

The drum major barked out an order and raised his mace. This time, one of the drummers began a steady roll as the entire group walked farther forward on the stage.

Silla lifted her head. I felt a low rumble as she began to growl. I laid a hand on her. "What's wrong, girl?" The hackles on her back rose. Tessa roused, unfolded herself, and laid her head on Drew's knee.

"As I'm sure you've already figured out," Shay shouted into the microphone, "one man has led the pack for the fifth year in a row!"

How would her voice ever last if she kept up this yelling?

At the foot of the stage steps, I saw Harper reach for his cell phone. There was a flash of light as the screen lit his face. I could tell he'd just gotten a text. He read it, did a double take, and then seemed to look at it again, just to make sure.

"Head on over here, Windsor Stone, and get what's coming to you!"

Nobody else seemed to notice what a strange invitation that was. Was Shay about to strip him of his past victories, the way Dirk had said she'd threatened to? Could she even do that? Windsor mounted the steps to the stage, his arms raised in victory, but he looked a little bit tentative as he strode across the stage, the drum echoing his footsteps. "Here I am!"

Dirk followed Windsor, his arms loose at his side, but his fingers tense. He was crouching slightly, as if ready to spring.

Harper shoved his cell phone into the holder at his waist and bounded up the stairs. "Robert Stone," he called. "You are under arrest for the murder of—"

Why did he say *Robert* Stone? The murderer was *Windsor* Stone. I saw the drum major's face, a mask of anger and disbelief. Dirk whirled around, his face a study in confusion.

In less than a heartbeat, the drum major swung his mace and knocked Harper off the edge of the platform.

Windsor Stone stood with his arms still up in the air,

the first two fingers of each hand still forming the V for victory, his mouth open in a silent O.

Mrs. Stone—the Mrs. Stone I'd known for most of my life, Andrea's mother, the woman who had welcomed me into her home when I was a kid, the woman who had smiled at me not half an hour before—screamed.

Silla bounded forward, barking, and the leash pulled me to my feet almost before I could think what was happening. People right and left drew back away from the Scottie's obvious fury. Silla jerked as she reached the end of the retractable lead.

Robert, his bearskin hat askew, bounded off the stage. Silla leapt to intercept him, snarling and wrenching the leash from my hand. I charged after her and threw myself onto her as Mr. Stone raised his mace for a vicious downward swing. "You stupid dog!" he yelled. "You gave me away, didn't you?"

Dirk flew off the stage at Stone and seemed to connect with his legs. The next thing I knew, the mace clattered to the ground next to me, and Mr. Stone was on his back, writhing on the grass. His tall hat had fallen off. Nearby I heard someone say, "Did you see that? Most amazing thing. One minute he was running hell-bent for leather, and the next his legs just went out from under him. I've never seen anything like it."

"No," another voice replied. "He was standing still when he fell. Ready to hit that woman with the business end of that stick of his, and it was like somebody tackled him."

I gathered Silla into my arms and smiled at Dirk, who was adjusting his plaid. "That was a masterful tackle," I said. In all the confusion, I don't think anyone else heard me. Silla added a deep-throated *woof*.

"I didna like the feeling, but 'twas important that he no could hit ye wi' the wee stick."

That *wee stick* was metal-tipped and longer than I was tall.

Fairing ended up being the one who snapped the handcuffs on the drum major. Murphy helped Harper to his feet. Harper limped back onto the stage and—I heard him because I'd edged close to him, wondering why he was so unsteady on his feet—he arrested Windsor Stone. Good. It looked like that man wasn't going to get away with stealing my necklace. Shay's necklace, darn it. Within moments Harper had motioned to one of the other police officers to lead Windsor Stone away, while Murphy had the long-haired wife in handcuffs and was herding her out of the meadow, following in the wake of the other two prisoners.

24

And let me speak to th' yet unknowing world
Of . . . purposes mistook.
ACT 5, SCENE 2

I can't say I'd ever wish to see Shay absolutely speech-less, but I have to admit to a minor gloat when I saw that she was. Two men in handcuffs, one for murder, one for theft. It did seem like the curse of the Hamelin High-land Festival had landed on Shay's Games once more.

But Robert? The drum major? Why? How?

"Dirk," I said, careful to keep my voice quiet and my mouth relatively still as I edged closer to the stage, "I thought you said Windsor did it."

"Nae. That I didna say. I said his wee wife said she thought he had, but he did deny it." He fingered the shawl, lifting one edge of it and rubbing the fabric between thumb and forefinger. "I didna believe him, howsoever. He sounded too . . . sincere. I thought 'twas Master Windsor who had done the killing."

"So did I," I said. "So did I."

"I did believe him, howsoever, whan that he did say he was glad to be shut o' the competition from Large William."

"Shut? Oh, you mean to be 'rid of.'"

"'Shut' is a much better word, would ye no say?"

But I couldn't get drawn into a discussion about the relative merits of his language versus my language. I didn't want anyone to see me talking to a ghost. Not here. Not now. Not when a few people around us were still discussing how the drum major's feet could have been swept out from under him like that. And anyway, I was even more concerned about Harper. The police officer at the bottom of the stage steps wouldn't let me through, but I called to Harper as he reached the top of them.

"Are you okay? Why are you limping?"

He stopped in front of me. "Nothing too serious. Just a couple of broken ribs, I think."

"You think? Did somebody call the paramedics?" I was already pulling out my cell phone.

He put a hand across mine. "I have to get to the station. I'll have somebody there take a look."

I doubted that would do much good. "They'll need to be taped."

"No, don't worry. Really. This isn't anything a good steak dinner won't cure."

"What on earth—"

"Or maybe a birthday party."

"I thought he hit you in the ribs, not in the head."

He laughed, quickly cut short—I should think so, what with his broken ribs—and headed toward the police station. Silla and I returned to Karaline and Drew's blanket.

After a quick consultation with her committee, Shay announced in a tight voice that the trophy for the Highland athletic competitions would go to the second-place contender. Once Senator Calais had shaken hands with the winner, Shay cleared her throat. "The People's Choice trophy"—she gripped the microphone in a white-knuckled fist—"will not be awarded this year, since both the first and second-place honorees are . . ." She shot a quick glance in the direction of the arch through which the police had ushered Robert and Windsor. "Since they are both unable to accept at this time." I did wonder which one of them had won first place. I supposed I'd never know, as I doubted Shay Stone Burns had any intention of telling me anything.

She switched the microphone from her right hand to her left, and her ring glinted. "And now, in the time-honored tradition of the Hamelin Highland Games, each clan here may send one representative to the starting point of our March of the Clans." She pointed toward the tall sentinel trees that overshadowed the opening to the Perth Trail, and a number of men—and a few women—began to make their way through the crowded throng. A few ragged cheers erupted, which gradually built into a general round of applause, but it was nowhere near the normal level that usually greeted such announcements.

"While we're waiting, lads and lassies, you're welcome to rearrange your chairs to face the stack of wood. Just don't sit too close to it." I think this was the first time I'd ever felt sorry for Shay. She was trying so hard, but I could hear the catch of the almost-tears in her throat. Or maybe it was rage at not having gotten her precious neck-lace back.

Stone was a fairly common last name. If it hadn't been for Dirk, I never would have made the connection of her being Windsor's sister. I doubt anybody had. I know she never mentioned it. The only reason I could see what strain she was under was that I knew. I wondered if she'd ever admit to it now.

I noticed, too, that Mrs. Stone was gone. She must have followed her husband to the police station. Andrea still sat in the fancy folding chair, with her bottle of Pepsi in the side holder. She sat as if turned to—oh dear, was I really thinking this?—as if turned to *Stone*.

Karaline jostled my elbow. "You're standing there like a statue. Would you like to join the three of us"—she gestured to Dirk and Drew—"while we find a place to watch the bonfire?"

I nodded, but my heart wasn't in it.

I guess it helps to have two dogs, a six-foot-tall woman, and a man with a wheelchair. Karaline and Drew found an ideal place for us, right in the front ring of the crowd. Karaline and I left plenty of room for Dirk. Silla sat be-side my stretched-out feet.

When the procession of the clans finally began, I joined in the collective sigh as we recognized the shape of a coffin being carried by the men who'd competed in the caber toss. It was second in line after Porter Mac-naughton, the lone piper, and was followed by a single drummer and the long line of clan leaders. They paced across the field and circled the bonfire. When they finally came to a stop, someone spread out a Clan Farquharson plaid, and the athletes set the coffin on it. Right in front of our blanket.

Someone had set up a portable microphone, and Shay gave a speech about William Bowman, the longtime competitor in the Hamelin Highland Games who had tragically lost his wife four years ago and had not competed since then. Never once did she mention her family connection with the dead man.

She then introduced a man I'd never seen before, the leader of Clan Graham, which had the largest number of attendees at this year's Hamelin Highland Games. "As many of you know," he said, "Big Willie's wife was a Graham." There were cheers from a fairly large contingent of voices. "When he lost his own life so recently, all the Highland Games lost a dear friend, and we choose tonight to honor him by dedicating this closing bonfire to the memory of Big Willie Bowman of Clan Farquharson."

The crowd was tired of sadness. The cheers started and kept going, particularly after Silla walked almost to the end of her retractable leash and jumped on top of Big Willie's coffin. Dirk stood and placed himself, like an honor guard, at the foot of his kinsman's coffin. Silla sat, unmoving, facing the stack of wood that would soon be ablaze. She waited until the cheering died down. After a few moments of utter stillness in which Dirk raised his dagger high above his head in an invisible salute, she raised her head and let out one long howl. *Ar-rooooooo*. When the echoes died away, she bent her head, licked the coffin once, and jumped down.

There wasn't a dry eye anywhere. I had never before seen such showmanship.

And then she returned to me.

After all of that, who even needed the fireworks?

Harper wasn't surprised when Shay Stone Burns answered his request with alacrity. This was a far cry from the way she'd come grumping into the station at his insistence the last time. A week ago, he wouldn't have believed that the smiling woman who sat across from him at the small table could possibly have been the same as the grasping woman who had backhanded her sister-in-law so viciously.

He knew, of course, as any police officer knew, that someone could—how had Shakespeare put it?—could smile, and smile, and be a villain, but it was hard to believe that Shay Burns fit into that category. And was she a villain? Certainly not in the same category as Robert, but maybe, most definitely, in the same category as conniving Windsor and Dolores. The trouble was, the necklace would have been in her possession all this time if Robert hadn't stolen it to begin with ten years before. And, he thought wryly, Robert would have had *all the silverware* at his disposal. Legally.

Harper couldn't, of course, tell Fairing or Murphy what had happened in that hotel room. He couldn't admit he knew anything about that side of the story. He wasn't even quite sure he believed it himself.

He could, however, make Shay squirm a bit before he told her the truth. And then watch her squirm even more.

He glanced at Fairing, who sat, notebook in hand, in a straight-backed chair against the wall, slightly behind Shay's line of sight, as if Shay Burns were a suspect here. It almost looked like Fairing didn't trust this woman.

Fairing had good instincts.

He cleared his throat. "Thank you for coming in when I asked you. This time." The pause had been minuscule, but Burns heard it. She narrowed one eye, and Harper was reminded again of a pirate in an old cartoon.

"I want my necklace," she said.

"Thank you for bringing that up. I wanted to talk to you about the disposition of the necklace."

"It's mine. You can't keep it."

"The necklace that was stolen from the ScotShop's owner is currently in our custody."

Shay crossed her arms over her chest. "It was stolen from me. I have a copy of my parents' wills."

"Yes, so you say."

"If that upstart little shopkeeper thinks she can keep my necklace, she has another think coming. I'll sue her for all she's worth."

Harper let the empty threat hang there unanswered. "Sergeant Fairing," he finally said, "would you please join us here at the table?"

"Yes, sir."

Shay Burns moved her chair back a few inches when Fairing sat down, as if to distance herself from—what?—contamination?

"Sergeant Fairing, would you explain to Ms. Burns the results of the investigation I asked you to pursue?"

"Yes, sir." She set down her notebook and pulled a sheaf of papers from a nondescript black briefcase. "Pursuant to your orders . . ."

She was enjoying this, Harper could tell.

"After consulting with a noted museum expert, I instituted a thorough Internet search for Ming dynasty silver-and-ivory jewelry."

Shay's leg began to twitch against the table leg. Harper could feel the table jouncing. "Internet? Museum?" Shay said. "What's this all about?"

Harper raised an index finger. "This will take only a few moments, Ms. Burns. Please continue, Sergeant Fairing."

"The necklace in question appears to be the only known example of this type of necklace in existence. Its provenance has been traced through hundreds of years—would you like the exact number?"

"That's not necessary, Sergeant."

"What's necessary"—Shay practically spit out the words—"is that you tell me exactly when I'm going to get my necklace."

"Exactly?" Harper kept his voice even, although he felt like cheering. This was going so well.

"Yes, exactly."

"Fairing, would you care to answer that question?"

"Yes, sir." She turned to face Shay Stone Burns and uttered one word. "Never."

Shay's face turned an ugly shade of red that migrated into an even uglier shade of purple. Well, mauve maybe. Harper liked that word, *mauve*. But he did hope Shay Stone Burns wouldn't have a stroke while he and Fairing were here watching her.

"Never? What do you mean, *never*? It's my necklace, you . . . you pipsqueak! It's mine—do you hear me?"

"I think probably everyone in the station hears you, Ms. Burns, but my answer remains the same."

"You're stealing my necklace!"

"Oh, you certainly would be welcome to have it," Fairing said, "if you are willing to purchase it from the rightful owner, the Chinese Art Museum, from which the necklace was stolen in 1957. The most recent appraisal of its value is slightly over seven point two million dollars. I'm sure they'd be happy to accommodate your request to open negotiations."

"You're crazy—do you hear me? My father bought that necklace in 1970. I remember the day he brought it home. And I inherited it."

Harper thought it best for him to intervene. "Your father bought a stolen necklace, Ms. Burns, and it will be returned to the rightful owner. We do not at this time know whether your father was aware it was stolen, although I can't see how he could have missed that detail. Nor do we know whether your father was a party to the original theft and simply kept the necklace hidden until 1970. But we have turned over the information we've gathered to the FBI and an international art authority. They will pursue the investigation from here on."

"You can't do this! That necklace is mine." She lashed out across the corner of the table at Fairing, but Harper was ready for her. He blocked her arm just inches before the diamond made contact with Fairing's face, just as Fairing's forearm collided with his hand. She'd been ready as well.

He'd been wrong. Fairing's instincts weren't good. They were great.

"Tsk, tsk, tsk." He'd always wanted to use those three little syllables. This seemed like the perfect time. "Assaulting an officer? You wouldn't want us to handcuff you, would you?"

"And, Ms. Burns?" Fairing said in a sweet voice. "I'll be looking into the provenance of that diamond as well."

Shay sputtered.

"And the ruby. And the tea service."

"The tea service," Shay growled, "was stolen."

"Ah, but we recovered it," Harper said.

"Where was it?"

Harper inclined his head in an easterly direction. "In Arkane. In a five-by-ten self-storage unit, the kind your brother—how did you put it?—isn't able to find his way out of."

Fairing gave him a funny look. Shay's look was priceless. Let her wonder for the rest of her life how he knew what she'd said about her brother. Of course, she'd probably just think Dolores had told him. What a shame to have a ghost and not be able to brag about him.

When Harper was fairly certain Shay wouldn't lash out again, he let go of her arm and asked if she had any questions.

"Yes," she hissed. "How did that . . . Peggy Winn get it?"

"Someone stole it from the museum in 1957; your father bought—or stole—it from that person either in or before 1970; Robert stole it and all those other valuable items from your father. He took the necklace one day to deliver it to a, shall we say, private collector, but he was waylaid by a couple of street thugs before he reached his destination and was robbed at gunpoint. Needless to say, Robert never received payment for it and naturally, he chose not to report the theft."

He waited a moment in case Shay wanted to make a comment.

She didn't.

"That thief obviously didn't know what he had," Harper continued. "He may have pawned it, but it's more likely he simply sold it on the street, since a pawn shop owner would know about the laws regulating ivory and probably wouldn't touch a piece without proof of its provenance. From there we're not sure, but we do know that Ms. Winn bought it at a flea market in Montpelier for . . ." He smiled. This really was priceless. "Three dollars."

25

Take up the bodies. Such a sight as
this . . . shows much amiss.
ACT 5, SCENE 2

I always closed the ScotShop on Mondays, and I had kind of hoped we could have a meeting that first day after the arrests, all of us who were involved in the final resolution, to discuss what the heck had happened. I know I still had a jillion questions. But it simply didn't happen.

Despite what Dirk said, I took Silla to the vet early Monday morning. I didn't like the way she'd sounded so hoarse on Saturday. He said he could feel a badly swollen place, about the size of her rabies tag, on her throat. Neither one of us could think of what might have caused it, unless maybe her collar had gotten caught somehow as she was wriggling her way through the wall. I spent pretty much the rest of the day around the house, talking things over with Dirk and comforting Silla. I texted Harper a couple of times. Told him about taking Silla to the vet.

Mentioned that I didn't want to bother him, but I did have some questions.

He hardly answered at all. Just texted that he'd get back to me.

Karaline couldn't have cared less about the delay. She was busy herself with wedding plans.

Harper kept putting me off, so I finally quit calling and texting him. If he wanted me—that is to say, if he wanted to meet with everybody—he'd have to make the first move.

By the time we all got together, more than a week later, most of our questions had been answered. All we had to do was read the paper or pay attention to the news. But we still had a few outstanding queries.

Karaline and Drew brought doughnuts, as well as a pan of lasagna for later. I made the coffee. The four of us gathered in my kitchen.

Shorty hopped up in my lap and Silla curled herself beside my left foot. Now that I was settled, I could start with the questions. "Just before the arrests, I saw you texting like crazy. What was that all about?"

Harper grinned. I loved that not-quite-a-dimple he had. "I was convinced Windsor was the murderer."

"Me, too," I said.

"But the only person who could identify him for sure was my sislaw, Amy, since she'd treated him in the ER when he went in with the dog bite." Harper leaned sideways—carefully, since his ribs were still taped—and looked at Silla lying by my feet. "Good dog!"

"You can say that again." I leaned down to stroke her back and she woofed gently.

"I couldn't figure out how to get a picture of him. Murphy tried, but Windsor was always slightly turned away from the camera, almost like he was afraid of having his picture taken, which of course just made me that much more suspicious. Finally, Murphy saw Robert's wife taking a picture of the two brothers together. Murphy stepped behind her, clicked the photo over her shoulder, and texted it to me." He stopped talking and pulled out his cell. "Here's the picture if you want to see it."

We all did, so he passed it around. "I didn't realize how much the two brothers look alike," I said.

Harper agreed. "If Murphy hadn't caught the two of them together, Amy said she might have thought a picture of Windsor was the one of *Smith*. But seeing them together, she said it was very obvious who'd been the man with the dog bite."

Drew grabbed another doughnut—with maple frosting, Karaline's specialty. "Was Amy there Sunday night?"

"No. She was working, so I texted it to her, asking, 'Is this the guy?' Of course, I meant Windsor. She was with a patient, so it took her a while to text me back with 'Yes. Smith is guy in tall furry hat.' That really surprised me. I got the text just seconds before I went up on the stage."

"And got whacked for your efforts," Karaline said.

"Otherwise," Drew said, "you would have arrested the wrong guy?"

"That's right." Harper sounded perfectly cheerful about it. "And now I owe my sislaw a steak dinner." He turned to me. "Do you want to come along?"

"I . . . uh . . . uh, sure."

"Good. I'll let you know when." He patted his shirt

pocket, for some reason, and I could see something lumpy in there. Before I could think much about it, he continued. "Of course, once we had him in custody, we had the evidence of the dog bite on his leg . . ." He reached down a little farther this time, slowly and gingerly, and ruffled the hair on Silla's head. She stood up, shook herself to resettle her coiffure, and laid herself back down. I handed Harper a doughnut drenched in dark chocolate. He'd just asked me out for a date. Those charcoal eyes of his were something else.

"Good dog," Karaline and Drew said at the same time, and Tessa added a canine vote of approval. They were all three going to have a great life together.

Harper ate the doughnut, watching me all the time. Karaline and Drew didn't notice a thing. They were too busy looking at each other.

"Is all of that enough evidence to get a conviction?" I sure did hope so.

"Yes," he said with a smile, but I had the feeling he was answering some other question, one that was just between the two of us. Then he turned serious. "We also had the bruises on his fingertips, which we photographed very carefully. Luckily, Amy had noted them on his hospital records."

Drew looked up from his fourth or fifth doughnut. "Bruises?"

"Remember how you told me that Silla could barely bark at all?"

"She sounded raspy," I said.

"And then you texted me that you'd taken her in to get her checked out?"

I nodded.

"I called the vet, and we had a long talk. Apparently, when Scotties bite, they hang on. They don't let go. So when she bit Robert's leg, the only way he could get her off him was to choke her until she passed out. Her rabies tag pressing against her windpipe constricted the airflow, and the vet said that could have caused her to lose consciousness. That's the only way Robert could have gotten out of that hotel room without a dog hanging on to his leg by her teeth."

"Good dog," Karaline and Drew said again, only this time they sounded like they really meant it.

"The pressure was enough to make her throat swell, which is why she sounded raspy."

Beneath the table, Silla let out a full-throated *woof*, as if to inform us that she was fully recovered.

After we all laughed, and after I gave Silla a special chewy bone treat and one for Tessa just to keep things even, Harper went on. "We found a clear half fingerprint on the chanter. It must have gotten in his way. He probably just pushed it to one side without thinking and forgot to wipe it down the way he did the drones."

"What I'd like to know," I said, "is why Robert trashed Big Willie's hotel room. What was he looking for?"

Harper scratched at his jaw, and I could hear the rasp of his five-o'clock shadow. I wanted to reach out and see what it felt like. I glanced up and found Dirk watching me watch Harper. His smile was wistful. What a good ghost. I was truly sorry he was so lonely for his ladylove.

"The best we can deduce," Harper said, "is that Willie found out what Robert had done, and Robert was afraid he might have left some notes about it. Motive for both the murder and for the frantic search."

"So, tell us," Drew said. "Where did you find the necklace, the one they stole from my twin?"

"You mean the one you helped Fairing track down the provenance on?"

Karaline reared back and studied that fiancé of hers. I studied my brother. He spread his hands. "I told you I wanted to be in on the action. I don't hang around museums all day for nothing."

"What would be a 'profenants'?"

Karaline and I both looked at Dirk. I couldn't think of a way to answer him.

Harper looked at me. "Did he just ask you something?"

"Yeah," said Drew, "I asked where you found the necklace."

I pressed with both hands along the ridge of my eyebrows and peeked at Harper between my fingers. "Things like this happen a lot."

"Like what?" Drew sounded bewildered.

I could see why.

"In case you're interested," Harper said, turning toward Drew, "it was in Windsor's sporran all the time."

"He lied to his wife?" Karaline sounded incredulous.

"He put a priceless Ming necklace in his sporran?" Drew sounded appalled.

"It was okay," Harper said. "He'd wrapped it in a couple of disgusting used handkerchiefs. I guess he thought nobody would want to touch it."

"I'm sure he had *that* right," I said.

"Good thing we had latex gloves on when we opened it up."

In between all the *eewww* and *yuck* sounds, I heard someone knocking on the front door. Shorty vaulted from my lap and ran upstairs. Silla looked up at me as if to ask what I was going to do about the excess noise. She unfolded her curled-up body and preceded me, looking much more impressive than a silly old drum major any day, with those natural tassels of her black hair swishing from side to side.

Paisley Mackenzie stood on the porch, wearing her long plaid skirt, a white blouse, and a green paisley scarf. "I'm ready for my tour," she said, "so I can see what you've done to my house."

Harper slipped his hand around my waist, and I leaned against him. Even Paisley Mackenzie couldn't dampen my spirits this evening.